CHARISMA

Also by Orania Papazoglou

SANCTITY

CHARISMA

Orania Papazoglou

CROWN PUBLISHERS, INC.
NEW YORK

This book is set in a real place—New Haven, Connecticut—but in an unreal time. Nothing in it is meant to imply that anyone in any way ever connected with the New Haven municipal government or its allied state agencies has ever behaved as any of the people in this novel behave. As far as I know, the New Haven district attorney's office has been a model of virtue and the Connecticut Department of Social Services has never made a mistake in all its long history. This is facetious, of course, but the intent is not. This book is *not* based on the facts from any actual crime that involves New Haven or anyplace else, and all the people in it are imaginary.

Copyright © 1992 by Orania Papazoglou

All rights reserved. No part of this book may be reproduced or transmitted in any form or by any means, electronic or mechanical, including photocopying, recording, or by any information storage and retrieval system, without permission in writing from the publisher.

Published by Crown Publishers, Inc.,
201 East 50th Street, New York, New York 10022.
Member of the Crown Publishing Group.

CROWN is a trademark of Crown Publishers, Inc.

Manufactured in the United States of America

Library of Congress Cataloging-in-Publication Data

Papazoglou, Orania, 1951–
    Charisma / Orania Papazoglou.—1st ed.
        p.   cm.
I. Title.
PS3566.A613C43   1992
813'.54—dc20   91-41469
                                                                           CIP

ISBN 0-517-57088-2

10   9   8   7   6   5   4   3   2   1

First Edition

Charisma

PROLOGUE

CHAPTER

ONE

1 He went to Mass that morning—seven o'clock Mass for the first Sunday in Advent, with the pink and purple candles rising from a nest of leaves at the side of the altar and the priest singing the preface in plain chant. It was a church he didn't know and a priest he had seen only once or twice before. The priest had never seen him at all. Still he thought it would calm him if he received Communion.

Outside it was a cold dark morning in early December, one of those days when it seems the sun will never rise. The wind blew sleet against the stained-glass panes of the windows along the church's north wall. The air-lock door in the foyer wasn't working properly, and blasts of cold came in with every late arrival. The church was filled with old women and couples with very young children. This was the Mass for people with something to do with the rest of their day.

He, too, had something to do with the rest of his day, but standing for the Lord's Prayer he could forget about that. What he couldn't forget about was the church itself, which was old and filled with statues. It was a small parish tucked away in a forgotten corner of the city. He thought the bishop had to be ignoring it. God only knew, the order to "simplify" had not been heard in this place.

When it came time for Communion, he slipped into the aisle behind a nun in a habit that made her look older and fatter than she was. He took Communion in the hand and walked back to his pew chewing vigorously. Chewing the Host was one of the revenges he took against Sister Mary Mathilde—who was probably dead and in Hell and watching his every move. He didn't take a lot of revenges against Sister Mary Mathilde. He recognized it was childish.

When he knelt down for his Communion thanksgiving, the knife in the pocket of his jacket knocked against his chest and he was brought up short. It was only for a moment, but it made him feel like an amateur. And that was bad. The one thing he had never wanted to be was an amateur anything.

The priest went back to the altar and began the prayer after Communion, slipping into plain chant again as if it were a habit he couldn't break. The sound was lulling but not really effective. Now that he had felt the knife once, he seemed to feel it all the time. The floor under his feet felt very hot, the way it would be if someone had lit a fire in the basement.

He stood through the Concluding Rite in a fog, wondering what in God's name he was doing in a church.

2   The parish was not only small but very old-fashioned. Its members lived in double- and triple-decker houses on the streets immediately around it, leftovers from a time when this city had been a Catholic stronghold and a seed ground for vocations. Now the neighborhoods that bordered this one were black or Hispanic or just plain bombed out. There was a crack house a block away from the rectory, and a chop shop for stolen cars across the street from the apartment where Mrs. MacGerety lived with her ninety-year-old mother. The United States Supreme Court had put an end to the crèche that had once stood in the small public park all through Advent and Christmas. The drugs had put an end to the crowds of children that had once choked the crosswalks on their way to and from the tiny parish school. This whole section of the city was in a state of religious civil war: church people against crack people, Christians against nothing-at-all. Even the Workingman's Club, that Depression-era fortress of proud atheism, had put mangers and angels on its windows for the season.

He left the church before any of the rest of them and stood

at the bottom of the steep marble steps, looking up at the blank faces of the houses around him. He was not afraid, but he could feel the wrongness of it. Everything here, even the church, was already dead—and it had been murdered. That was what he thought of to describe it. It made him feel instantly better. He wasn't losing his grip on things after all.

He waited until the rest of them started to come out and then moved away. He turned down a side street he had never been on before and looked at the statues of the Virgin on the tiny front lawns. This close to the church, everyone was Catholic and everyone was poor. The neighborhood was a great square marked off for half a dozen games of tic-tac-toe. He was in no danger of getting lost.

He made a turn and then another turn and then another turn again. When he had done all that he found himself in front of a tall green triple-decker with a dove-of-peace plaque on its worn front door. The plaque was hung inside the glass, to save it from being stolen. He looked up at the windows of the second- and third-floor apartments and saw that they were dark. He was beginning to wonder if they were abandoned. He'd been in the ground-floor apartment four or five times already, and he had never heard a sound above his head.

He waited anyway, for caution's sake, while the rumble of distant traffic made him think about storms. They had cut a highway through the deserted neighborhoods half a mile from here. The highway was always full of tractor trailer trucks. He started to get itchy, and moved to relieve himself. The lock on the back door was solid, but the locks on the windows were useless. He broke a pane of glass and climbed inside.

Three blocks away, the church started ringing its bells. It was eight o'clock in the morning, and he was very cold.

3 Fifteen minutes later, she turned onto the street: the woman who lived in this apartment. She was a more-than-middle-aged woman with a body rapidly melting into shapelessness and a round, oddly innocent face, one of those "good Catholic women" who baked cakes for the rectory and looked after children whose parents wanted to go to Confession. At Halloween, she put laminated pictures of the Sacred Heart into little orange-and-black bags full of candy corn. At Christmas, she bought hand-painted cards from the Benedictine nuns and sent messages that said "May the joy of Christ be with you all this season." Once, every parish had had a hundred women like her. They came to every seven o'clock Mass and every parish Rosary and every Fatima novena. Now they were mostly gone, to the suburbs or the grave, and nobody knew why this one was still around.

But he knew. He watched her come up the street, stopping every once in a while to rub the joints of her fingers where her arthritis bothered her. He knew this woman very well, even though he had spoken to her only once. Her name was Margaret Mary McVann. Every Monday afternoon she served lunch at a soup kitchen two parishes away.

She stopped at the wrought-iron gate, rubbed her hands again, then pushed the gate open and came inside. He was standing just inside the door, one of his arms brushing against the curtains that covered the living-room window that faced the street. He was cold. The window he had broken had dropped the temperature in this apartment to something close to freezing. She started to come up the steps. He held his breath.

Damned idiot, he thought. He didn't know if he meant Margaret Mary or himself.

She let herself into the vestibule, fumbled around for a moment at the bottom of the stairs, and then put the key into the lock of the apartment's front door. He held his breath again. When the door swung in, he went rigid.

In the silence, the cuckoo clock on her kitchen wall sounded maniacal.

4 He had laid her things out on the coffee table, all her religious things from when she had been a nun. There was no habit—they were never allowed to keep their habits—but there was a fifteen-decade rosary and a heavy brass medal and the leather-bound copy of the Little Office she had been given when she entered the novitiate. There was even a picture: three nuns in old-fashioned habits, all of them very young and all of them smiling. On the back of it someone had written, "Sisters Ruth, Peter and Innocentia— in Rome!!!"

He had meant to lay out the rosary he had sent her, but he hadn't needed to. It had been on the coffee table when he came in.

5 She came through the door and stopped, staring at the things on the table. He was still behind the door, so he couldn't see her. He did hear her. She sucked air and reached automatically for the holy water font on the wall just inside the door. She crossed herself and started saying the Hail Mary.

The rosary he had sent her was made of real amber. It glowed oddly in the not-quite-light that came through the living-room curtains.

He had the palm of his hand flat on the door. He pushed the damn thing shut and it slammed. That was when he felt himself losing it.

6 *Damnherdamnherdamnherdamnherdamnher,* he thought. The blood rushed into his head. Something inside there was getting bigger and bigger and bigger, pushing against his skull, making him blind. He kept thinking of amber as a death trap: prehistoric insects caught and suffocated, drowned in glue, petrified. He kept thinking of dinosaurs stripping the leaves from trees and leaving behind them barrenness.

Damnherdamnherdamnherdamnherdamnher.

She turned toward him and put her hands to her face. He saw her skin go white and her eyes grow larger.

7 When she saw who and what he was, the panic drained out of her and the confusion began, raw confusion like the addledness of someone who has woken up in the middle of a dream. She hesitated, seeming to want to come toward him. He came toward her instead and she stepped away.

He got one hand around her jaw and the other on her shoulder. He dragged her to him and spun her around. She got a hand inside his jacket and pulled.

He tore her neck just as she tore his jacket. The sounds were strangely similar.

A moment later, she was on the floor, dead.

8 The blood drained from his head and his eyes cleared. She had a piece of his jacket lining in her hand. He took his jacket off and left it folded over the back of a chair. He was wearing two sweaters over a shirt and undershirt. He'd survived like that before in the cold. Besides, it had never really been his jacket anyway.

Somewhere outside, the church bell rang again, a single solemn gong marking the half hour. It had taken no time at all. He hadn't been too weak for it. He had only to worry about finishing up, and about the weather. He hadn't noticed it before, but the sky had opened. There was snow coming down as thick and fast as summer rain. Through the crack in the curtains he could see it piling up on the dead branches of the yard's one tree.

He picked up her nun things and put them back in the drawer where she'd kept them, the third one from the top in her bedroom bureau. He went back into the living room and rescued the knife from his discarded jacket. The rosary he had sent her was still on the coffee table. It had been jogged out of place. It looked as if she'd been saying it and then put it down, carelessly, on her way to do something else.

The cold was still slipping through the window he had broken, dropping the temperature lower and lower, making everything frigid.

9 She was lying on the floor with her head tilted too far around, with her legs spread apart as if someone had tried to rape her. But he hadn't tried to rape her. He didn't want to rape her. She was an old woman. Sex had never held much interest for him anyway.

10 What he really wanted to do was cut.

CHAPTER

Two

1 Sometimes, Susan Murphy thought her life would have been easier if she had been able to look at it as a series of grievances. God only knew, her history entitled her to one or two. Standing in this stone-floored foyer, looking out at a landscape she had once known more intimately than she had ever wanted to know anything, she could count out the things that would have turned any of the women she knew into raging shrews. Her father, her mother, her order, her Church: Dena, who had been a Franciscan before the ravages of Vatican II, would have taken any one of these things and run with it. In fact, she had. The last Susan had heard, Dena was down in South America somewhere, trying to bring contraception to women who only wanted to know how to have more babies, and communism to farmers who had their minds on jungles and rainfall.

One wall of the foyer was a great glass window, leaded and paned. Susan looked out of it at trees and rocks and curving stone walls. It was a beautiful place, Saint Michael's. Its fidelity to the spirit of the medieval Church was absolute. So was its fidelity to the spirit of nineteenth-century capitalism. What it reminded her of, more than anything, was home the way home had been before the real trouble started: that massive house on Edge Hill Road; that endless dining room with its forty-chair table set with silver; her mother in pale pink taffeta and too many pearls. One of the reasons she was leaving the convent was that too much had started to remind her of home as home used to be. Sometimes, waking up in the morning and not quite rid of sleep, she thought of herself not as Sister Mary Bede, but as the woman her mother had once told her she would be. What scared her was the possibility that that woman was what, in spite of everything, she really was.

Silly ass, she thought. She heard sounds above her head, heavy shoes on wrought-iron spiral stairs. She looked up to see Reverend Mother coming down to her, moving painfully, stopping on every riser to catch her breath. The black folds of an only-slightly-modified habit shifted and swirled in the air around her, making her look like a moving cloud.

"Are you all right?" Susan said.

"I'm fine." Reverend Mother came down two more steps, stopped, and sighed. "If you wouldn't wear a jacket, you could at least have let yourself into the office. There's no heat in that foyer."

"I'm not cold, Reverend Mother."

"Of course you're cold. Everyone's cold."

Susan started to fold her arms under the short cape of her habit, realized it wasn't there, and stuck her hands into the pockets of her jeans instead. The jeans were new, and stiff. They scraped against the skin of her legs and made her wonder if she was bleeding.

It was seven o'clock on the morning of the Monday after the first Sunday in Advent, December 2. She had just spent half an hour in this foyer, trying to be angry. There had been days lately when that was all she ever did.

She crossed the foyer and opened the door to Reverend Mother's office, mostly to give herself something to do. Then she let herself slip into her favorite fantasy.

She was driving along the road somewhere, sliding through small towns full of small stores and twenty-five-dollar-a-night hotels. The snow was thick and absolutely white, just fallen. The thin branches of the trees were encased in ice, so that the trees looked decorated. The sun was shining.

Up ahead, just coming into view, was a wide open Dunkin Donuts.

2 The meeting in Reverend Mother's office was a ritual, like Mass. Every nun who left this order had to have one, even if she left before Profession. Susan had never understood what for. In her case, at least, there was nothing unexpected or inexplicable. She and Reverend Mother had been talking it over for months.

Of course, it was hard to pin down what they'd said to each other, or what they'd understood. Susan decided she was here because she was supposed to be here. To have left any other way would have been rude. Neither Sister Mary Bede nor the Susan Katherine Murphy of Susan's mother's fantasies would ever be rude.

She sat down facing the oversize crucifix at Reverend Mother's back and stretched out her legs. She had to, because she found it hard to bend them. Her brother Dan had sent her the jeans. She had sent him her measurements. He liked clothes tighter than she did.

Reverend Mother poured two cups of coffee from the pot on the tray Sister Martina had brought in and handed her one.

"Did you get it all straightened out about the car?" she said. "I heard you on the phone last night. What makes them think nuns have credit cards?"

"They don't think nuns have credit cards, Reverend Mother. They just don't rent cars to people who don't."

"There probably are nuns who have credit cards," Reverend Mother said. "Out there, somewhere."

"Out there, somewhere" was Reverend Mother's code for what other people called "the spirit of Vatican II." It took in a lot of territory. Susan drank coffee and put her cup down on the edge of Reverend Mother's desk.

"My brother Dan straightened it out," she said. "He called and rented it himself. I think he used a little pull."

"Pull."

"He's the district attorney for the city of New Haven, Reverend Mother. And it is a local rental company. Local to New Haven County at any rate."

"You should have joined an order with a Motherhouse farther

away," Reverend Mother said. "Maybe that was the problem. Usually, I think it's better for women to be close to home, but in your case—"

A look passed between them, something that said they both knew everything there was to know about "this case." And would rather not talk about it. Susan had a sudden, vivid memory of the day she had told Reverend Mother what had happened in her life. She had sat in this chair in her novice's habit and talked for six hours.

Reverend Mother poured more coffee, which Susan knew she wouldn't drink. Reverend Mother never drank more than one cup a day.

"Do you know what you're going to do with yourself?" she said. "I can't imagine you want to work for the district attorney's office. I can't see you as one of those new women lawyers with their suits and their athletic walking shoes."

"I'd have to go to law school for that, Reverend Mother. And I don't think Dan could hire me even if I wanted him to. They have rules about nepotism, you know."

"How old are you?"

"Thirty-five."

Reverend Mother nodded. "I think I've heard of your brother. There was a case, about two years ago. It was in all the papers. About child abuse in a daycare center."

"That was Dan," Susan said. "And it was certainly in all the papers."

Reverend Mother shot her a strange look. "What's the matter, Sister? Don't you get along with your brother? The papers at the time made him sound like—well, like a crusading knight."

"I like my brother just fine, Reverend Mother. I suppose I don't know him all that well. He's ten years older than I am. He's never even been to visit me up here. I'm closer to the younger one."

"Younger than you are?"

"A little."

"And?"

Susan shrugged. "His name's Andy. You may have seen him once or twice. He's been up here on visiting days."

"What does *he* do?"

Susan smiled. "Reverend Mother, the three of us were brought up with a lot of money. Sometimes, with people who have been brought up like that, it's better not to ask what they do."

"Meaning he doesn't do anything," Reverend Mother said.

"Meaning he thinks he's an artist," Susan said.

Reverend Mother sighed. "I think you should have taken that job with the archdiocese," she said. "I know it was social work and you're not trained for that, but you could have handled it. It would have made a good transitional phase. Halfway in and halfway out."

"Except that sometimes it's not so transitional, Reverend Mother. Sister Davida took a job with the archdiocese in 1972. She's still there."

"Nineteen seventy-two was a very different year."

"An entirely different decade."

"And Sister Davida was a very different kind of nun."

"Reverend Mother, Sister Davida was a psychopath."

Reverend Mother got out of her chair. She was a huge woman, tall and grotesquely fat, except that under the folds of a conservative habit nobody ever looked really fat. Just tented.

"Susan, Susan, Susan," she said. "You've got to stop saying things like that. Seventeen years, and we didn't even make you circumspect."

"Maybe," Susan said, "but I can recite the Litany of Loretto from memory. And I can recite the Miserere from memory in Latin."

Reverend Mother turned away, opened the top drawer of her filing cabinet, and went rooting around for Susan's papers.

In the seventeen years she had known this woman, Susan had never once seen her put anything in its place.

3 Fifteen minutes later, Susan climbed into the convent van next to Sister Mary Jerome, stuffing the things she was taking with her on the dashboard over the glove compartment. There wasn't much. A dwarf manila envelope held her fifteen-decade rosary and the brown scapular she had worn under her habit. A larger manila envelope held a small packet of unopened mail. The Miraculous Medal she had worn around her neck was still there, under the shirt and sweater Dan had sent her. God only knew why.

Sister Mary Jerome sat in the driver's seat, stiff and cold and disapproving. She was a young nun with an uncertain vocation and a sour face, a well of bitterness that could not be excavated because it had no bottom. Defections always threatened her.

She pointed to the manila envelopes and said, "If we go up a hill, that stuff is going to fall on the floor."

Susan took the manila envelopes and put them in her lap. Sister Mary Jerome frowned at them.

"I can't believe you aren't going to open your mail," she said. "I always open my mail. We only get it once a week."

"And there's never anything in it," Susan pointed out.

"There's a lot in yours."

"It's just circulars, Mary Jerome. Religious publishing houses wanting to sell me catechisms. Religious supply houses wanting to sell me First Communion gift sets. It's because I was principal of a school."

"You get mail every week," Mary Jerome said. "I see it stacked up on the table in the living room. Sometimes I go months without seeing an envelope."

"I'll send you some," Susan said. "I'll even get my brothers to send you some. Don't you think we ought to get moving?"

Mary Jerome turned the key and shifted into gear. "I can't believe you're not going to open your mail," she said again. But she had pulled the van into the drive, and they were moving.

Through the windshield, Susan could see snow beginning to come down, white against the black bark of naked trees. Saint Michael's had nearly two acres between it and the road. Standing on the porch at the front of the Motherhouse was like looking into primeval forest. The lawn could have been endless.

Today the drive itself was slicked with ice and looked dangerous. Mary Jerome was alternately humming the alleluia and muttering under her breath about "we."

When they made the first turn of the three that led to the gate, Mary Jerome said, "Some people just don't know how to *appreciate* that mail."

4 Halfway to town, Susan finally opened her mail. She did it because she was nervous, and because Mary Jerome kept staring at it. Mary Jerome kept staring at her, too, but there was nothing Susan could do about that.

They were rolling along on ice and snow, going much too fast, skidding across streets that dipped and curved and plunged between white Protestant props. A Congregationalist church. A gambrel colonial built before the Revolution. Susan had never noticed before how deliberately picturesque this town was, as if a Norman Rockwell aesthetic had been imposed on it by legislation, from above.

"People just don't understand," Mary Jerome said. "About mail, I mean. I tell my family and I tell my family, but they just won't listen. They think just because we're not allowed to write more than four times a year, they shouldn't write to us more than four times a year."

"My family never wrote to me at all," Susan said. "They certainly wouldn't be writing now."

"I think now was exactly when they'd write."

"I don't want to talk about it, Mary Jerome."

Mary Jerome stared at the pamphlet Susan was unwrapping, glossy and four-colored and crammed full of pictures of the Virgin on a cloud. GOOD NEWS FOR CATECHISTS, was written across the top of it. "I would never have entered the kind of order where I'd be the one buying catechisms instead of Reverend Mother. I mean, why would I have bothered? What's the point of being a nun if you're going to run around in makeup and live in an apartment?"

Susan almost said: What's the point of being a nun? But she had answers to that question, better ones than Mary Jerome had, and she could only have asked it out of spite.

She dumped the circulars back into their manila envelope and took out the only interesting thing, a small box wrapped in brown paper, the kind of box samples of toothpaste came in when you lived in a suburban house. It had been addressed by hand.

Mary Jerome eyed it, the envy plain on her face, turning her ugly. "Is that from one of your former students? If it is, it'll be a tube of hand lotion. That's what they always send. Scentless hand lotion."

It wasn't a tube of hand lotion. It was a five-decade rosary, made out of amber, a slightly more expensive-looking version of the kind of thing laypeople used when they said "a third part." Mary Jerome's eyebrows climbed up her forehead to the edge of her veil, making her look Neanderthal.

"Good Lord," she said. "Who'd send a rosary to a nun?"

Susan closed her eyes and told herself: I am not a nun.

I.

Am.

Not.

A.

Nun.

CHAPTER
THREE

1 Years ago, long before he was even old enough for high school, Pat Mallory used to come up to Edge Hill Road to see the houses. In those days, New Haven was a "nice" town, a half-city with an urban feel but a country rhythm. It was also solidly Catholic. With the exception of Yale, an Anglo-Saxon fortress spread out across Prospect and Chapel streets and tucked into the trees on the narrow offshoots of the business district, New Haven then might as well have been dedicated to the Immaculate Heart of Mary. Maybe it had been. What he remembered most about those trips up the hill were the names on the mailboxes. Meehan, Carroll, Hanrahan, Burke: all those great stone houses, seven and eight and nine thousand square feet big; all those broad front lawns; all those long black cars; all of it, every piece of it, Irish. A year or two later, when Kennedy was inaugurated and the nuns at school opened every class by thanking God for putting a Catholic in the White House, Pat had thought he'd finally understood. Edge Hill Road was the kind of place people like the Kennedys came from.

Now, getting out of the car into the cold stiff wind of the dark December 2 morning, he half wished he were ten years old again. The great stone houses were still there, but they meant less to him than they once had. Everything did. Three abortive years on scholarship at a very expensive Jesuit college in New York had taught him that Edge Hill Road was not the kind of place Kennedys came from. It didn't represent enough money, and it was too close to town. Seventeen years with the New Haven Police Department had taught him that New Haven wasn't a very "nice" town, not anymore, and that it was getting less nice all the time. Lately he had begun to wonder why he was living in it. The neighborhood where he had grown up, with half a dozen brothers and sisters stuffed into seven rooms and a statue of the Virgin on the front lawn, was now a crack alley. The street in front of Holy Name School was lined with prostitutes. The Green was full of bums. Sometimes he felt like a science-fiction version of Rip Van Winkle: a man who has been asleep just long enough for his world to have turned into the antithesis of itself.

Still, it looked strange, a body stake here at the bottom of Edge Hill. Edge Hill might not be the kind of place Kennedys came from, but it was rich enough. There wasn't a child on the street who went to a public school, and most of the girls "came out" in the most publicly possible way. Every spring, the backyards were full of striped caterers' tents and dance bands imported from New York City. What they usually got up here was burglaries and break-ins and driving-under-the-influence after nights on the town.

He slammed the door and waited for his driver to come around the car and join him. Now that he was chief of Homicide, he always had a driver, although he never had a car much better than the Buick unmarkeds he used to drive when he first got out of uniform. This driver was a boy named Robert Feld, still in uniform, black and much too young. *Much* too young. Sometimes the NHPD managed to sign on reformed street kids, hard boys who'd gotten religion, and they were always perfect. They knew the territory and they'd been leached dry of sentimentality in the womb. Robert Feld was the other kind. He had a degree from Storrs and a commitment to Positive Attitudes.

Pat let Feld come up to him, then pointed across the street. He looked away as he did it. Like most people, Feld made him nervous—because, like most people, Feld made him feel outsized. Pat Mallory was six feet six inches tall, two hundred and forty pounds, naturally bulked in the shoulders and naturally broad across the chest. He had never really worked out, because he had always been afraid to. In high school, he'd spent a year in mortal terror, convinced there was something wrong with his thyroid gland that was going to make him grow and grow and grow and never stop.

"Look," he said. "Who caught this thing? They've got one of their lines tied to a lamppost."

Feld blushed, then went patting around in his jacket pockets until he found a steno pad. He squinted at it. It was ten o'clock in the morning, but it wasn't exactly light. The sky was crammed black with clouds. The streetlights, primed to turn off automatically every morning at seven, were giving off something like shade. It could have been the middle of a night when the moon was full, or the street was having a block party.

On Edge Hill Road, they didn't have block parties.

Feld was getting into gear. "Conran and Machevski," he said finally. "They're who caught it."

"They're not Homicide," Pat said. "Who do I have down here?"

Feld squinted again. Then he sighed. "I don't know if I took this down right," he said. "Ben Deaver. That's right."

Pat was sure it was. Ben Deaver was the highest ranking black in Homicide. He was also among the two or three smartest officers, of any color. Someday, soon, if Pat did twenty-five-and-out, Ben Deaver was going to have his job.

"The other one," Feld said, "is a little fuzzy. Debero?"

"Dbro." Pat sighed. "Jesus Christ."

"Excuse me?"

"Never mind."

"I've never heard of this—Dbro," Feld said. "I've been driving you for five months, I've never heard of him. Is he new?"

"No," Pat said. He looked across the street again. It was wide and deeply guttered. On any other day, it would have been choked with traffic. This morning it was choked with slush, a black river disappearing into blacker grates. The temperature was dropping again, just enough. In an hour or two, it would start to snow.

Pat left Feld where he was and crossed toward the line of

police cars that had been parked to block the flow of cars and tourists. In the pocket of his jacket he had the note his secretary had written him after she'd taken the call that brought him down here: the first call, not the second. The first call was from Dan Murphy, the New Haven district attorney, the man in charge of media hype. He'd been on his way out of the office when that second one had come in. Now he wondered if he should have taken the time and answered the second call himself. It would have been Deaver, and Deaver always had something to say.

But the first call had been bad enough, even though it had been filtered through his secretary. He kept thinking about the note in his pocket and the fact that it would have to say now what it had said then. Dan was on the warpath, looking for a way to make the papers. That, coupled with Dbro, was the kind of disaster he did not need right before Christmas.

There was a body stake here at the bottom of Edge Hill Road, and the body staked had belonged to a nine-year-old boy.

2 Ben Deaver had taken his jacket and laid it across the hood of one of the black-and-whites. When he saw Pat coming, he picked it up and started to put it on. It was an automatic gesture, not meant. Pat shook his head slightly and Deaver put the jacket down again. Pat knew what was going on here, with Deaver at any rate. There were things you got used to after a while—things that, when you started out, held all the nauseating terror of the climax scenes in the horror movies you'd watched as a teenager. The things you did not get used to made you hot. Pat could remember himself in the back bedroom of that nursery school on Pinchard Street, looking at the pool of blood on the floor, at the smear of feces on the wall, at the cigarette butts clogging the drainhole in the sink. He had stripped off his jacket and his sweater. He had wanted to strip off his shirt. He had thought his skin was going to boil. Now, he thought, Ben Deaver was literally radiating heat.

At the other corner of the stake, Dbro was wearing his heavy sheepskin-lined jacket zipped to his chin and a pair of dogmuffs over his ears. Deaver kept darting little glances in his direction, startled, as if he'd been presented with a giant amoeba pretending to be the Ghost of Christmas Past.

"Jesus," he said. "Nothing ever touches him. *Nothing* ever touches him."

"Nothing ever did."

Deaver nodded and sat down on his jacket. He looked tired and angry and half ready to cry. He'd looked much the same the first time Pat had ever met him. That had been ten years ago, when Deaver had been sixteen and of the (highly erroneous) opinion that he could turn himself into a creditable bag man.

These days, Deaver looked like he could have graduated from Yale. His hair was clipped short. His shirts always seemed to have just the right amount of starch in the collars, and they were always white. When he did paperwork he wore heavy black glasses and smoked a pipe.

He kicked the heels of his wing-tip shoes against the black-and-white's fender and said, "I called that priest. You know, the one with the place down in the Congo. I thought he might be able to give an I.D."

"Father Thomas Burne," Pat said.

"Yeah. That's the one. The kid—" Deaver looked over at Dbro again. The technical people were beginning to wrap up, beginning to move out, leaving a clear path to the body. They had been here for an hour, and they hadn't been allowed to accomplish much. The photographers had gotten their photographs. The rest of them had been more or less on hold. They couldn't do much work until the body was picked up. The body couldn't be picked up until Pat had had a look at it. He had had his secretary call in and tell them that.

"The kid," Deaver said, picking up the thread again, "has that look to him. The kind they all have over here. At Burne's place. That look that seems to say 'Victim for Sale.' You know what it's like. They all end up over at Burne's place one way or the other."

"When they're this young they usually stay."

"I know. But I had to try something. Christ, Pat, this is—I had to try something. I saw what we had and I nearly—"

"What?"

"I don't know." He had stopped kicking his feet. His hands were splayed out over his knees, twitching. "When we first got the call, I thought it was going to be, you know, one of them." He gestured up Edge Hill. "I thought, Jesus, that's what we need. Some little rich kid getting mugged, some little rich kid dealing dope. Then I got here and—"

"You're sure it's not some rich kid?"

"Positive. You look at him."

"I will," Pat said. "I don't want to rag your ass, you know, but I've got a reason for asking. You're not the only one who called me."

"Who else called you?"

"Dan Murphy."

Deaver's face started shading into purple. The muscles in his neck were beginning to bulge. "Crap," he said. "Crap and double crap."

"I know."

"What the hell did he want?"

"A chance to hog the publicity and make himself look like a crusader."

"We don't need him in this, Pat, we really don't need him."

"I know," Pat said. "When I saw the address, I thought it must have been a kid from the neighborhood. Who else would get killed on Edge Hill? I thought it was because it was close to home."

"I heard he lived up here," Deaver said.

"Stone house right up there at the lip of the ridge. The one with the turrets." It was a house Pat remembered from his childhood walks, but he wasn't going to tell Deaver that. As far as he knew, he had never told anyone about those walks. He just took them again and again, in his dreams.

He flapped his arms against the cold and said, "So? You were telling me—"

"I was telling you," Deaver said, "yeah. So. I got here and Machevski was puking all over the scene. Just sick inside out. That's one thing. I thought we must have had a slasher, because you know how Machevski is about slashers, there's just something about knives with him he can't take, but—"

"Ben," Pat said, "what do we have?"

Ben wrapped his arms around his chest, looked into the sky, looked uneasy. By now the technical men had all drifted away. The tourists on the edges of the police lines were starting to get bored. The body was lying in its aura of chalk, made difficult to see from where they were standing by the restless pacing of one of the medical examiner's men. Deaver bit down on the inside of his cheek, hard enough so that Pat thought he was going to bleed.

"It was a hit."

"What?"

Now that it was out, Deaver seemed to feel better. At least he had stopped biting the inside of his cheek.

"It was a hit," he said again. "It was a classic hit. Gun to the back of the head. Kneeling position. The whole thing. If the kid had been nineteen instead of nine, I would have said high-level dope and old-line connections. Pat, go look at him. I know it sounds nuts, but it was a pro job. It was an expensive pro job."

"On a nine-year-old kid?"

"Yes."

"On Edge Hill Road?"

"Yes."

"For Christ's sake."

"I know." Deaver pulled on his jacket. He turned his back on the scene and looked down into the heavy brownstone Victorian buildings that blocked his view into the center of town.

"There's something else you ought to know," he said.

Pat wanted to say "now what?" He left off the "now."

"Dbro knew him," Deaver said.

"Dbro knew the kid."

"That's right."

"Fucking shit," Pat said.

"You know what it means that Dbro knew him? You know?"

"I know."

"His name was Billy Hare," Deaver said. "Dbro drives me crazy. Someday he's going to drive me crazy enough."

Pat unbuttoned his own jacket. "Don't let him. Let him drive Dan Murphy crazy enough."

"Nothing drives Dan Murphy crazy. Except us. And those." Deaver pointed down the hill toward the television cameras, parked at the line, going full blast, and waiting for their chance.

Already.

3 Usually, Pat Mallory did a lot to avoid television cameras. He didn't like them, and they didn't like him. Today he barely noticed them, although there were two that seemed to be hanging out of the sky right over the stake and another with a light aimed right for his eyes. For the next fifteen minutes he didn't notice much of anything, not even if Conran and Deaver were right about the hit. What he noticed when he got to the body was the clothes.

In the time he had been talking to Deaver, the wind had risen. It was blowing down the hill at him, unobstructed, forging streams of ice under his hair. He stopped just outside the chalk outline and looked down.

The boy was delicate, small-boned and fine, the kind of boy who had trouble in school playgrounds and on the rougher city streets. He was blond and small and gentle, even covered with blood and broken into pieces of bone. He had no coat.

What he did have was a heavy wool sweater and a button-down cotton shirt and a pair of corduroy pants, all perfectly matched, all taken straight out of an ad for Ralph Lauren Polo for Boys. Expensive clothes, but the wrong kind of expensive clothes, the kind that made you feel the kid had been dressed up as a preppy for a round of trick or treat. There was only one place in this city where the boys wore this kind of clothes and wore them new and always neat. The words that came into his mind and that he couldn't get rid of were: hooker's clothes.

It took him a while to understand why he was so sure of the hooker part, even though it was right in front of him. The clothes had been a little tight. When the kid had been bent over to take the hit, his pants had ripped along the seam. Now the seam was gaping. Through it, Pat could see a pair of bikini underpants.

They were bright red silk, almost translucent, and stretched as tight as skin. On the hump of the boy's right cheek, the logo winked through a thin film of blood and snow.

It said CHRISTIAN DIOR.

CHAPTER

FOUR

1   Sometimes, Bishop John Martin Kelly thought he knew more than he ought to about schizophrenia. Sometimes he simply thought he had two souls operating in one body: the one he was aware of, and the one that sneaked up on him when he wasn't paying attention. For the past thirty-six hours, he had been living with that other one. Now it was ten o'clock on the morning of the Thursday after the first Sunday in Advent and he was standing at his office windows, looking out over the city of New Haven, feeling dizzy and exhilarated and scared to death. Spread out in front of him was Yale, its spires and crenellated towers, its turrets and air of always being safe. When he'd first seen it, he'd thought he'd wandered into Oz. It was even better than the Jesuit seminary, maybe because it was older. And richer. There were people who talked about the great wealth of the Catholic Church, but John Kelly knew it couldn't begin to compare with the wealth of the Protestant Establishment. Those people ran the world. Besides, being Catholic had its drawbacks. It could be dangerous. Being a Jesuit could be more dangerous still. It always surprised him that he hadn't thought of that when he joined the order. In those days, he'd been very hardhearted about his search for security.

His search for security. He got his cigarettes out of the long center drawer of his desk and lit up. He hadn't slept at all the last two nights. His brain was reeling, and when it reeled it tended to give him flash-picture shows that made him unbearably uncomfortable. One minute, he saw pictures of the future: Bishop John

Martin Kelly, a real bishop instead of just an auxiliary, plastered across television screens from one end of the country to the other. The next, he got pictures of the past, of the place he had left to accept the embrace of Holy Mother Church. That place had been a single two-bed room in a cheap motel on the outskirts of Elyria, Ohio. His father had just gone into bankruptcy for the fourth time.

His cigarette had burned down to a long column of ash. He tapped it into the ashtray and took a deep drag. His father had been a man of enthusiasms, a manic without a depressive phase, and because of that John Kelly distrusted enthusiasm in himself. His childhood had been an epic nightmare of instability and insecurity. First they would have a house. Then the house would be foreclosed on and they would have an apartment. Then the apartment would be snatched away for nonpayment of rent and they would have a motel room. Then the cycle would start all over again, or not. He could remember once or twice when he'd thought they were going to die. They had spent a memorable Christmas Eve sleeping in boxes on the streets of Chicago, curled up against the wind behind a warehouse near the stockyards. For weeks afterward, he'd imagined the smell of blood.

It was after that Christmas Eve that he'd started to go to church. On Christmas Day, his father found another sucker. She was an old woman with a big house and rooms to rent on Chicago's South Side. She took pity not on the man, but on his wife and children. By then, John's mother was a kind of ambulatory catatonic. She literally walked into walls. His brothers were well on their way to what seemed then like their inevitable ends. Charlie was a proto-delinquent, criminal already at the age of eight. Bobby was coughing with the start of the tuberculosis that would kill him before his seventh birthday. His father was hale and hearty and full of plans. They were disintegrating around him and he didn't see it.

The rooms the old lady let them have were small and on the third floor. They had to climb three flights of steep back stairs to get to them. When they did get there, John's mother went into the smallest of the bedrooms and curled up on the cot that had been shoved under the one small window. John knew she was going to stay just like that for a day or more. He went into the kitchen and looked through the empty cupboard, the clean, unstocked refrigerator, the oven with its polished metal racks. The whole place smelled of ammonia and his father. His own clothes smelled of dirt. Through the high window over the kitchen sink, he could see the city, black buildings and even blacker snow, grime and noise and mindless machinery. Everything was moving and moving and moving, moving without end. Someday they would be caught up in it again, swept out into the sea of cold.

His father was in the shower, splashing water and singing. After a while, the water shut off and the plastic shower curtain rattled over its hollow tin rod. The walls up there were so thin, you could have heard a butterfly fart from two rooms away. John even heard the towel coming off the rack, a fat slap of cotton like a backbeat. His father was singing "Peg o' My Heart."

Then the bathroom door opened, and John realized his father was about to come out into the kitchen, wrapped in a towel and singing. He panicked. He was only ten years old. He had no idea how to deal with this man or the woman in the back bedroom or the two boys who always seemed to be getting sick or acting crazy. They'd been on the run this time for two months. He was tired and scared and sick himself. He was very nearly starving.

The door to the stairs was in a hallway off the kitchen. He ran back there and then down, down and down and down, going so fast and so fluidly that when he hit the cold of the street it almost didn't touch him. He kept running, too. Usually he was worried about getting lost. They'd been in a few shelters in their travels, places where bodies were stashed when they were too poor to afford places to live, too sober to be dismissed as bums, and too stupid to be dead. In those places, he had learned to fear one thing more than he feared the amusement park ride of his own life: the Department of Welfare. To his ten-year-old mind, Those People were the Gestapo, the Devil, and the Wicked Witch of the West all rolled into one.

He ran anyway, down streets and up avenues, through small parks that looked cramped and overcrowded even without any people in them. The South Side was a rough section of the city. It always had been. In 1961, it was a rough section that happened to be white. After a while, he began to realize he was being watched. The buildings around him were shabbier than the ones he'd left, marked with paint and dotted with splinters. The stoops were full of men and teenage boys, out on the watch no matter how cold it was. His flesh started to crawl.

In spite of the way his family lived, their roots were in the middle, not the working, class—and they looked it. One of John's grandfathers had been an engineer. The other had been a teacher. John himself was growing into a body that was almost stereotypically "bookish." He was thin and tall and delicate, and if they'd had the money for it he'd have been wearing glasses. The boys around him now, even the boys his own age, were altogether different. They were bulked up in the shoulders and thighs. They had a lot of energy. They were watching him and he didn't think they liked what they saw.

He knew he was going to have to do something when he started to be afraid. When he was afraid he couldn't think, and thinking was all he had. Being afraid was what had gotten him into this mess to begin with.

He didn't know where he was, so he didn't know where to go. He didn't want to turn around. That would only make the boys think they'd gotten to him, which was a bad idea. He kept looking for a side street to turn into. All the side streets were narrow and dark. The street he was on at least had Christmas decorations.

He had gone two blocks when he saw the church. Unlike the buildings around it, it had a lawn, two small squares of snow on either side of a narrow concrete walk. He was surprised to see its doors were open. His father had been baptized Catholic and his mother had once been devout, but it had been years since either of them had seen the inside of a church. They'd certainly never taken him to one. He stopped at the edge of the walk and tried to see through the peaked double doors to whatever was inside, but all he got was the impression of tiny flickering lights. Candles, he thought, and then: at least it would be warm.

He went up the walk, then up the steps, then into what seemed to be a vestibule. He didn't know what to call the parts of a church. There was another set of double doors inside and he went through those, too. The ceiling seemed to lift off above his head like a rocket ship. The building seemed to stretch all the way to California. It was the biggest room he had ever seen, and for a while that was all he was able to take in. Height, width, breadth: it was a room for multitudes or giants.

Then he began to calm down—he thought of it as his brain beginning to thaw out—and he started to notice what was around him. The flickering lights were a bank of candles in front of a tall statue of a woman in blue-and-white robes. He thought she must be the Virgin Mary. In the back where he was were tall curtained boxes with panels between each set of curtains and crosses embossed on the panels. He had no idea what those were. He counted pews and came up with twenty-six on each side.

At the front, on the other side of the altar from the statue of the Virgin, there was a small curtained cabinet with a light hanging over it, a candle burning in a little red jar. It fascinated him. He went up the aisle toward it, ignoring the pictures that had been placed at intervals along the walls. They were all pictures of Jesus Christ in terrible agony: carrying his cross; falling on stones; bleeding. It hurt him to look at them.

He got to the rail that divided the pews from the things at the front—the statue, the altar, the candles, the little curtained cabinet—and stopped. He told himself he wasn't allowed to go any farther. The truth was, he didn't want to. It was scary up there. There was a crucifix on the wall behind the altar, a dozen times larger than life size, made out of stone, and carved with every detail. His eyes kept going back and forth between it and the little red light. Back and forth. Back and forth. Back and forth. He kept thinking it was trying to tell him something.

A Catholic with any training at all would have knelt down. He didn't know enough to do that, so he was still standing at the rail when a man came through the side door, threw his right hand around in front of his face and chest, then did a quick bobbing kneel in front of the altar. John almost laughed. The man was wearing a robe that only sort-of fitted him. The sleeves were too long and fell down over his hands. It gave them something in common. John's shirt was too long, too. His clothes were always the wrong sizes, because they were always picked off the rag tables at Goodwill.

That's a priest, John thought. Just as he thought it, the man held out his hand and said:

"I'm Father Carnetti. Can I do something for you?"

Later, he would think of all the answers he could have made to that question. God only knew, he had enough that needed to be done. Standing there in the church, he could only think of one thing to say, and it didn't make any sense.

"What was that you were doing with your hand?" he asked the priest. "That thing when you first came in."

"You mean the Sign of the Cross?"

"I don't know."

Father Carnetti made the Sign of the Cross again, slowly this time, so that John could see exactly what he was doing.

"That was it," John said.

"I take it you're not a Christian," Father Carnetti said.

"I don't know."

"Well, certainly not a Catholic."

"I don't know," John said again. He hesitated. "My father was a Catholic once, I think. A long time ago. I think I was too little to remember."

"What about your mother?"

"She used to go to church." John coughed. He could only vaguely remember his mother going to church, mornings when she left him alone with his father or just alone. He couldn't have been more than two or three years old. Then he remembered something, and brightened. "She used to have beads she carried around. Beads with a cross on the end of them. That's Catholic, isn't it?"

"That's right. That's a rosary."

"So she must have been Catholic once in a while."

"What is she now?"

"The next best thing to dead."

"Ah," Father Carnetti said. "I see."

John held his breath. He had no idea what he'd meant by what he'd said. He had no idea how to explain it. If Father Carnetti asked him about it, he was going to have to turn and run.

But Father Carnetti had turned back to the crucifix. He had his hands behind his back and his chin down so that it tucked into his high collar.

"I came over here to get away from the rectory," he said. "My housekeeper made my dinner for me and then went home. She's got six grandchildren. Do you want to come and eat with me?"

"Eat?"

"Well, it is Christmas. I hate eating alone on Christmas. My family's out in Oregon and I couldn't get away."

"Do you have children of your own?"

"Priests don't have children of their own. We don't marry. I have a sister in Portland. She's got the children."

"I'm sorry you couldn't—get away."

"So was I. Now maybe I've changed my mind. Will you come and eat with me?"

"Yes," John said. At that point, he would have gone to eat with vultures in a lion's den. His stomach felt like one of those black holes they'd told him about in one of the schools he'd attended in those intermittent periods when his father had money.

"Good," Father Carnetti said. "I'll tell you all about the Catholic Church. When we get to the pie, maybe you can tell me about that look you had on your face when I came in here."

"Look?"

"Never mind. I used to walk around with that look on my

33

face once, when I was your age. I think we'd better get moving. The stuffing's sitting out on the table getting cold."

Father Carnetti turned and started walking back toward the side door, his robe flapping around his legs. John stood watching him for a while and then followed. The only choice he had was dinner with the priest or those rooms his father had found them where there was going to be no dinner at all.

Besides, there was something else, something he couldn't pin down but something that made him feel good.

He was interested.

2   Interested. The buzzer on his intercom was going off like a third-rate smoke alarm. His cigarette had burned to cinders in the ashtray. Here he was, forty years old, an auxiliary bishop, vicar of the bishop of Bridgeport for New Haven. It wasn't the best he could have done. There was a vast field for ambition in the Church, a veritable Jacob's ladder of preference and preferment. He could have been assigned to a more important diocese or even sent to Rome. Still, considering who he was and where he'd come from—*what* he'd come from—he hadn't done badly. He could have been sent to South America or imprisoned in a boys' school in the bowels of the Bronx. Either of those things could happen to him yet. He was successful and he was safe. The safety was the important part. The Church wouldn't let you go bankrupt. The Church would always give you a home. He had to be losing his mind.

Sometimes he thought Marie was going to make him lose his mind. He'd told her a hundred times. Buzz once and then stop. Considering the noise that thing made, if he didn't answer he wasn't in the building.

He flipped the damn thing to talk and said, "Yes?"

"Mr. Murphy's here," Marie said. "I know you told me to send him right in, but I thought I ought to buzz."

"Send him right in," John Kelly said.

"I will. Now that I've buzzed."

"Marie—"

She flipped off with an angry little click. The office was silent.

Bishop John Kelly sighed and stood up. He rarely wore full clerical dress, but he was wearing it today. He'd always considered it good policy to meet movers and shakers in the costume of a prince of the Church. He wasn't a prince of the Church, not really, not yet, but all this time in the Jesuits had taught him the importance of image. Dan Murphy would have understood. He wasn't really a mover and shaker either, but when he came through Bishop John Kelly's door he looked like one.

He also looked a little amused. He had a Kevin McCarthy kind of face, what John thought of as "upper-class Irish," and it was pulled into a smirk.

"Well?" he said. "Have you thought it over?"

John Kelly sighed. He liked Dan Murphy, maybe because Murphy was a known quantity. He always knew what Murphy was going to say and do and want and think. Unlike someone like, say, Father Tom Burne.

He pushed thoughts of Tom Burne out of his mind—Burne was a bad subject for contemplation at any time—and said, "I've thought it over six or seven times. Are you sure this Cometti person doesn't have ties to the Mafia?"

"Coletti," Murphy said. "Victor Coletti. If Coletti had ties to the Mafia, I'd know about them. And I wouldn't know him."

"I suppose that's true."

"A district attorney has to be careful."

"You have to be careful, at any rate," John said. He thought of asking Dan if it were true that he wanted to run for governor some day, and decided against it. Dan would deny it, and he already knew the answer. He took the letter Dan had sent him off his desk and flattened it out against his hand.

"Let me get this straight," he said. "Tuesday and Thursday nights at seven thirty. On WNHY. Which is a network affiliate."

"Right," Dan said. "I told you it was going to be good exposure."

"It's impossible exposure. Seven thirty is when the affiliates make all their money off the game shows. I asked."

"Victor Coletti is a good Catholic layman," Dan said.

"If he's that good a Catholic layman, the Pope is a South American nun."

John Kelly sighed again and sat down.

All other considerations aside, there was the religious situation to consider. If he took this offer, he'd spend an hour a week explaining Catholic theology over the air. What would they do to him if he didn't get it right? The Bronx? Worse? He'd never been popular with his bishop. They were from different backgrounds and didn't get along. That's what he was doing in New Haven.

He was successful and he was safe. That should have been all that mattered to him. Unfortunately, the idea of this project kept making him high.

If he did it right, he could be the next Fulton J. Sheen.

Ambition.

He folded the letter and stuck it in his letter holder. He trusted Dan Murphy as much as he trusted anyone. Murphy had more to lose than he did. The Church might send renegade auxiliary bishops to the Bronx, but she didn't throw them out on the street.

"Look," he said, "let's be intelligent. Before I agree to this thing, let's you and me figure out what Victor Coletti wants."

CHAPTER
FIVE

1   For the longest time, the Congo was the only name he had
for it. It was only later he realized that it must have been
built for something better. It was a wide street, lined by tall buildings that had once been handsome, or at least imposing. In the
period before this present incarnation, it had been the place where
"good" black people lived. Now the quietly decorated apartments
of quietly industrious Baptists had been handed over to the con-
noisseurs of neon. The small stores that hung back from the curb
were called Silver Balls and Passion Pit. Every once in a while, two
or three of them had been knocked together to make a movie theater.
In the dark like this, with the lights flashing and the fuck meat
picking its way over the bodies of bums, it seemed impossible that
the Congo had ever been anything but what it was.

    He had a newspaper in the pocket of his new jacket, the one
he had boosted out of Macy's on the afternoon after the morning
he had killed Margaret Mary McVann. The jacket was long and
warm and stodgy. He knew better than to boost anything with
style—or to wear anything with style either, at least down here,
where style usually translated into the announcement of a drug deal
successfully completed. It was like the man said: this was not his
place and these were not his people. When he had a lot of luck,
they thought he was invisible. When he had less, they thought he
was harmless. He didn't want to know what would happen to him
on a day when he didn't have any luck at all.

    Harmless.

The street sign above his head was bent, tilted, and out of true. When the lights flashed the right way, he could just see the words CONGRESS AVENUE in black letters on a white background. They were filmed over by electric-blue paint.

He started walking into the light, up the street toward the Stick Up Theater and the crowds of girls who hung out in front of the laundromat. It was cold and he was colder. The knife was colder still. He had stuck it under his clothes, deep into his underwear, caught by the waistband of his jeans.

Every time he moved, it pricked him in the hip.

2 At the place where Congress Avenue intersected with Duval Street, he stopped. There was a street lamp there that was actually working, and a garbage can, and a little bump in the sidewalk where a newsstand had once been. The newsstand had disappeared around the time the Baptists did. The garbage can was empty, although the gutters around it were full of trash. He took the newspaper out of his pocket and dropped it neatly into the can. He was getting into dangerous territory here. Even the girls refused to go this far out.

He had been searching for something about Margaret Mary McVann for five days, but until today there had been nothing. It had made him very nervous. Margaret Mary had lived alone. She had had few friends. She had talked to nobody at all in the building where she lived. Even so, she hadn't been a hermit. There were the people at the soup kitchen where she worked and the people at the church. Somebody should have noticed she was gone. He kept thinking of her lying in the living room like that, her neck bent too far to one side, the cold streaming in from the broken window at the back. He kept thinking about the rosary on her coffee table, too, and how hard it had been to find it. He had to steal the rosaries from the Daughters of Saint Paul bookshop, one by one. The two things seemed linked together somehow, or maybe not. It had gotten to the point where the only thing he was absolutely sure of was his charism.

A charism was a gift of the Holy Spirit. Someone with charisma was filled with the Holy Spirit: he glowed with an inner light. That was why they liked to use the word for politicians. They mistook a talent for television for the Spirit. They mistook ambition for a righteous fire.

He had meant to leave the newspaper folded open to the story about Margaret Mary McVann, a small square of story on page three, without a picture. Instead, he'd dumped the paper into the can with the front page facing out. There was another picture of Billy Hare on that page, and a bigger one of the district attorney. The boy had been dead for twenty-four hours. Attention was beginning to shift to the living.

And the interesting.

He started to reach into the can to rearrange the paper and stopped himself. One thing he never wanted was to be caught rooting around in a garbage can. It was a line you crossed that you could never cross back again.

He crossed the Congo instead, and walked into the blackness of Duval Street.

3 Like many of the streets off the Congo, Duval was deserted. The process that had only started farther down the avenue was completed here. Windows gaped, clear of panes. Here and there an entire wall had fallen in, as if demolition had been begun and then abandoned. To someone who knew nothing about places like this, it would have sounded as silent as a void.

Since he was very familiar with places like this, he could hear what there was to hear. The buildings were full of people, junkies on the run from rehabilitation. If he'd gone through any of the doorways, he would have found a litter of broken needles and bent spoons and crack vials. He would have found bodies, too. When junkies started dying of AIDS, they did one of two things. They either got themselves to a hospital and got religion, or they got themselves to a dealer for one last rush. The ones who wanted to rush curled themselves into hall closets or the corners of staircase landings and pumped themselves into convulsions.

He passed a building that sighed like Spanish moss in the breeze and turned down yet another street, a worse one, called Amora. At the end of Amora there was a building with all its doors and windows intact and lights on in every room. Glowing alone in the gathering night, it looked like a fairy castle or a prison. At one time or another, he had thought it was both.

It was called Damien House. Once, years ago, he had known it well.

4   The first time he had gone to Damien House, he had gone to the front door. There was a sign there and a bell to push. It had seemed like the right approach. Now he went around to the back. There was a little garden there with a wrought-iron gate and a door that led to the kitchen. He let himself through the gate and stood on the kitchen steps.

It was only six o'clock in the evening, only December 6, but it was already full dark. It was darker than it might have been because of the clouds that covered the sky. The bad weather they'd been having all week was set to continue. There was a smell of snow in the air. There was a bite, too, just to let him know something was coming.

All the buildings for blocks around were deserted. The only light came from the bulb above his head, screwed into the outer wall above the kitchen door and protected by a net of plastic-covered wire. He thought about using his key and decided against it. He could hear her moving around in the kitchen, moving slowly as she always did when she didn't have much to do. It was Friday night. Most of the rest of them would have had their dinner at a pizza parlor up on Chapel Street and gone on to Saint Bartholomew's for a dance.

Father Tom would be in his office on the third floor, worrying about money or the latest letter from the bishop.

He took off the fuzzy woolen gloves he'd been wearing and knocked on the kitchen door.

5 Her name was Theresa Jane Cavello. When he first met her, she'd been a Franciscan nun. In those days she wore a little veil on her head that barely reached the bottom of her short hair and a big silver cross around her neck and cheap dresses of brown and navy blue and black. She still wore the dresses—this one was a dull matte gray—but the rest of the costume was gone. Two years ago, she had left her order and returned to ordinary life.

Now that she had made the change, he found it hard to understand what change she'd made. It was odd how the demonic could mimic the sanctified. She still worked at the same place, doing the same things, seeing the same people. For awhile, he'd thought there had to be a man. Then the man had failed to materialize, and he'd decided she was too old. She was forty-one.

She came to the door and looked out its window, tense. The window was a web of barbed wire pressed between two panes of glass, but the glass was not bulletproof. God only knew what she was going to find out here. Then she saw him and her face relaxed. He stood in the cold listening to her unbolting all six of the locks, one after the other.

"You," she said, swinging the door open.

"Me."

She stepped away, letting him come in. "Is it asking too much to think you've come to stay?"

"Much too much."

"I was afraid of that." She closed the door behind him and started locking up again. "Father Tom's upstairs. You could go up and say hello."

"You know I don't want to see Father Tom."

"Oh, I know."

The kitchen door opened on a small vestibule. She walked through it into the kitchen proper and turned the burner on under the kettle. She always kept the kettle full and ready, in case of emergencies.

"Father Tom was talking about you just last week," she said. "He worries about you, you know. Whether you believe it or not.

Especially when you disappear for six months and nobody's seen or heard of you."

"I've been all right."

"I can't believe that."

"It's true."

"You look all right, but I know what it's like out there. We all do. Are you at least going to let me make you dinner?"

"If you want."

"I want. The gang had dinner out but I've got pot roast left over from yesterday. Why don't you sit down and take off your coat?"

"I want to give you something first."

She had been standing at the refrigerator door, looking through the food, her back to him. Now she turned around, curious and a little wary. So many of the things people wanted to give her these days were stolen. She'd gotten out of the habit of looking on gifts as unalloyed joy.

He reached into his pocket and pulled out the rosary—which was not stolen, but might as well have been. Its amber beads looked even more amber in the yellow light from the overhead lamp.

Theresa blinked and said, "Oh. It's lovely. It's really lovely."

"You don't think it was stupid, bringing a rosary to a nun?"

"No. Of course not. I'm not a nun anymore."

"I know," he said.

6 This was his charism, the light that illuminated his life. He felt it as heat. He felt the kitchen as heat, too, with hot air pumping through its radiators and bright blue-based flames flickering up around the kettle. There was a large magnetic cross tacked on to the old-fashioned refrigerator door: Father Tom's doing. There was a picture of Our Lady of Fatima on the breadbox: Theresa's. He still thought of her as Sister, but he was trying not to.

She had sat down at the kitchen table. She was fingering the rosary, running it through her hands, looking at each and every bead. It was as if she'd never seen a rosary before. The heat was suddenly more than he could bear, a fire. It licked up from the pale green squares of linoleum on the floor and ran across the soles of his feet.

He thought of Sister Mary Mathilde and the book she had carried under her arm. He had tried and tried to see the title of it, but the spine was always wrong way round. She disappeared down hallways with her veil flapping across her back, hiding it. He wondered what she had thought of him when he had finally gone out of her life.

7 Theresa got out of her chair and went back across the room, back to the refrigerator. She was holding the rosary balled up in her right hand, her middle finger threaded through it. She was a small, compact woman with the muscular thighs of a field hockey player. She moved as if she expected a puck to smash into her knees at any moment.

Without the veil, her gray wiry hair was tangled and dry. She ran her hands through it and said, "I wish you'd come back. Everybody wishes you'd come back. We talk about you all the time."

"I can't come back."

"Anyone can come back. Especially you. We're so short-handed and you were always so good about things."

"I made a mess of everything I touched. You remember."

"I remember the time you fixed the boiler. Minus twenty degrees with the wind chill and we had no heat."

"You needed a new boiler."

"We still haven't got one."

"Then you need a new mechanic."

"You're not a mechanic. You're just—talented."

"Is that what it is?"

"You weren't taught to do those things. You just knew."

"I just used common sense. Anybody would have known if they'd used common sense. You people just don't have any."

Theresa laughed. "They breed it out of us in convents and seminaries. It's the first principle of religious formation."

Is that why she had left her order, because they hadn't let her use her common sense?

He watched her turn away from him, pivoting on a single heel.

8 This was his charism, the light that made him what he had not started out to be. When it was in him, he could come down to the Congo without fear. He could walk anywhere in the envelope of its protection.

He listened to the wind rising outside, beginning to batter at the windows and rattle the door. It reminded him of the wind Moses had heard when he first knew the voice of God.

9 When Theresa finally had her back to him, he took out the knife.

PART ONE

CHAPTER

ONE

1 One week and one day after Susan Murphy came home, on Tuesday, December 10, there was a story about her brother Dan in the New Haven *Register*. In a way, there had been stories about Dan in the *Register* ever since she left the convent. The Billy Hare investigation was a media event. It had made the local news on all three network affiliates and both cable channels. The *Register* had run with it because it had the advantage of being able to print what television was afraid to show: pictures of a child dead and bloody in the snow; fragments of bone and a face made into marble by the cold of a morgue. This story was different because it was about Dan himself instead of Dan-as-spur-in-the-behinds-of-a-compliant-police-department. From the headings, she could tell the *Register* was trying to establish Dan as a champion of child protection. It made a lot of references to the Domeneck case.

The story was on page one of the living section, and the living section had been left lying face out on the kitchen table. Susan paused to look at a picture of Dan that must have been taken at his law-school graduation—Yale, of course, because he wanted to go into politics and needed to show some loyalty to the state of Connecticut to do it—and then drifted across the kitchen in search of the tea kettle. The kitchen was cold, but that didn't bother her. This kitchen was always cold. Like a lot of kitchens in a lot of houses on Edge Hill Road, it was a vast place designed to allow half a dozen servants to work at once. The stove, the refrigerator, and the sink each commanded their own room-size corners. The fourth corner was free of cabinets and held a heavy round oakwood table, large enough to seat ten. The nineteenth century had never heard of the thirteen-foot work triangle.

Outside, it was cold and dark, only six o'clock in the morning. Through the windows over the sink, she could see the trees that ran in two neat rows on either side of their lawn, leaving the center clear. The trees were covered with snow that seemed to have congealed on them. It was the worst weather she could remember in this part of the country at this time of year, and it both depressed and annoyed her. The depression was simple: she had always imagined herself coming home in the spring, as if the freedom she would feel on leaving the constraints of convent life would be reflected in the weather. The annoyance was harder to figure. It had something to do with the fact that constant onslaughts of snow and ice made her feel trapped.

She found the kettle behind a pile of bread pans Andy had used to make Anadama loaf, filled it at the tap, and put it on to boil. She had come downstairs without shoes—jeans and a turtleneck, kneesocks and one of Andy's plaid flannel shirts, but no shoes—and as she stood at the cupboard next to the stove it began to bother her. She had a lot of reflexes left over from seventeen years at Saint Michael's and places like it. She got up at five no matter when she went to bed, and she was on her feet and halfway through the Litany of the Holy Names of Jesus before she knew what she was doing. Worse, she found it almost impossible to talk at meals. It had been so long since she was allowed to, she'd forgotten how. Lately, Dan and Andy had been looking at her as if she were diseased—brain damaged, maybe, the way people got on too much booze and dope. Well, it wouldn't be the first time someone in this house had been brain damaged as the result of an addiction, although she didn't think she was. Religion wasn't that kind of an addiction.

(*Right.*)

She got out a cup, a saucer, a spoon, a tea ball, and the tea.

The tea was an expensive blend, ordered from Fortnum and Mason in London. The spoon was from her mother's second-best set of silver. The cup and saucer looked like they'd been picked up on sale in Sears.

She stuffed the tea ball full of tea and threw it in the yellow teapot she'd unearthed her first night home. Then the kitchen door swung open, and she turned around to find herself face to face with Dan.

"Good grief," she said. "You look like the man in the Arrow Shirt ad."

Dan flicked a finger at the lapel of his suit, which was gray and lightweight wool, as if he were setting out for the office in summer. All his suits were like that. He had them made to order at J. Press.

"I've got a press conference at nine," he said. "Did you see the paper? I left it out for you."

"I saw it. I haven't read it yet." Actually, she had no intention of reading it. The idea of a child murdered turned her stomach. The fact that it had happened right down there, at the bottom of this street, made it worse. Edge Hill Road was always full of children. They were one of the things the neighborhood specialized in, like Chanel suits and Bentleys.

The idea of Dan making his career out of this kind of thing revolted her even more, but she wasn't going to tell him that. She didn't think he'd have the faintest idea what she was talking about.

"I really just got up," she said. "I mean, I've been awake but I just got down. The two of you moved everything while I was away."

"The cleaning lady moved it. She doesn't think. She just puts things away the first place she finds room for them."

"Whatever." The kettle was whistling. Susan got up to take it off. "I just feel like I'm stumbling through an obstacle course around here sometimes. I'll get used to it."

Dan dropped into one of the kitchen chairs and picked up

the paper. His face creased, running little lines like fleshy shelves across his forehead. "All this publicity and it's going to go to waste," he said. "It's a shame, isn't it?"

"Why will it go to waste?"

"Because in about three days it's going to disappear," Dan said. "The media are going to figure out what's happening and then it won't be happening. As far as they're concerned, anyway."

"I don't understand." Susan brought the teapot to the table and set it down. "Why wouldn't they go on with it? They've made such a fuss about it already. It seems like just their kind of thing."

Dan gave her a funny look, funny-cynical. It was an expression of his she especially disliked. "They think the kid's a kid," he said.

"What's that supposed to mean?"

"It means they think they've got a nice little ordinary nine-year-old with a bullet in the back of his head. What they've really got is a hooker."

Susan blinked. "A hooker? Do you mean a prostitute?"

"Of course."

"That nine-year-old child was a prostitute?"

"Of course."

"Don't just keep saying 'of course,'" Susan said. "How could a nine-year-old boy be a prostitute? Who would he prostitute himself to?"

"Men." Dan folded the paper and slapped it back onto the table. "You really have been in a convent. Billy Hare prostituted himself to men, to pederasts. He'd been doing it since he was six or seven years old. His parents were a pair of prize junkies. They managed to bring him into the world clean. He was their asset. One day they probably got tapped out completely and sold him off."

"Oh, sweet Jesus Christ," Susan said.

She felt as if she'd just inhaled a lungful of natural gas, but Dan was going on, pouring himself a cup of tea from her pot, reaching for the sugar bowl at the center of the table. She didn't remember him getting up to get the cup, but he must have. She couldn't understand why he didn't sound upset. It was as if he dealt with this sort of thing every day.

"That's why the media are going to lose interest," he was saying. "Murder in the middle class is news. Murder in the under-class is invisible. Especially if it's politically sensitive."

"'Politically sensitive.'"

"I don't mean the governor's running a meat shop," Dan said patiently. "I mean the whole thing gets into areas the press doesn't want to deal with. You ever hear of a man named Father Thomas Burne?"

Father Thomas Burne. The name rolled around in Susan's head and finally poked a hole through the fog it was in. She had heard of Father Thomas Burne.

"I think we used to get brochures for his place at Saint Mi-chael's," she said. "Requests for money and food. Damien House. A place for runaway children."

"What they're mostly running away from is pimps."

"Are you sure?"

"Yes, Susan, I'm sure. And I personally think Tom Burne is a saint. The problem is, every time they give him air time he starts talking about pornography, and every time he starts talking about pornography he starts talking about censorship. And that—"

"What does censorship have to do with turning children into prostitutes?"

Dan smiled. "Go down to Congress Avenue and take a look at the pornography he's talking about."

"Pornography about children."

"Of course."

"Is that legal?"

"Probably not. The legality of it isn't the problem here. The existence of it is the problem here."

"I don't understand."

"No," Dan said, "I don't suppose you do."

"What about all those investigative reporters I've heard about? Wouldn't they be interested?"

"I don't know that either, Susan. They haven't been so far. And Tom Burne has certainly tried. Hard."

"Obviously not hard enough."

"As hard as anyone could. Look, I'm sorry. All right? I keep forgetting how long you've been away and what kind of an environment you've been in. I didn't mean to upset you."

"I don't care if you *upset* me." Actually, she wasn't upset anymore. The fog was gone, and so was her nausea. In their place was a hard little clicking computer, making calculations.

She looked into the clear brown water of her tea. It was getting cold. She ought to drink it. She just wished she could remember pouring it.

"This Damien House," she said, "is it here in New Haven?"

"Off Congress Avenue on Amora Street."

"Do you know if Father Burne is a diocesan priest or from an order?"

"No." Dan was amused. "Does that matter?"

"It might."

"I'll find out for you if you want to know." He got out of his chair and stretched. "Just do me a favor, if you don't mind. Don't go wandering down to Amora without a police escort. One of Burne's people was murdered in the kitchen down there less than a week ago. That didn't make much splash either. Maybe the press doesn't like the feel of Father Tom Burne."

"Where are you going?"

"To the office. It may be seven o'clock in the morning, but I do want to be out of the district attorney's office one of these days. That takes work." He straightened his suit jacket and tucked his shirt a little more neatly under his belt. "Do me a bigger favor," he said. "There are a pile of invitations cluttering up the mantel in the living room, all of them for you. Answer a couple of them in the affirmative."

"It's a lot earlier than seven o'clock in the morning."

He made a face at her. "There's a dinner party at the Hanrahans' next Friday night at eight. Go out to Lord and Taylor or one of those places and buy yourself a dress. Katie Hanrahan thinks you've spent the last seventeen years growing mustaches and a butt."

"Have I?"

"You look like Mother, Susan. You always did."

He turned around and walked out through the kitchen's swinging door, letting it swing back after him, like a wave.

Susan finished her tea, poured herself another cup, then went searching around in the breast pocket of Andy's shirt for her cigarettes. She lit one and coughed. She wasn't sure why she was smoking again. Cigarettes tasted terrible and they made her chest ache. Maybe it was some kind of reaction to leaving the convent.

After a while, her cigarette grew a long column of ash and she had to get up. The ashtray was tucked away in the cupboard with the teacups and the bowls.

2   Andy didn't wake until quarter to ten. When he came down, she was waiting for him, not in the kitchen but in the foyer. He had to pass through that after he came down the stairs. She had exchanged his flannel shirt for a plain green sweater. It had been hard to find. Most of the sweaters in the drawers of the cedar chests upstairs were either her own from her days at boarding school—and therefore too small—or her mother's. Her mother's looked much too rich. She might be going crazy, but she wasn't going stupid yet.

Andy stopped at the bottom of the stairs when he saw her and raised his eyebrows. He was good at it, and Susan laughed. He had always been her favorite brother. Unlike Dan, he was short and stocky and powerful, a throwback to ancestors who had come over on the boat and never expected to have any money. And he was fun. Dan was always so serious all the time, so driven. He would go to the Hanrahans' dinner party, but that was probably because Dec Hanrahan was a power in the Democratic State Committee. He would buy her a beautiful dress, but only so that she could look good for a purpose. Andy was a float.

Andy crossed the foyer to her, an oversize leprechaun under the shower of rainbows sent out by the prisms on the chandelier.

"What's the matter? Has the Catholic representative of the Puritan Ethic made you so crazy you want to go back to the convent already?"

Susan laughed. "He left at six forty-five. He had a press conference at nine."

"That's our Danny. Two hours to rehearse the six words it takes to make a sound byte."

"Maybe you ought to take some time to rehearse something. Don't you ever do anything, Andy?"

"No. And I don't intend to. You want to do something, though."

"You're right, I do."

"If it requires physical labor, I won't help."

Susan had been sitting on a loveseat, the only piece of furniture in the foyer. She stood up and started walking around the checkerboard marble floor. "Do you ever think about it? About Mother and Daddy and everything that happened?"

"No," Andy said. "You shouldn't think about it, either."

"I know. I don't, usually. Something Dan told me this morning got my mind on it."

"Well," Andy said, "that makes Dan a jerk, but we always knew he was a jerk. You don't have to be a jerk along with him."

"Maybe I can't help myself. I told Reverend Mother all about it when I was, I don't know. A novice. A canonical novice? A senior novice? I don't remember. I thought I'd tell her and then she'd kick me out."

"She didn't, though."

"No," Susan said. "I should have known better. I'm sorry. I know I'm acting morbid. And I want a favor from you, too."

"What kind of favor?"

"I want to go downtown. I want you to come with me."

Now it was Andy who was sitting on the loveseat. He always claimed he was indolent. He didn't like standing up for long. "If you want to go buying dresses," he said, "I don't want to come. The last time I did that with a woman, I ruined a beautiful relationship."

"I don't want to buy dresses."

"What do you want to do?"

"I want to go down to this place off Congress Avenue. It's called Damien House."

Andy tilted his head back and stared up, at the chandelier, at the domed ceiling beyond it. His body had gone very still.

"Does Dan know you want to do this?"

"He probably suspects."

"He probably told you not to go."

"I'm thirty-five years old, Andy. I'm not a baby."

"You're not a baby, but this is a bad idea. A very bad idea. You don't know the half of what you're getting yourself into. They had a murder there last Friday night."

"Does that mean you won't take me?"

Andy sighed. His head was at a normal angle again. His arms were wrapped around his chest. Susan thought he looked infinitely tired, as if he'd taken a sleeping pill when she wasn't looking and it had just started to hit him.

"Oh, I'll take you all right," he said. "But I want you to know up front I think you're crazy."

CHAPTER

Two

1 Susan had driven to New Haven from Saint Michael's. She could remember it in detail, mostly because she had been so terrified. Nuns in traditional orders weren't handed car keys as a matter of course. There were designated drivers and designated riders. Susan had always been one of the latter. Getting into a car again, bumping along beside the Housatonic River on the Derby Road, had been the second most frightening thing Susan had ever done. She'd thought the particulars of that trip had been burned into her brain: the shacks that had once been summer cottages now lying in ruin next to the water; the patches of ice in front of every stoplight along the new six-lane stretch between Derby and New Haven proper; the car dealerships that cluttered the intersection at the turn-off to Orange and promised Mazdas and BMWs for practically no money at all. Searching her memories of that trip, she came up with a picture so complete it was almost documentary footage.

Sitting in the bus next to Andy, she realized she didn't really remember anything. She'd been so wrapped up in her fear, she'd barely taken anything in. The people around her, on the bus and at the curbs where the bus stopped, were so alien they made her dizzy. Most of them were black. A fair proportion of the rest were Hispanic. What few whites there were were all men and all what her mother would have called muscle-headed Irish, or some other ethnic culture's version of the same: big, fat, ham-handed, rough, and obsessively reading the numbers on their lottery tickets. Among these people, she felt like Tinkerbell. Worse. She felt like a fraud. The clothes Andy had made her change into—all of them worn and all of them pulled from the junk closet in the service hall—made her feel as if she were wearing a sign on her forehead that said SLUMMING.

"We can't take my car," he'd told her, back at the house. "It's a Porsche and it's practically brand new. It'd get ripped off with us in it before we got halfway to where we were going."

Now he sat with his legs stretched out across the aisle, just a little too broad for the plastic seat he was sitting in. If it hadn't been for the intelligence in his face, he would have looked like all the other white men here. Susan thought the white men might not notice the difference. They weren't staring.

"We're going to have to make a transfer," Andy was saying, "and then when we get to Congress Avenue we're going to have to get out and walk. That's what I'm worried about."

"There isn't a bus that goes to Amora Street?"

"There isn't anything that goes to Amora Street. Except for Damien House, there isn't anything on Amora Street. The place was abandoned years ago. It looks like those pictures you see of the South Bronx."

"Oh."

Andy shook his head. He'd already told her he wouldn't have come with her at all if she hadn't "still looked so much like a nun." Whatever that meant. Susan supposed he was thinking now that she still thought like a nun. She pressed her great mass of black hair more firmly into her combs and twisted until she could see out the window behind her. The view was dislocating. There was Yale: a medieval landscape of turrets and lawns. Then there were the bums. A little colony of them had set up a cardboard housing project under cover of a stand of leafless trees on a street off Prospect. Every one of them had his own brown bottle and his own paper bag.

Susan turned back. "I don't know," she said. "It's not the New Haven I remember."

"It hasn't been the New Haven you remember for ten years."

"I guess not. I'm surprised you and Dan haven't sold the house."

"We can't sell the house," Andy said.

Susan flushed. "The Hanrahans could have sold theirs, and they haven't. Dec is living where he grew up. I saw the address on that invitation Dan is so crazy about. Why haven't they moved to the suburbs like everyone else?"

"Maybe Edge Hill Road is a special case."

"Why? We had a murder at the bottom of it the day after I got home."

"Is that what you want to talk about? Murders? If I'd wanted to talk about murders, I could have gone into the D.A.'s office and had a chat with Dan's secretary. She's got a running file in her head of every death in the city of New Haven back to 1962. She's especially fond of murders."

Susan turned away again. This time, the window behind her looked out on the passing of small, neat streets of two-story houses. The houses were old and painted strange pastel colors, but they were reasonably well kept up. She turned back again and folded her arms across her chest.

"I don't understand you," she said. "I don't understand either of you. How can you live together in that house?"

"It's convenient and it's cheap."

"A lot of things are convenient and cheap. What do you two do when I'm not around? Fight?"

"I haven't had a fight with Dan since Mother died."

"Mother or Daddy?"

Andy didn't look at her. The bus was pulling up to the curb. They were at the Green, and the Green was where half the people in the city changed directions. Andy stood up and zipped his jacket shut.

"This is where we get off," he said. "We've got to hurry. If we miss our connection, we get stuck in the cold for half an hour."

But Andy wasn't really hurrying, so Susan didn't hurry either.

She just wrapped her scarf more tightly around her neck and thought: We're going to have to talk about this sometime. I haven't had seventeen years to get it out of my system. I haven't had seventeen years to make myself forget.

Of course, she should have had. That was what she'd gone into the convent for, something she hadn't realized until much too late. But going into the convent hadn't worked, and coming home hadn't worked so far either. She still found herself tripping over it all at the most unlikely times, like now. She'd have her mind on something else and it would sneak up behind her, just to kick her in the rear. She was surprised she hadn't started imagining things, like ghosts rattling chains through the hallways of the house on Edge Hill Road. Ghosts would have been appropriate in more ways than one.

Maybe she was a ghost of a kind herself.

When the bus stopped, it skidded into the curb and cut off abruptly. Andy fell halfway over, saving himself from landing on the floor only by keeping both hands wrapped around a metal pole. Susan didn't, only because she hadn't yet stood up. Seconds later, she was not only standing but running, chasing Andy down the ridged metal steps into the wet and slithering wind.

The Green would have been beautiful in the snow, except that its benches were covered with bums.

2 There were no bums on Congress Avenue. Like Edge Hill Road, its sidewalks were clear of all but businesslike traffic. Unlike Edge Hill Road, on Congress Avenue there was a lot of it. Susan saw a line of girls standing under the chipped blue paint on a plate-glass window that said WASHCENTER, a man changing a movie marquee from SOMETHING-PASSION to HOT-GIRLS-SOMETHING-ELSE, another man laying out watches on an orange crate covered with a piece of turquoise felt. It was early. Congress Avenue didn't really get moving until after dark. Even so, the girls were wearing skirts that barely reached the tops of their thighs and fishnet stockings that revealed more skin than they covered. Susan

thought they had to be freezing. She also thought they had to be fourteen.

Andy tugged on her arm. "You can't stand around and sight-see, for Christ's sake. You'll get them nervous. Either that, or they'll think you're buying."

"Do I look like someone who's buying?"

"Why not?"

Susan let him pull her along. There might be a point to that "why not." She'd never been in a place like this. There were orders that sent their sisters to work among the poor in red-light districts, but hers hadn't been one of them. She'd done her time at the Motherhouse and in parish schools. Oddly enough, though, this place bothered her less than the Green had. She liked the rhythm of it. There was music blasting out of a window somewhere, a big radio turned up loud and pushed against a thin pane of glass. She didn't recognize the song, but the backbeat was eternal. It reminded her of the Chuck Berry records they'd played in their rooms at Sacred Heart when the madames were all safely tucked in bed.

"It doesn't look anything like those pictures of the South Bronx," she said. "It looks—happy."

"Anything would look happy on three vials of crack a day. A rock would look happy. That's why people take crack."

"I thought you could tell when people were on dope. None of these people look like they're on anything."

"Maybe they're not, at the moment. Will you come on? If you keep this up, we're going to get mugged."

"I know why people come down here," she said. "If I was stuck in New Haven and I didn't have anyplace to go, I'd come down here too. It would be better than staying in the middle of town."

Andy stopped. He had to. Susan had stopped already. They were standing in front of a movie theater called the Snake Charmer. A poster in a frame beside the ticket booth showed a woman in stockings and garters and no underwear, her legs spread wide. She was holding her ass in the air with hands tipped by sequined fingernails. Her face rose in the background, not quite clearing the knobby mountains that were her knees. Susan stepped closer and read the teaser line, half-obscured by a wash of mud at the bottom of the frame.

"'They can't get enough and they like their men rough,'" she said. "Wonderful."

"Wonderful?"

"I was being sarcastic, Andy."

"You were getting suckered." He took her arm again. "You can't walk around this place and look at these people as if you were walking through a zoo. They won't like it. And they're not stable."

"I'm not looking at these people as if they were in a zoo. I like it here."

"You like the exoticness of it."

"That's not true." It wasn't, either. Andy had dragged her along a little farther. They were standing in front of a shop door covered by a hinged iron gate. The gate had been pushed open a little and the glass door beyond it propped back. Susan came to a stop again, to watch a frazzled old woman push a rack of Indian print shirts out onto the sidewalk.

Andy was getting angry. Susan knew that. She was going to have to say something, but she didn't know what. She didn't know Andy very well anymore. She didn't know anyone. She'd gotten out of the habit of talking about herself. That was one thing nuns were never allowed to do. They were supposed to take the lives they'd lived in the world and lay them down on Christ's altar, to burn them as sacrifices in the fire of religious meditation. God only knew she'd never been able to do that, but she had learned to fake it very well. Her self was in a box somewhere, buried out of sight.

She started moving on her own this time, but slowly, so she could take it all in. She did like it here. In fact, she loved it. It was like a heart that never stopped beating, but pumped up, fast—a runner's heart hitting its stride in a marathon. The music had changed into something that really wasn't music at all, just a voice talking in endlessly relentless meter and a background of percussion sticks. A bookstore was opening across the street. A young man with a cigarette hanging out of the corner of his mouth and a black leather jacket torn at the shoulder seams was dragging a stand-up board onto the sidewalk. When he got it where he wanted it, he took out a handkerchief and tried to wipe it off.

"Ever since I got here," she said, "not just since I got home, but ever since I got back to New Haven—the whole place has seemed dead. At first, I thought it was just the house. I wasn't even surprised. I kept asking myself what else I could possibly expect. I mean—"

"You mean nothing." Andy had his arm braided around hers now. He was doing more than just pulling her along. She resented the hell out of it. "The house is not dead. The house isn't anything. You're making all this up."

"No, I'm not. But when we got to the Green today, I changed my mind. It isn't just the house. It's the whole city. It's as if sometime while I was away the place lay down and turned over and decided to sleep its way to the grave. It just decided to give up and check out."

"This is where people give up and check out," Andy said. "This is Suicide Hill."

"Don't *pull* me."

Andy stopped instead. In anger, he looked like their father. His face got as red as if he'd drunk a quart of vodka in the last half hour, straight.

"I'll tell you what they didn't do for you in that convent," he said. "They didn't make you grow up."

"Which means what?"

"Which means they sell people down here, Susan. This place is a fucking slave market. Come six o'clock there are girls on this street not fifteen years old who'll blow you off for a ten-dollar bill and let you cram your prick up their asses for forty. They don't do it out of a dedication to black-market capitalism. They do it because if they don't their pimps will cut them up."

"And there are the boys," Susan said.

"Yeah," Andy said. "There are the boys. Most of them are only ten."

"Let me tell you what they don't do," Susan said. "They don't buy a bottle and sit down and let themselves go. They don't pickle themselves into insensibility and call it relaxation. They don't—"

"They do. They just don't use booze."

"Like Daddy," Susan said.

Andy blew a stream of white breath into her face. "Jesus Christ," he said. "I should have known. All the way back at the house, I should have known you've got to talk about Daddy."

"No, you shouldn't have. I didn't know it myself."

"Yes, you did."

He turned his back to her and started walking up the street, away from the bus stop, away from the Indian print shirts and the bookstore with its stand-up board and the movie marquee that now read HOT GIRLS, HOT CITY. Susan stood where she was for a moment and wondered what she was supposed to do, as if she had a choice. Then she followed him. After a while, she even picked up speed. She knew there were people watching her, faces behind curtains at the windows of apartments on the upper stories of the buildings across the street, but she couldn't make herself feel afraid.

When she reached Andy she took his arm and said, "It's just that back there on the Green everything seemed hopeless. Nothing seems hopeless here at all."

"I'll show you hopeless," Andy said. "Hell, I'll show it to you like you've never seen it before."

3 Later, she had to admit he'd been right. It got bad, and not long after it got worse. First the stores and theaters and laundromats petered out. Then everything did. It was eerie, like walking through an abandoned movie set. The buildings were all there, intact and solid, but there wasn't anyone in them. There

wasn't anyone anywhere. The weather was clearing. The wind had pushed back the clouds and the sun was shining through. It illuminated nothing.

They turned onto Amora Street, and the landscape changed again. The buildings were no longer intact. Whole walls had collapsed into vacant lots. There wasn't a pane of glass in a window anywhere. Even so, Susan could tell the street was inhabited. There was laughter everywhere, high hysterical laughter bubbling up out of the ground, floating into the wind, sounding insane. Sounding insane and homicidal.

She stopped in the middle of the street, finally scared to death, wanting nothing except to go back.

"I have to get out of here," she said.

Andy tugged at her arm. Again. "Look up there."

She looked. Two blocks away there was a building with a sign in front of it, a plastic cross lit from the inside by fluorescent bulbs. Under the cross a smaller sign spelled it out in heavy black letters:

DAMIEN HOUSE.

Andy tugged at her arm one final time and said, "If we're going to get there, we've got to go."

CHAPTER

THREE

1 The boy who answered the door at Damien House was tall
and thin and wrapped in uncertainty. He couldn't have been
more than twelve years old. For a while, Susan thought there had
to be something wrong with him, that he was retarded or a deaf-
mute. She and Andy were standing in the cold on the stoop. The
boy was standing in the doorway, blocking their path in. He seemed
to be staring at Andy, but he might have been staring into space.
It was impossible to tell. He wasn't saying anything.

Susan heard the sound of heavy walking coming out to her
from deep within the house, and a moment later the boy stepped
back—proving at least that he was not deaf. The space he'd left at
the door was filled with the body of a thickset woman with gray
hair and patched black plastic glasses. Her face was set into a mask
of distrust she seemed to have to work at to maintain. It held for
Susan, but it slipped a little when she first saw Andy. Then it
dissolved altogether. A smile like melting butter spread across her
face.

"Andy *Murphy*," she said. "Good Lord. Mark, what's the
matter with you. You know Andy Murphy. He was here the last
time you were here."

"I know Andy Murphy," the boy said. Still, he hung on to
his place at the door. It was only when the woman nudged him
that he moved back.

"I think Mark must be a little tired," the woman said. She
propped back the door and shooed them in. "Lord only knows,

we're all tired around here these days. After what happened to Sister Theresa, we can't sleep nights. Sister Theresa. Listen to me." She turned back to the boy. "Go get Father Tom, Mark. Or go get someone to get Father Tom. He's going to want to see Andy."

"Right," Mark said.

"Right is right," the woman said. "If you don't want to go upstairs yourself, you can get Kirsten to go. She's in the library."

"Right," Mark said again. Susan thought he was going to move right away. His body seemed to shift into flight mode, to become fluid. Instead, he stood his ground, giving her a long look and Andy a longer one. It was only when the situation became completely uncomfortable that he made his escape.

The woman with the gray hair stared after him, watching him disappear under a staircase at the back of the hall. They were standing in a small foyer, long and narrow, with the front door at one end and a collection of other doors—metal, by the look of them—at the other. The front door was metal, too, and bordered by thick metal panels painted to imitate mosaics. The only light came from an old-fashioned frosted fixture on the ceiling above their heads. It was, however, a very bright light. It lit up the foyer like an interrogation room.

The woman started locking the front-door locks, shooting in one dead bolt after another, mechanically. "It was because of Theresa Mark came back," she said. "The word's out all over the street. Business has been terrible. They know what it's like when things like this happen. They know the police are going to be in and out of the house for weeks. So they don't come, of course, but Mark—"

Andy cut in. "Francesca, this is my sister Susan. I don't think you've ever met."

Francesca stopped in the middle of throwing the last bolt and flushed. It was a bright, painful, adolescent flush, and Susan suddenly felt sorry for her. She had known women like this in the convent, women who had never quite gotten over the awkward confusion of puberty, who still didn't know what to do or what to say or where to put their hands and feet. Francesca covered it by securing that last bolt and wiping the palms of her hands on the skirt of her gray flannel dress.

"I'm sorry," she said. "I've just been babbling along, and I haven't even said hello."

"That's all right," Susan said.

"It really has been very hectic around here." She stopped wiping her palms and looked directly at them, more relaxed now. The hump had been gotten over. She was on familiar ground. She gave Andy another big smile. "And I was so surprised to see your brother," she said. "The last I remember, he was threatening never to darken our doors again."

"Well," Andy said. "That was a long time ago."

"A long time we haven't seen you in. Did you come because of Theresa? Pat Mallory's here, you know, up with Father Tom. He's taking an interest."

"He would," Andy said.

"Who's Pat Mallory?" Susan said.

Francesca sighed. "He's the chief of Homicide for the New Haven Police Department. And he means well. We all know he does. But when we have police in the house the children are afraid to come, and the children are the point."

"Better him than whoever killed Terry," Andy said.

Francesca shrugged. "We all know who killed Terry. Some poor child on crack. She was in the kitchen by herself and she let him in and that was that. Father Tom was in the study when it happened and now he's having a nervous breakdown. She should have known better not to let in someone she didn't know on her own."

"Tsk, tsk," Andy said. "Aren't you blaming the victim?"

Francesca shook her head. Then she went to a door Susan hadn't noticed before and opened it.

"Maybe you ought to wait in here," she said. "Mark came back because of Theresa, but he's very skittish about being here. He doesn't want to talk to anyone and I don't think he's going to stay. I think I'd better go up and get Father Tom myself."

2 The room Francesca showed them into was small and square and crammed with furniture. It reminded Susan of convent parlors as convent parlors had been when she first entered her order. It held none of the icons of the New Church: no bright banners or watercolor murals, no doves of peace or names of Jesus spelled out in psychedelic letters. There were two couches, four overstuffed chairs, five straight chairs, and a coffee table with a Bible on it. There was a brass-and-walnut crucifix hanging from a nail on the wall between the two front windows. That was it.

Susan circled the room, checking it all out, and then turned back to Andy. He had taken up residence in one of the overstuffed chairs, and he was looking distinctly uncomfortable. Susan didn't blame him. If her day had been a series of shocks—and even pleasant surprises, like the rhythm of Congress Avenue—then this was the biggest shock of all. She had known her brother Andy literally all her life. The last thing she'd ever expected to hear of him was that he'd spent significant time in a place like Damien House. And yet he had to have spent significant time here. Francesca knew him well. Susan tried to imagine the possibilities and couldn't. Andy volunteering to counsel down here two or three nights a week? Andy couldn't counsel anyone. Even as a child, he'd been a perpetual, deliberate mess-up, an apostle of the futile gesture. Andy running donation drives for canned goods and thermal blankets? Andy hated to work, and donation drives took a lot of it. She ought to know. She'd run a couple of dozen herself.

She dropped down on one of the couches and looked across the room to him. "Well?" she said. "Are you going to tell me about it? Why were you never going to darken their door again?"

Andy was peeling a roll of Life Savers, peeling it strip by

strip, as if engaged in some esoteric form of origami. "I had a fight with Father Tom Burne," he said.

"Why? What were you doing down here?"

"I was living here," Andy said.

Susan stared. "But what were you living here for? What could you possibly have wanted here? Did Dan throw you out of the house?"

Andy put the Life Savers down on the coffee table. "No, Dan didn't throw me out of the house. It was Dan's idea, if you want to know the truth about it. I don't think anyone here does. I lived here for two years: 1982 and 1983."

"Why?"

"Because that's what people do," Andy said. "Oh, there are people who come in by the day, run programs, take the kids to the movies, that kind of thing. But the core group lives in. That's what I was doing. I was part of the core group."

"What does the core group do while it's living in?"

Andy grinned. "Serves as role models, basically. Can you imagine me as a role model?"

"No," Susan said.

"Neither can I." Andy sighed. "Maybe that's why I didn't last. I did all the work, made dinner and cleaned up and taught some of the kids how to read, but I always felt like a phony doing it. And the religion. You know how I am about religion."

"You believe in the great god Pan."

"If I believe in anything. This is a very Catholic place. Considering what goes on here, you'd think Tom Burne would be a hip priest. He isn't. He's straight out of the Baltimore Catechism."

"Dan says he saves boys from prostitution."

"Boys and girls both. Sometimes he just saves kids from social workers. After two years in this place, I hated the social workers more than I hated the pimps."

Susan got off the couch and went over to look at the crucifix. The wood of its walnut base was chipped, but it had been expensive once. She wondered where it had come from.

"Why would Dan send you down to a place like this?" she asked. "He has to know you're not suited for it. He isn't suited for it himself."

"Do you think he's suited for the governor's office?"

Susan turned to look at him. He had scrunched down in his chair. His legs were extended halfway across the room and his feet tucked under the coffee table. He had his chin on his chest and his eyes closed. Susan felt the irritation bubbling up inside her, the way it had when she had to deal with parents who refused to discuss the truth about their children. There were people in this world who not only didn't want to think, but didn't want to know. It made her a little crazy to realize her brother Andy was one of them.

She went back to the couch and sat down again. "I know Dan wants to be governor," she said. "I don't know what that could possibly have to do with Damien House."

"Think about it," Andy said. Only his lips moved.

"I have thought about it. Wouldn't it have been more to the point for Dan to place you with the state Democratic Committee?"

"No."

"Why not?"

Andy opened his eyes. It made Susan feel better. For a while there, talking to him had been like talking to a corpse.

"Back in 1979," Andy said, "when Tom Burne opened this place, he was practically proclaimed a saint. The next year, Reagan got elected, and the Democratic Party needed saints. Every jackass in the state was trying to cram money down his throat. Even though they knew he wouldn't take it."

"Why wouldn't he take it?"

"He said he didn't want to get tied up with the bureaucracy. He still says that. You start taking money from the government, you start having to follow government rules. And there are a lot of government rules."

Susan stared at him with exasperation. "A lot of rules you

don't think make any sense. You never think rules make any sense. I suppose your Father Tom is exactly the same way."

"He isn't at all that way. That's why we had a fight."

"What about, Dan?"

This time, Andy sat up. "Dan is still trying to get himself connected to this place," he said. "He has to. Like I said, the Democratic Party needs saints. It's too bad it was Theresa that was killed. Fran's right—it'll turn out to be some kid on crack. If it had been something a little more interesting to the media, Father Tom offed by Mafia dons, Dan could have jumped in and made network with it."

There was a clatter on the stairs, then a clatter in the hall. Then the door opened and a man walked in. He was tall and broad, as shaggy as a mountain man, dressed in a frayed arctic parka with ratted fur along the edge of the hood.

"They're in here," he said to someone behind him. Then someone behind him made a strangled little noise, annoyed.

Susan sat on the couch, her hands folded in her lap, her legs crossed at the ankles, feeling like a dowdy ex-nun and an imbecile at the same time. The words she could not get out of her mind were so familiar she could hardly believe them—stupid words, used by Catholic laywomen from one end of the country to the other, the litany of women who had never been in religious life and could not understand.

Here she was, face to face with Father Thomas Burne, and all she could think of was:

What a waste.

3   She was not face to face with Father Tom Burne. She found that out quickly enough. The big man came into the room, cleared the path to the door, and another man came in behind him. He was wearing a Roman collar and a distracted expression, and Susan remembered what Andy had said about him: *he's straight out of the Baltimore Catechism.* If the big man was a priest, he was

anything but straight out of the Baltimore Catechism. He was some kind of renegade.

Andy was on his feet, holding his hand out to Tom Burne, looking a little embarrassed. "I read in the paper about Sister Theresa," he said.

"Everybody did, on page three," Burne said. He turned to the big man. "Do you know Pat Mallory?"

"Yes," Andy said. He held his hand out again, looking a little relieved when the big man took it. "I know him through my brother, Dan. You remember."

"What? Oh. Yes. Your brother's Dan Murphy. Who is this?"

"This is my sister, Susan," Andy said.

Tom Burne looked her over and said, "Nun."

Susan had been sitting on the couch through all of this. Now she stood up and began to pace around, bumping into furniture, finding it an agony to sit still.

"Actually, I'm an ex-nun," she said. "I left my order—last week."

"It could have been last year, or last decade," Burne said. "It wouldn't matter. Nuns get trained and they never lose it. If they've been trained right." He considered it. "Theresa was an ex-nun," he said finally. "Andy might not know about that."

"I do now," Andy said.

Father Burne sighed. "They're all ex-nuns these days. I can't believe it. They pop in and out of habits the way Imelda Marcos changed shoes. They pop in and out of the seminary that way. It makes you wonder what's going on in the real world."

"Father Tom refuses to believe this is the real world," Pat Mallory said.

He'd sat down on the other couch, the one Susan had not been using. Susan made herself stop pacing and look at him. He looked as big now as when she had first seen him, which surprised her. She'd been sure at the time that his size had been at least partially her imagination. On the other hand, he looked relaxed, which he hadn't when he first came in. It was as if he'd been expecting a problem he now knew wasn't going to arise.

"I tried to tell the good Father once that this was the only real world," he said, "but he gave me a lecture on the joys of Heaven. I won't do that again."

Susan smiled. "I'm sorry if we came at a bad time. I did know about the murder. I've got to admit I didn't realize there would still be so much going on."

"There usually isn't. Mostly we get done whatever we're going to get done the first few hours after we're called. I probably shouldn't even be here."

"You can be anywhere," Burne said. "You're the chief."

"Being chief amounts to being a glorified office boy, and you know it."

"I'm glad you came anyway," Burne said. "It was a terrible thing."

Mallory shifted his attention back to Susan. "If you've been in a convent, you wouldn't have known her, but we all did. Theresa Cavello. Unless you were a Franciscan?"

"Immaculate Heart of Mary," Susan said.

"Oh. Well. She was a Franciscan once, and then she quit. She was killed last Friday night, in the kitchen here."

"I found her," Burne said. "I came downstairs at ten o'clock and there she was, all over the kitchen floor."

Mallory stood up. "He got on the phone and called me. There's a precinct house three blocks away, and still he called me. And I came, didn't I, Father?"

"Yes, Pat, you came."

"I always do," Mallory said. "I even come back. But I've got to go now. You'll do those things I asked you to?"

"Of course I will."

"Good. When you get the information, call me. Call me at home if you have to."

"I will," Burne said. "But Pat, you've got to understand about the precinct. You know we think they're linked to—well, everything that goes on down here."

"I *do* understand. Christ, trust me. I understand." He turned to Susan and Andy, aiming for a place between them, talking to neither and both of them. "Good to see you again, Andy. Nice to have met you, Miss Murphy. I'll tell Dan I ran into you both. I gotta go."

He went out of the room, shaking the house as he walked. They all watched him until he disappeared.

When they heard the front door closing, Father Tom shook himself, blinked, and seemed to come out of a trance.

"Pat always says he understands about the precinct, but I don't think he does. I don't think he understands at all."

"Understands what?" Andy asked.

Burne waved him quiet. "Never mind about all that. I'm sick of thinking about all that. Let's see what we can do about *you*."

The "you" was directed at Susan, and so was the smile. Its wattage rivaled the light in the foyer and seemed to send out sparks.

For the first time, Susan understood why people talked the way they did about Father Thomas Burne.

CHAPTER
FOUR

1 Headquarters was one of those buildings, built in the fifties and sixties of concrete and plate glass, that was faintly reminiscent of a parking garage. There were others that looked like prisons. The fifties had been big times for New Haven. Korea followed on the heels of World War II, and the combination acted like an amphetamine cocktail. There were new schools, new hospitals, new police stations. There were even new residential colleges at Yale, although Yale had more sense than to build in concrete. Now it was forty years later and the town was a checkerboard of Victorian Gothic and Prison Camp Aesthetic. Only the Gothic looked like it was going to last another decade.

Usually Pat Mallory didn't notice any of this. As a man, he had grown up to be what his parents had wanted him to be, and what all those brothers and sisters had taught him to be. They had crowded his life then and they crowded it now, even when they lived a thousand miles away. Eileen the nun, Kathleen the nurse, Maureen the housewife, Jack the plumber, Dick the accountant: workaholics every one of them, although *workaholic* wasn't the word for it. Work, Pat's mother had once told him, was identity. What you do is what you are. How well you do it is like the carat stamp on gold. It tells you how heavy you weigh in the scales of God.

Since he had gone out to Damien House on his own time, he had also gone in his own car, and without a driver. He stopped his little Toyota at the gate to the parking garage, signed in with the patrolwoman on duty, and slid down the ramp to the underground. This was one of those days when everything bothered him, when even work couldn't stop him from getting irritated by inessentials. Headquarters building was ugly and moronic. Nobody with a brain in his head could have thought for a moment that the place would be a congenial one to work in. His car was a mistake. He had a log cabin out in Oxford and a closet full of outdoor clothes. He was six feet six. He should have bought a Wagoneer. At least that would have fit him.

He pulled into one of the overflow spaces next to the west wall, cut the engine, and got out. Then he went back and locked up the car. Here was another source of irritation: this garage was one of the least safe places to park your car in the city of New Haven. A Jaguar would have better luck propped against the curb on Congress Avenue. The gate was guarded twenty-four hours a day. There were always a dozen police officers on the premises, going in and out from one thing to another. It didn't matter. *They* always got in here, and *they* always did significant damage.

Them.

Once, when he was eight years old, his mother told him a story about *them*. Her *them* in those days was different from his *them* now—her brain nattered away at her about Protestants; his was an equal opportunity employer—but the two *thems* had a great deal in common. They were Other and they were Bad. He was in the kitchen, eating toast, feeling sick, home with a cold. He never knew what had started his mother talking.

She got the toast out of the broiler, laying a layer of margarine across each piece as thick as the apron under a Christmas tree. She put that down in front of him and took a seat on the other side of the table.

"Do you know anything about Protestants?" she said.

He knew something about Protestants. He'd heard all about them, at school. He was in the third grade at Precious Blood Parochial School.

"Protestants are traitors to the true Church," he told her dutifully, and she smiled.

"It's not their treachery to the Church I'm worried about. Do you know what they used to do in this country, back when your grandmother was a little girl?"

"I guess they used to do a lot of things," he said.

"When your grandmother was a little girl, I'm talking about Grandma Reilly now, my mother, when she was a little girl there were no parish schools in New Haven. There were only public schools. There was a law then, just like now, that everybody had to go to school somewhere. Since there weren't any parish schools, Catholics went to public schools with everyone else."

"Did they lose their faith?" Sister Catherine had told them about people who lost their faith. She'd described the tortures of Hell in detail.

"Some of them did," his mother said. "Most of them didn't. There were Sunday schools even then. The children were brought up right and everyone said family rosary. The problem was that the Bible was taught in the public schools, but it wasn't the real Bible. It was the Protestant Bible with things left out and other things changed around. One of the things the Protestants changed around when they wrote their Bible was the Lord's Prayer. They added something to it."

"I know about that," he said. "Sister Catherine told us. For thine is . . ."

"Shh," his mother said. "Listen. They taught this Protestant Lord's Prayer in the public schools, and every morning they made the children stand up and say it. They still do. It's a terrible thing. There are Protestants in the public schools, but there are other people, too. Not only Catholics, but Jews, and it's against the religion of the Jews to say the Lord's Prayer at all. But they make all the children stand up and say it anyway.

"Your Grandma Reilly said this Lord's Prayer in school for a whole year, for the first grade. Then that summer she started catechism with the nuns to prepare for First Communion. The nuns told her about the real Lord's Prayer and the Protestant one, and why saying the Protestant one was wrong. Of course, everybody said the Protestant one in school anyway, just not to cause trouble, but your Grandma Reilly wasn't like that. She thought if it was wrong she shouldn't do it.

"When school started the next year she went to her class, but when the teacher stood up to lead the prayer your Grandma Reilly only said part of it. She left the part the Protestants had put in off. She did this for two weeks before the teacher noticed. Then he did. When the prayer was over he made the whole class stay standing and went down to her desk and asked her why she hadn't said the whole prayer. And she told him."

"Did she shake her cane at him?"

"She didn't have a cane then. She was only a little girl. A very little girl. The teacher looked at her and said they were going to say the prayer again, and this time she had to say the whole thing. He went back to the front of the room and made them pray all over again. But when it came to the Protestant part, your Grandma Reilly still left it off.

"I think the teacher must have gone a little crazy. He made the class pray and pray and pray, again and again and again. It went on for hours. No matter what he did, he couldn't make your grandmother say what she didn't want to say. The teacher was very angry. Finally he took his pointer and stood right next to her desk, stood right over her to frighten her. Still, when the time came for the Protestant part, she put her hands flat down on her desk and didn't say anything. That was when he lost control of himself. He lifted the pointer up over his head and brought it down on Grandma Reilly's hand, brought it down hard, so that it broke her fingers."

"*All* of her fingers?" Pat said. He was appalled. The nuns would whack away with their rulers now and again, but they never hit hard enough to break anything. They just made your fingers sting and your heart burn. Somehow, getting a nun angry at you was a shameful thing. Especially if she was little and old.

"I don't know how many of her fingers he broke," his mother said, "but it was more than one, and it was on more than one hand. She had to go to the hospital and have the bones set and the hands bandaged up. While she was there, the principal called her father and asked him to come into the school. Her father thought the principal was going to apologize, or maybe even fire the teacher who had broken Grandma Reilly's fingers. It would only have made sense.

"But when your Grandma Reilly's father got to the school, he found the principal very angry. 'You Catholics,' the principal said, 'you're going to have to decide what you want. You're just going to have to decide if you want to be Americans.'

"Grandma Reilly's father didn't know what the principal was talking about. He was an American. He'd been born right here in New Haven in a house on Clark Street. But the principal said, 'No man can be Catholic and American both. Americans don't go in for superstitions and sell their souls to a pope. Americans don't grovel around on their knees in front of a priest who's a man no better than he should be.'

"Your Grandma Reilly's father was a very pious man. He said, 'But what about God?' And the principal said, 'Oh, God. God is the God of the powerful. Look around you and see who he loves best.'"

Pat looked down at his toast, half eaten, and his tea, half drunk. His head was spinning. He was only eight years old and he was sick enough to be confused on general principles. Half of what his mother had said he hadn't understood. The other half had given him the first real shock of his life.

"I don't understand," he said again.

She nodded at him. "You don't have to understand it all. You just have to understand this. There's a difference between them and us. Our God is the God of the poor and the meek. Their God is the God of the powerful. You can see who He loves best."

"I don't understand," he insisted.

She got up. "Don't understand then. Just remember. There's a difference between them and us."

Them and us. Ever since, his world had been divided into them and us.

2   The elevator had bounced down in front of him and opened its doors. Since he was leaning on the button, it was staying where it was. Its inner walls were covered with spray paint and scratch marks: FUCK THE PIGS; UP WITH ASSHOLES; LUIS 86.

He looked around to make sure there was no one watching him and stepped inside the elevator. He punched the button for the eighth floor and leaned against the handrail while the cage took him up. The people who worked in this building always called the cab the cage even though it wasn't one. The damn thing shook as violently as the pen of a mistreated tiger in a third-rate traveling zoo.

On the eighth floor, he got out, shrugged off his jacket, and folded it over his arm. He had been subject to more and more of these reveries lately, these daydreams, these walking trance-states into the past. Certain things, like the deaths of Theresa Cavello and Billy Hare, just seemed to set them off. Part of his mind told him that was reasonable. You had to process the things you couldn't stomach as well as the things you could. Your body got rid of waste one way and your mind had to get rid of it in another.

Unfortunately the rest of his mind wasn't so reasonable. It was as irritated with him as he was with the building, which made for the beginning of a very bad day.

On his desk was the file marked "McVann, Margaret Mary." It was a crime he hadn't been called to the scene of, and not one he'd expected to be involved in, but a passing memory of the details had made him leave a message with his secretary to have the file brought up. Now he sat down and flipped through it, to the picture of Margaret Mary with the Eucharistic symbol on her forehead, to the notation in grease pencil in the photograph's corner: "temp in apt at disc 4°F." The rest of the photographs detailed bruising—on the neck, on the back of the hands.

The Eucharistic symbol made Margaret Mary McVann and Theresa Cavello connected.

How?

The bruises on Margaret Mary and the lack of them on Theresa made the two cases different.

Why?

Did he have a nut here or something more banal, a mugger with a sense of humor, an individual with a grudge?

It was the kind of thing he would never be absolutely sure of until the cases were closed.

CHAPTER
FIVE

1   If Pat Mallory hadn't known the people at Damien House, he would never have become involved in the Theresa Cavello case. It wasn't the kind of thing he was supposed to get involved in. Chief of Homicide was essentially an administrative position. His job was to "stay on top" of duty rosters and case assignments and ongoing investigations. What this meant was that he was supposed to have answers to the idiotic questions Dan Murphy or the mayor decided to ask at irregular intervals: why had this been done here, why hadn't that been done there, why couldn't his people come up with a single viable suspect in this other place. Since the answers were always the same, but nobody wanted to hear them, he spent a lot of his time inventing euphemisms. It was amazing what the single word *crack* could be turned into, when he put his mind to it.

Every once in a while, for things like the Billy Hare case, he was dragged out for show. Years ago, he'd had a reputation as a first-class detective. He was the man who'd solved the Jug Killer case and managed to get the Church Street Slasher safely into jail. His name appeared in the *Register* and his picture appeared on the local television news. That was how he'd ended up in this office, even though he didn't play politics—even though he didn't know how. Crack had brought with it a crime wave that made all previous crime waves seem unreal. Compared to a machine-gun drug battle in broad daylight on a street four blocks from the New Haven Green, the Church Street Slasher was Saturday afternoon at the movies. In the wake of the bad publicity, the mayor had thought it would be a good idea to promote him. He was known to the public, and he wasn't a party favorite of the other side.

Now he sat down on his desk and looked at the mess on it— the mess of a Tuesday morning when he'd been late getting in to work. In the upper-left-hand corner were two stacks of pink message slips. The taller stack would be messages he didn't have to answer: civilians with bees in their bonnets; social workers with Good Liberal speeches to deliver about Bad Reactionary police officers; magazine writers with questions about his childhood that sounded like they'd been cribbed from a textbook for Abnormal Psych III. The shorter stack would be messages he did have to answer. Some of them would be just as irrelevant as the messages in the taller stack, like the ones from Dan Murphy demanding to know what he was *doing* up here. Others would be serious news. He had fifty-four detectives under his authority. All of them were working.

He reached for the shorter message stack and then stopped. He was not a man who resented riding a desk, or got irritated by the constraints of it. He thought it was a nice way to go on working without getting shot. Not getting shot was just fine with him. He'd been shot a couple of times, and shot at a couple of dozen more. He hadn't liked any of it at all. Still, there were times he got tired of the bureaucratic pace of it. This was one of them. The shorter stack would be full of information about the progress of the Billy Hare case. It would say what he expected it to say, which would depress him beyond reason. He didn't care how many front-page stories they printed in the *Register*. He'd seen cases like this before. They were unsolvable, but they were impossible to process. The chances that he'd ever have what he needed to arrest somebody were practically nil.

Although he wished they weren't.

He really wished they weren't.

The upper-left-hand corner of his desk contained one file folder, marked CAVELLO/DAMIEN HOUSE in royal blue Flair across its broad front flat. It was marked with ordinary police code on its tab, but he didn't pay any attention to that. He pulled it to him and opened it. There were witness statements. There were reports from the two patrolmen first on the scene. There were photographs. There was even a computer printout nearly an inch thick, containing the raw data the Mobile Crime Unit had collected to write its reports with. What there wasn't was a report from the morgue.

Pat closed the file and tapped his hands against it, distracted. Then he punched his intercom and said, "Andrea? Are you there?"

"My God," Andrea said. "You're in. I didn't see you come in. When did you come in?"

"About a minute ago. You must have been in the john."

"I don't go to the john. I was just about to bring in more messages."

"Important?"

"Crap."

"Keep them for a while. Who do we have on the Cavello/Damien House?"

There was a rustle of paper, Andrea going through the duty book. "Markham and Halt," she said finally. "I think they're down in the pen."

"Did you tell them I wanted a morgue report?"

"Of course I did. I even talked to them myself."

"Did you tell them I wanted a back check?"

"I just told you I—"

"I know, I know," Pat closed his eyes. No matter how hard he tried, he couldn't bring up the faces of Markham and Halt. That meant they weren't very good or very bad. He knew all the good ones by name, and he thought he had enough on the bad ones to keep them in line. It was just too bad he wasn't political. If he had been, he could have had the bad ones transferred out. He thought about Dbro and shook his head.

On the other end of the line, Andrea was getting restless. "Pat?" she said.

"I'm still here," he said. "I'm just trying to think of what to do."

"I'll get Markham and Halt up here for you if you want."

"Maybe that would be a good idea." No it wouldn't. He sighed. "Never mind. Did anybody tell you anything about this thing? About Cavello?"

"Was there something they shouldn't have told me?"

"No."

"The word around here is that she was marked. Not just cut but marked. With some kind of Devil worship symbol or something."

Pat looked at the statue on his desk—a six-inch-high porcelain of Saint Michael the Archangel, patron of policemen, sent to him by his sister the nun—and stifled a laugh. "Well," he said, "she was marked with something. Are you sure Markham and Halt are in the pen?"

"They were the last time I looked."

"What about Anton Klemmer? Is he on duty today?"

"Anton Klemmer is always on duty. He sleeps in one of his cold drawers."

"He sleeps with his children's nanny. She's twenty-two years old and from Sweden. Call Anton and tell him I'm coming down. I want to talk to him."

"All right."

"Call Markham and Halt and tell them to meet me there?"

"All right again." A pause. A cough. A paper shuffled. "What about you?" she said.

"I'm fine."

"Maybe. But you just got in and you're going out again."

"I'm feeling restless," he told her.

"I know that." Another cough. Another shuffle. Another pause. "Forget I mentioned it," she said. He heard her nails click against the intercom button as the line went dead.

Outside, the weather that had been getting better was getting worse again. Pat stood up, put on his jacket, and went to the window to look at it. The sky was jammed shut with clouds again, and big snowflakes were drifting down, round white mats as big as drinks coasters. He ran his hand through his hair. He really was restless. He couldn't stand the thought of not moving something.

Andrea was sixty-three and fat as Oliver Hardy, the proto-typical secretary of a man with a jealous wife. But he didn't have a wife. He'd never had one. His brothers and sisters had all gone on to build families like the one they'd come from, but for some reason he'd never been able to connect. Even his lovers never lasted long. Women drifted in and out of his life like cases, rearranged his furniture, then disappeared. He couldn't remember having wanted one to stay.

He couldn't remember what had started him on this train of thought, either. Like the memory of his mother, it had just hit him.

He zipped his jacket shut and headed for the door. Once he got to work, he would be all right. He told himself to think about Theresa Cavello and Billy Hare.

What he thought about instead was Dan Murphy's sister, her black hair and the serious attentiveness of her face, the tense watch-ful stillness that surrounded her like a halo. Nuns were always like that, and they never stopped being nuns. It got into their skin and stained them.

Stained them.

He hated to admit it, but he was burning out.

2   The problem with the New Haven morgue was that it wasn't in a basement. Part of it was. Most of it—the offices, the tech rooms, the computers, and the files—was on a first floor of broad hallways and wide plate-glass windows. It didn't even have the virtue of being dark. Walking down to Anton Klemmer's office was like wandering through a particularly peppy grammar school.

Anton Klemmer didn't do much for Pat's prejudices, either. By tradition, he should have been an old man with an immigrant's accent, puttering around a shade-darkened room and cackling over skulls. In reality, he was young, and very American. His name was a sop his mother had thrown to her husband's father. It had worked. Anton had grown up on Noble Street in West Haven, gone to a local public school and the University of Connecticut at Storrs. He'd led a perfectly normal life until medical school, when he'd marched into Johns Hopkins without a single loan to his name. His grandfather hadn't left him much, but he'd left him enough.

When Pat came in, Anton was sitting in a gray swivel chair, his feet up on his desk, his nose buried in a book whose cover read: *Microscopic Spectography in Investigative Analysis*. As always when he wasn't doing an autopsy, he was dressed in part of a three-piece suit. The pants and vest were there, although the vest was unbuttoned and hanging open over his white shirt. The jacket was nowhere in evidence.

Pat closed the door to the hallway, and Anton closed his book, not bothering to mark his place.

"My secretary got a call from your secretary," he said. "We should be in the Fortune 500."

"What's the book for?" Pat asked him.

Anton shrugged. "They send them to me. They want me to write blurbs. I never write blurbs, but sometimes I read the things."

"Is it any good?"

"The guy who wrote it knows as much about criminal investigation as I do about cooking." Anton threw the book on the desk. "So, what's this all about? I gave you everything I had on Billy Hare, but you know how that kind of thing is. Nothing makes any difference."

"This isn't about Billy Hare. I came about Theresa Cavello," he said. "I got your note."

"Ah," Anton said. "Did you understand my note?"

"Maybe." Pat leaned over and took a pen and a piece of paper off Anton's desk. There were plenty of both. Anton seemed to live in a sea of Southworth and Bic. Pat put the paper on his knee and drew carefully. "She was marked. With this. And you're upset about it."

Pat threw the paper back onto the desk. Anton picked it up and let it flutter in the air. It said this:

Anton let the paper drop. "Very good," he said. "Do you want to see the mark?"

"I've seen it," Pat said.

"I suppose you would have. You knew her."

"I knew her very well. She'd been at Damien House since the place opened."

"Yes," Anton said. "Well. I knew there had to be something. You wouldn't have asked for information otherwise. Do you know what was strange about this mark?"

"It's a Catholic mark," Pat said. "A Church mark. The symbol for the Eucharist. It's also the second one we've had."

"So?" Anton shrugged. "She was a Catholic nun—excuse me, ex-nun—living in a Catholic religious house. Everybody in the neighborhood knew that. As to her being the second one—well, the second of two women who live not a mile from each other and spend their time helping the poor. Find somebody they both knew. On crack."

"If you believed that, you wouldn't have written me that note."

"You're right." Anton took his feet off the desk. "I'll tell you what I found strange about this mark. In the first place, it was on her forehead, just about where you'd have put ashes if you were a priest and this was Ash Wednesday."

"Not so strange," Pat said.

"No, it's not. But now consider this. First, it was the only mark on her."

"I knew that."

"And second, it was neat."

"What do you mean, neat?"

"Neat," Anton insisted. "Have you ever watched a crackhead move? They jerk. They shudder. If they're high enough they bounce off the ceiling. They don't carve Eucharistic symbols into nearly live flesh so *neatly* they could have been making an etching for a lot of Benedictine nuns. Just a minute." He got out of his chair, went to his files, and pulled out a folder. On his way back to his desk, he dropped the folder in Pat's lap. "Read that. He used a knife, not a razor blade. We know that from the width of the cuts. But he used the knife well. He didn't snag the skin. He didn't tear her. He made perfectly straight lines except for the curve of the P. Then he made a perfectly symmetrical curve. What does that sound like to you?"

"Psychopath," Pat said, and then realized with a shock that he hadn't been expecting it. Even with the McVann death nagging at his memory, he hadn't been expecting it. When he'd read Anton's note, he'd thought he was going to get a crime of passion, religious for once instead of sexual. He'd thought he was going to find that one of the people at Damien House had cut her, for reasons that were now obscure but would someday be clear. Now he was being presented with a death that might have had no reason for happening at all.

The Jug Killer. The Church Street Slasher. Serial killers were every police department's ultimate nightmare. Pat felt a little sick.

"Jesus Christ," he said.

"Wait," Anton told him. "You're going to feel worse. I feel so bad I can hardly look myself in the mirror."

"What do you mean?"

Anton got up again. This time he didn't bother to walk over to his file cabinet. The folder he needed was right on his desk. He could have reached it sitting down. Apparently he hadn't wanted to.

He dropped the folder into Pat's lap, on top of the one on Theresa Cavello. "That's the file on Margaret Mary McVann. Her body was found in her apartment over on Dee Street the day before Theresa Cavello died."

"I know." Pat squirmed. Serial killers had cycles. First there was a long time between each kill, then a shorter time, then a shorter time still. What did they have if this guy was killing one a day?

Anton reassured him. A little. "She wasn't killed the day before Theresa Cavello died. She was found. She'd been dead about a week."

"That can't be right, Anton. I've seen the file. There wasn't that kind of mess."

"Look at the folder. There was a broken window. Temp down below twenty-five. It was a refrigerator in there."

Pat looked. The picture Anton wanted him to see was right on top, probably because Anton had been looking at it himself, frequently. It showed a middle-aged woman with her hair fanned out behind her, lying on a rug. Her neck was broken. Her forehead was marked with the ♃, carved into her flesh as neatly as if it had been stenciled on.

Pat put both folders back on Anton's desk and took a deep breath. "Shit," he said. "Bruises here, no bruises on Terry—what do we have?"

"Don't start swearing yet," Anton said. "You don't have anything to swear about yet. Wait till you hear the kicker."

"What kicker?"

"We don't have the body."

Pat stared. This is impossible. In a case of violent death, morgues kept bodies for weeks. Sometimes for months. Even with a loving family clamoring around for a chance to hold a funeral, the body should have been kept for seven days.

"You have to have the body," he told Anton.

"We ought to have it," Anton said, "but we don't. In fact, we don't have a number of bodies we ought to have. We had a new girl in processing last weekend."

"What's that supposed to mean?"

"It's supposed to mean she mistook the overtime drawers for the holding drawers and shipped the wrong set out for cremation. By the time anybody knew what had happened, it was Monday morning. All we have are ashes."

"Shit," Pat said again. He wondered if he was getting angry. Listening to Anton this morning had been like taking body blows.

He was punchy, and he couldn't get through that to what he actually felt. God, it was incredible. First life looked like it couldn't get any worse, and then it did.

"Shit," he said for the third time. "Anton—"

The phone on Anton's desk rang, tinkling like a bicycle bell. Anton picked it up and waved him quiet.

"Bitching about it isn't going to change anything," he said. "It's my ass we're talking about here, not yours."

Actually, it was the ass of that new girl in processing, but Pat didn't say that. He just sank more deeply into his chair and started trying to work it all out. Billy Hare. Theresa Cavello. Margaret Mary Whoever she was. Two big messes, when last week he had had none.

A moment later, Anton put the receiver on the desk and shoved it across to Pat. He was wincing.

"It's for you," he said.

CHAPTER
SIX

1 When Pat picked up the phone, he expected to hear a voice he didn't know: Markham's or Halt's, telling him why they weren't already at the morgue. Their absence had ticked away at him all the way through his conversation with Anton Klemmer. Andrea had gotten back to him after she'd called down to the pen. They had definitely been there and they had definitely gotten his message. Where were they? Their absence linked up with the processing girl's stupidity. It was all incompetence and indifference, the way everything else in life was these days. He couldn't understand it. He remembered his mother cleaning, his father making a high chair in the back bedroom: the tension and seriousness, the undiluted dedication. He'd grown up with people who cared, about everything. He cared about everything. When things got crazy the way they had these last two weeks, he began to take it personally, as guilt. He kept thinking that if he had worked harder, thought smarter, stayed awake longer, none of it would have happened. It was some lack in himself that made violence possible. People like Markham and Halt and the processing girl cared about nothing. They didn't see themselves responsible for the state of their own teeth. Most of the time they just made him tired. They became part of the nothing-in-particular that was drowning him in exhaustion. Every once in a while, like now, they made him impossibly angry.

He put the receiver to his ear, telling himself he didn't know Markham and Halt. They could have been held up by a break in another case. They could have stopped on Chapel Street to prevent a robbery. They could be going to the aid of an officer in trouble, taking a heart attack victim to the hospital, delivering a baby. It wasn't fair to people to judge them without knowing the facts of their case, and Pat Mallory liked to be fair.

Still, when he spoke, his "Yes?" had the bite in it that was only there when he was ready to kill somebody. Every officer in Homicide knew it well.

There was a pause on the other end of the line. Then a cough and a sigh, and Ben Deaver said, "Pat?"

"Oh," Pat said. He literally felt the heat leaving his body, lifting off from his forehead and spinning out into the air. It left a wash of embarrassment behind, because he'd been a jerk. "Sorry. I thought you were somebody else."

"I guess," Ben said. "I almost feel like somebody else. We've got another one of the boys."

"Oh, Jesus," Pat said. He looked at the ceiling and sighed. "I'm in Anton Klemmer's office," he said, although Deaver must have known that. "I'm here on the Cavello thing. What did you want?"

Deaver took a deep breath, sucking into the phone. "I'm down on Whalen Avenue, down by the theater. You know where that is?"

"Yes." Deaver was too young to remember, but there had been a time when the movie theaters on Whalen Avenue were a Mecca for every high-school student in the city. Pat had seen the first four James Bond movies there. He'd even seen the first re-release of *Gone with the Wind,* with a girl from Saint Mary's he was hoping to talk into necking with him.

"I'm in a phone booth about a block west of the theater," Deaver said. "About a block north of here there's a vacant lot. Can you find it?"

"Of course I can find it. If you're there the place has to be full of cops. Anyone could find it."

"The place is full of cops," Deaver said. "I've done as much damage control as I can—"

"Damage control?"

"Keeping the techs away from the scene. It would be easier if Dbro wasn't here. Every time I tell them to pack up and wait, he tells them to unpack and work. Can you get down here right away?"

"Ben, for Christ's sake—"

Anton Klemmer had a crystal paperweight on his desk, made in the shape of a round cut diamond. Without realizing it, Pat had picked it up in his free hand. Now he put it down again, carefully, as if he were afraid he was going to break it.

"Do you have anybody there besides cops and techs?"

"Some civilians standing on the sidewalks, trying to figure out what's going on. That's it. So far."

"All right."

"I've got to go back and make sure Dbro isn't making mud pies in the middle of the mess. Get down here right away, all right?"

Pat started to say "All right" himself, but Deaver had hung up. He stared at the receiver for a moment and then put it back in its cradle.

On the other side of the desk, Anton Klemmer sat with his arms folded over his chest, his head cocked. "Bad news?" he asked.

"Yes," Pat said.

"What do I do with your two detectives, if they ever get here?"

Pat was already reaching for his jacket, trying to remember if he'd brought along a pair of gloves. He had a vague memory of very bad weather waiting for him on the outside, terrible weather he had to protect himself against. His incipient burn-out seemed to be in full gear. He felt like his head was stuffed with cotton candy.

"Get them to do a back search," he told Anton Klemmer. "When you've got them safely into the cold room, stuff them in a drawer and lock them up."

2 Because he had been in a hurry, Pat Mallory had come down to the morgue alone. Coming out, he knew he ought to call for an official car and a driver to take him to Ben Deaver. That was the way things were done. It was incredible how many people got crazy when you skirted protocol, as if not wanting to be driven around like a kid too young for a license was an insult to all the people in the Department who wouldn't mind a bit. Even the uniforms sometimes took it that way. Either that, or they hated you for what they thought was your attempt to play Good Buddy.

Dbro was going to hate it if he showed up on the bus, but he didn't care about Dbro. Deaver wouldn't even notice. Besides, Pat was antsy. The shock-feeling had worn off, and he was already thinking of the dragging feeling as "his burn-out," the way another man might think of "his marriage." There was a lot of adrenaline left in him yet. He wasn't panicking, but he thought he could, if he let himself. What was going on here was an avalanche. There was too much of it, coming too fast, flowing over his head in soft cold waves that threatened to suffocate him.

There was a bus stop two blocks from the morgue's front door, and he caught a northbound there, wedging himself into a seat between a young girl with her arms full of packages from Macy's and an old man who smelled of muscatel. The old man's jacket had been torn nearly in strips. It hung down from his shoulders like a fringe. Pat watched the other passengers watching him: a black woman with a choir robe over one arm and a Bible in her hands; a black man in a good suit with a briefcase between his feet; a college boy in a Harvard sweatshirt and a pair of Maine hunting boots pretending to read a textbook on sociology. They were all sitting very still, as if any movement on their part would flip the old man's switch and turn him into a bellowing maniac with a taste for human blood.

The northbound had a long way to go. By the time it got halfway to Pat's stop, the old man was the only other passenger on it, and he had fallen asleep. Pat got up and went to sit behind the driver. By law, that seat was a handicapped space, extra-wide to accommodate wheelchairs and walkers and canes. He stretched out his legs and looked through the oversize windows at a city that was rapidly dwindling into rubble. Small streets full of smaller houses that, farther south, had been brightly painted and well kept up were, here, small streets with smaller houses in decay. Then the houses stopped and he was surrounded by blank brown brick buildings that could have contained anything, or nothing. New Haven was getting to be like New York: a place where turning the corner was a kind of teleportation.

He saw the theater ahead in the distance and stood up. He wanted to walk a couple of blocks. The driver braked for a light and looked up at him.

"Cop?" he said.

"Yeah," Pat said. "I'm a cop."

"I thought you were a cop," the driver said. "I wasn't sure you were a cop. Mostly you get a cop, he'll flash his shield."

Pat had thought about flashing his shield, but he'd decided against it. Cops were allowed to ride city buses free if they were on Department business. A lot of them rode free all the time. It was one of those situations that was impossible to untangle honorably, so Pat didn't untangle it at all. He just carried a lot of change.

The driver went through the intersection and pulled up at the stop on the opposite curb, pulling his doors open as he went, even though that was more illegal here than smoking marijuana. Pat was halfway down the steps by the time the bus stopped, which was illegal too. It brought a satisfied little smile to the driver's face.

"It's always one thing or the other," the driver said. "Don't I *know*."

Pat jumped onto the sidewalk and started walking north.

3 Right around the corner from Whalen on Belknap Street, just out of sight of the avenue behind an outcrop of brown brick, the world was full of police. Obviously, while Deaver had been trying to keep things calm, Dbro had been sounding alarms from one end of town to the other. Two black-and-whites, two unmarkeds, the Mobile Crime Unit, an ambulance, a medical examiner's van: it looked like the scene of a high-level political assassination. Pat kept expecting to see a brace of FBI agents talking into walkie-talkies.

The vacant lot stretched between two buildings that had been built to look like squared-off, tiered wedding cakes. Pat walked past the first one and looked into the clearing. The civilians were being held well back, possibly because there weren't that many of them. Ben Deaver had managed to do at least one of the things he had set out to do. There was nobody who looked like a reporter in the small crowd. There were no television cameras at all.

Pat made his way through the line, past little clots of officers and technicians who first stared at him and then stared away. In outdoor clothes instead of the regulation suit, he wasn't instantly recognizable. Deaver was pacing back and forth in front of a large pile of equipment that was still packed into black boxes. His feet kept scuffing across the hard shell of the frost and making it spark. Pat saw him look up and waved.

"Jesus Christ," Deaver said when Pat finally got to him. "Where have you been?"

"I took the bus."

Deaver turned around and swung his arms in the air, over the boxes and toward the open space beyond. "I managed to keep them out of there. Just. I told one of the patrolmen you'd suspend him and I told one of the M.E.'s men you'd have his nuts. I told them anything that came into my head."

"I take it Dbro made a few phone calls."

"Six."

"Was one of them to Dan Murphy's office?"

"I don't know."

"One of them probably was."

Deaver shrugged. "All I care about is that you're here and it hasn't been fucked up yet."

Pat walked around him and around the boxes. As soon as he got clear of the equipment, he saw a single shoe attached to a single foot, sticking out of a clump of low thorny brush. Weeds grew fast everywhere, but in vacant lots they grew stunted. These would not have been high enough to hide a full-grown man.

"Who found the body?" he asked Deaver.

"Guy runs a junk store out on Belknap. He says he comes out here a couple of times a week to see what he can find."

"You don't believe him?"

"Who knows?"

"Then what?"

Deaver had turned his back to the scene. "He called 911. He even stuck around. Dubrowski and Pierce caught it and came on out."

Pat went in a little farther toward the brush. Something had gone right. That made him feel better, but not good. It was impossible to feel good about anything while you were staring at that shoe, a perfect miniature Gucci loafer whose brass horsebit winked and glittered even though there wasn't any sun. He went in a little farther and found himself staring at a black sock with the words *Christian Dior* embroidered on the heel.

"Ben?"

"Somebody dumped a load over there on the other side of those bottles," Ben said. "Dbro kept wanting somebody to clean it up."

Pat said nothing. The dump would belong to a junkie or a wino who'd gotten too high to make it to a bathroom, or hadn't had a bathroom to make it to. Even if it belonged to their executioner, they wouldn't get anything out of it. You couldn't analyze feces the way you did blood types or fingerprints and come up with a match. It might have made some difference if it was a trademark. Since there hadn't been any feces at the first site, it wasn't.

He went right to the edge of the brush, got down on his haunches, and parted the weeds. In life, this boy wouldn't have been anything at all like the boy they'd found at the bottom of Edge Hill Road. Billy Hare was small and blond. This boy was dark and already muscular in a babyish way that promised real power when he reached adulthood. Except that he was never going to reach adulthood, and in death he was Billy Hare's twin. The same off-the-rack designer clothes. The same careless hairstyle, cut too well to have been picked up at the local barbershop. Pat checked and found a pair of bikini underpants, made of silk in bright electric blue.

He stepped back and let the weeds fall into place again. Pieces of the boy's head had been shot out all over the lot behind him. The gray of the brain matter was still gray and the red of the blood only slightly brown. He hadn't been here long, even if you factored in the effect of all this cold.

Pat turned around and went back to Deaver, still standing with his back to the scene.

"Did Dbro know the name of this one, too?"

"I didn't ask him," Deaver said.

"Ask him. Then get the techs here to do what they're supposed to do."

"I want *you* to do something," Deaver said.

Pat almost asked him what. Instead he unzipped his jacket and started heading back to the line. The snow that had started falling when he was still back at Headquarters had turned into something so fine it felt almost like rain, but not quite. It clung to the windshields of the cars parked on the sidewalk in thin sheets, making them look frosted.

Deaver caught up to him. "Are you going to do anything? Anything at all?"

"I'm going to do something."

"What?"

"Do what I asked you to do first."

"What?" Deaver insisted.

Pat looked at Dbro. He was standing next to one of the patrol cars, bundled up like an Eskimo, whacking his hand against the hood while he told one of the uniforms where to get off. Or something. Christ. Dbro was always telling somebody where to get off.

Pat stopped when he and Deaver were still far enough from the line not to be overheard.

"There's going to be a meeting in my office tonight at ten o'clock. You, me, Anton Klemmer, then pick somebody you trust and bring him along. Pick somebody you like."

"Not Dbro?"

Pat blew white breath into the air. "Not anybody who's going to talk to the district attorney before I want him to."

CHAPTER

SEVEN

1 That morning, Friday the 13th, he stopped first on Edge Hill
Road. He'd been stopping there first every day for a week.
Now the rhythm of the neighborhood, so different from that of
the rest of the city, was beginning to sink into him. He liked watching people in the not-quite-dawn. Downtown, morning reminded
him of a conspiracy of pod people. The streets were empty and the
buildings seemed uninhabited—and sometimes were—but every
once in a while flat unmarked trucks pulled in and out of underground garages. Their grilles looked sentient and their drivers
looked dead. Morning on Edge Hill Road was more like a ballet.
Between five-thirty and six lights began to go on at the back of the
biggest houses: maids getting up to clear living rooms of abandoned
glassware and warm kitchens for the start of breakfast. Between six
and six-thirty the street was full of women: maids who "lived out"
coming in to work. The maids who lived out always looked cold.
No buses ran on Edge Hill Road. The maids had to get off on
Prospect and walk the rest of the way up. They wore black rubber-
soled shoes and thin black cotton uniforms, no matter what the
weather.

He was sitting in the tree closest to the house on the left side
in the backyard of the house he knew best, cross-legged on a branch
that hung closest to the kitchen's corner window: the one that
belonged to Daniel Murphy. This house was the exception, even
though it was one of the biggest and best kept up. The Murphys
had a maid who lived out, but she didn't come in until nine. Instead,

it was Susan Murphy herself who came to the kitchen at six. He could see her moving around in there, getting out the tea things, running her hands through her hair.

It was Susan Murphy who had started him toward his charism—the mention of her, and who she was the sister of, in the small diocesan newspaper that was scattered like leaves through the vestibule of every parish church. Up until then, he had felt the power without knowing what to do with it. He had seen the evil without knowing what could be done to defeat it. Then he had realized what was happening, all the nuns leaving their orders, bleeding the church white, a kind of willful hemophilia. They willed themselves out of the church and changed everything and everyone around them in the process. She had changed her brother Dan. She had been false as they were all false. Everything was jumbled up together and confused in his mind, but one thing at least was clear: it was wrong of them, the ones who were leaving. It was wrong of them and they had to be stopped. In the beginning, she had carried a lot of her convent with her. She had kept her arms close to her body and her head down. She had moved quickly but without any suggestion of haste. As the days passed, she became more like a normal person. Worse, she became more like a normal person as "normal" was defined on Edge Hill Road. He wondered what God thought of what she was doing: the immense amount of tea she put in the tea ball, always a waste, because she never drank more than two cups and nobody else drank tea at all; the thick dark cashmere sweaters she wore over her jeans, belonging to her brothers and much too large, that she treated as if they'd cost nothing at all; the food she made and didn't eat and finally threw away. Like everyone else up here, she had become addicted to waste, and to casual luxury. Sometime while he wasn't watching, she'd had her ears pierced. Now she wore a fat pearl in each one. On the days when he was much too tired, he thought she looked like those old pictures of Frankenstein, with knobs on the side of her head to cover the bolts that held her together.

The bark underneath him was iced-in and as hard as stone.

Susan Murphy took her tea things to the kitchen table, sat down, and stretched her legs onto an opposite chair. Her hair had lost the dull flatness that came from years of being held down by a veil. She picked up the pad of paper and the pen she had put down on the table when she first came in. In the glare of the overhead kitchen light, the T of the Tiffany T-clip looked like a bar of gold.

Somewhere beyond the trees, in the house that belonged to the family called Burke, the pool house was being readied for a party. There was a floor in there over the pool that could be kept open for swimming or closed for dancing. It was closed now and covered with large round tables that seated eight people each. He had counted them. The Burkes were having a hundred and four people in to dinner.

It was getting late. He was always safe in the tree, but he wasn't always safe out of it. If he waited too long, he would have to stay up here until dark. Unless he wanted to get caught.

He listened to the bells of the churches down on Church Street, ringing out their short codes for the half hour. Then he looked down at Susan Murphy again. He had sent her a rosary, but he didn't know what she had done with it. Sometimes he was afraid she'd thrown it out. He didn't know what he'd do if she had. He only had six more, and the damn things were hard to get.

She was staring into space, drinking her tea from a Royal Doulton cup. Royal Doulton cost two thousand dollars for a place setting, but he had once seen her take one of these cups and throw it in the garbage. It had had a chip the size of an atom in it.

He went a little farther up into the tree, then a little farther left. Then he started to come down. On that side he was far enough from the window so he wouldn't be seen. He thought about God again and about the Royal Doulton cup. Sometimes he thought he knew about everything in the world and sometimes he thought he knew nothing at all.

He headed across the lawn and stopped at the board fence. There were a pair of boards there he had loosened himself, and he pulled them out. It was six thirty and just getting light, but it was all right. The maids who lived out were all at work now. Even if they saw him, they would treat him as if he were invisible.

Sometimes he thought he was invisible. God, sending him on another errand, made him transparent.

2 Once he got downtown, he began to feel a little better. The Green looked good. The bums had disappeared, as they did every once in a while, for no good reason he could see. Yale looked magical, like the kingdom in a fairy tale. He imagined a dragon in the Old College yard. If there was one, he would turn himself into a knight and slay it.

He crossed Chapel Street and walked uptown, faster and faster, until he could turn and then cross again and get himself on Clark. The rosary in his pocket clicked as he walked. The knife under his shirt pricked him only dully, because this time he had remembered to wrap its point in tissue paper.

Everything on earth was speaking to him in God's voice.

3 She was alone when he came in, fussing around behind the counter with a big plastic bag full of sugar packets. It was quarter to seven. At seven thirty, the place would start to fill up. This was the only cheap place to eat for blocks and the neighborhood was full of working bachelors. They commuted to Sikorsky or the copper-plate plant in Bristol. They were men who would have drunk beer for breakfast, if it had been legal.

She looked up when he came in and smiled. She was a young woman—no more than twenty-five—but she seemed older. She lacked the energy other people had. She wore a blue glass Miraculous Medal around her neck and her dull brown hair pulled back by an elastic band. She had been out of her convent for over a year, but she was nothing like normal people at all.

He climbed up on the counter stool in front of her and she said, "I was wondering where you were. I haven't seen you in weeks."

"I've been busy."

"You're always busy. Sometimes you're busy eating here."

He took his wallet out of his back pocket and laid it on the counter. It was a good one, real leather, that he'd boosted out of Malley's. You could boost style if it was the kind of style you concealed. Wearing fancy underwear was one way. Walking around with a six-hundred-dollar wallet in your pocket was another. He opened the wallet and pulled out the bills in the fold.

"Look," he said. "I actually have money."

"I see that."

She was giving him a funny stare. He looked away. "I was just trying to let you know I didn't always come just to get some free food."

"I know you don't," she said.

"I come to see you," he said.

"I know you do. I'm not going to let you pay for breakfast anyway."

"You'll get fired if you get caught."

She shrugged. She had tucked the sugar packets neatly into wire holders. She swept the holders away with the side of one arm to clear the space in front of her.

"I'm not so sure it would be a tragedy if I did get fired. I've been walking around this morning wondering what I'm doing in this place, waiting tables by myself. Trying not to care that the only help I've got is reading *Rolling Stone* in the ladies' room. It wasn't exactly what I thought I'd be doing when I left the convent."

"What did you think you'd be doing?"

She shrugged again. "I don't know that I know. I wasn't in one of those orders where they lock you up all the time. I wore normal clothes and I got to go to restaurants. It all felt—pointless, somehow." She laughed. "This feels pointless, too."

"Do you ever think of going back?"

"To what?"

"To God."

"I didn't leave God. I left a lot of self-righteous social workers who wanted to get themselves ordained as priests."

"You didn't want to be ordained a priest?"

"No. Good Lord, no. That's all I would have needed."

She reached to the shelf over her head and brought down a paper place mat, then to the shelf at her knees for the silverware. The silverware was wrapped in a paper napkin that had ARLIE'S RESTAURANT printed on it in blue.

"I'm not going to get fired," she told him. "Arlie's wife left him. She went out to Oregon with her exercise teacher. He drinks himself under the furniture every night and doesn't get in till ten."

4 From the back, her hair looked like a tangle of spiderwebs made of wire. It sprung when she moved, and he sat watching it. Once she had sat him down in a booth in the back and showed him all the pictures she had of herself as a nun. The only difference in her between then and now was that now she wore a uniform. The nuns in her order all seemed to dress in jeans, with peace symbols instead of crosses around their necks.

"We took a vote when the Pope visited America and I was the only one who wanted to go see him," she had said. "The rest of them wanted to picket. They were always picketing about something. South America. The death penalty. Catholics for Choice. There was a woman named Sister Jennifer Streem who kicked a parish priest in the knee because he told her she couldn't distribute Communion."

"Maybe you were sent there to bring them back to God. Like Theresa of Avila and the Carmelites."

"I'm no Theresa of Avila. And nobody could bring them back to God. They don't believe in God. Never mind the one Holy Catholic and Apostolic Church."

"What do they believe in?"

"Politics."

"I know another nun who left her order," he had told her. "She left because where she was they didn't believe in politics."

"Maybe it's like being married through a matchmaker," she'd said. "Maybe you don't do so well when you marry something blind."

5 Now he sat on his stool and thought: a vocation is a call from God that must not be ignored. Every nun in the world would tell you that, even the ones who believed in politics.

She had made eggs and toast and sausage and put them on a plate. She put the plate in front of him and turned around to get orange juice. She knew he didn't like coffee. She'd asked him about it once and he'd told her.

"So," she said, "what have you been busy with? Have you been sitting all day in the movies again?"

He hadn't seen a movie in three months. "I went to *Batman,*" he lied, knowing she'd never see it herself. "They spent a lot of money on it but I didn't think it was very good."

"My nephew didn't think it was very good, either. He liked something called *Roger Rabbit.*"

"I didn't see that one."

"At least you're not spending all your time in dark rooms anymore. I used to worry about you. I used to think you'd go blind in those places."

"You can't go blind in the movies."

"You can go blind anywhere. Aren't you going to eat your breakfast?"

He looked at his plate, then at the clock on the wall to his right. It was ten minutes after seven, getting late. He wasn't hungry. He was never hungry when he was filled with the Spirit. He looked at his hands and thought he saw them glowing.

"Are you all right?" she asked him.

The knife nicked him. Its point was beginning to tear through the tissue paper.

"I'm fine," he said. "Come in back with me. I've got something to show you."

"Something I have to go all the way out back to see?"

"Someone might come in and see me giving it to you."

"What is it? A dirty book?"

"Of course not."

"I've never read a dirty book. My sister keeps telling me I don't know what I'm missing."

"This is a religious thing."

She gave him another long look, fond this time, and then started off toward the back, where the garbage cans were. There was a small courtyard out there, blocked from the street by a high solid fence. It had a door in it to let the garbage trucks in, but the garbage trucks only came on Thursdays.

He wrapped his fingers around the rosary in his pocket and slid off his stool. He saw her disappear between the refrigerators just as the knife began to prick him again.

"I wish I knew what went on in your head," she was saying, in a high clear voice that carried. "First you're here. Then you're there. Now you're everywhere. You remind me of this television show I used to watch. It had a genie it in. I used to camp out in the living room with a bag of potato chips and wish I could be one."

He caught up with her. He stepped past her into the courtyard and waited until she got outside. Then he slammed the door behind them both.

"Look," he said, holding the rosary out to her. "Real amber."

6   Three minutes later, she was dead, lying with her arms spread out across the concrete and her feet in the trash. He got a handful of snow and pressed it down on her forehead, making her cold, making her freeze. He would hold the snow to her forehead until her skin was just a little stiff. He had learned with Margaret Mary McVann that human flesh was very hard to cut when it was warm.

Her name was Ellen Burnett. It was engraved on a plastic pin she wore on the pocket of her uniform.

PART TWO

CHAPTER

ONE

1   The rectory where John Kelly lived with four other Jesuit
priests was not really a rectory at all. To be that, it would
have had to be attached to a parish. Instead, like most Jesuit houses
unconnected to a Jesuit university, it was attached to nothing. He
was there because, as auxiliary bishop and vicar for New Haven,
he had to live somewhere. The Jesuits interpreted their vow of
poverty as a sacrifice of ownership. As a member of the Society of
Jesus, there was literally nothing in the world that was actually
"his." Even the clothes on his back belonged to his order. On the
other hand, he lived in this house, built in 1891 by a man who'd
made a fortune out of the Civil War. The hallways were wide and
the bedrooms were oversized. Downstairs, there was a living room
that had once been the Great Hall of a castle in Bavaria. It had been
moved stone by stone to New Haven and reassembled on the spot,
complete with gold-leaf-painted mirrors and sculpted marble col-
umns that held up the fireplace mantel. Being here, he could almost
imagine himself a different kind of man in a different kind of time:
a man poverty inspired instead of paralyzing; a time when inspi-
ration was applauded and might have done some good.

     He went down the curving staircase to the foyer, then across
the foyer to the dining room. The dining room had a convex ceiling
lined with miniature imitations of the foyer chandelier. Underneath
it, a black walnut table stretched out to the length of fifty feet. As
always, his fellow priests were clustered at the far end of it. They

always jammed themselves together as if they were having breakfast in a small diner's even smaller booth.

He walked down to them and picked up the plate that had been set at his place. Along one wall there was an oversize sideboard. On the sideboard were half a dozen sterling silver serving trays, each set in a sterling silver frame that held it over a glowing pink candle. The pink was their housekeeper's idea of piety. Pink—old rose really—was the liturgical color of the first three weeks of Advent.

He got toast, scrambled eggs, and bacon. Then he sat down next to Manuel Rodez and his Siamese attachment, the daily newspaper.

"Isn't anyone going to say good morning?" he said.

Rodez looked up. "It isn't a good morning," he said. "In fact, it's a perfectly lousy morning. And it's Friday the thirteenth."

On the other side of the table, Bill Keeler coughed. "I think you're exaggerating that," he said. "We've got better weather than we've had for a month."

Rodez pushed the paper across to Kelly. "Look at this," he said. "This was on the doorstep when I got up."

"The paper's always on the doorstep when you get up," Jim Barnes said.

"The paper's usually a lot of dreck about local politicians." Rodez pushed the paper at Kelly again. "Look at it," he insisted. "You're the vicar around here. You ought to have known this already."

"The vicar is not supposed to spend his time hanging around in morgues," Keeler said.

Rick Borden laughed. "John'd probably have a better time if he did. It has to beat trying to explain to the bishop why some priest in the Congo is saying his Mass in Esperanto."

"That's not what John's trying to explain to the Bishop," Keeler said. "He's trying to explain how being a television star is theologically equivalent to bloody martyrdom."

Rodez was still pushing the paper out. John took it, sighing a little. Since he'd first mentioned Victor Coletti's offer, he'd been under almost constant attack from these four men he lived with. Coupled with the attacks he made on himself—What was he doing? Why was he doing it? Why was he taking risks?—these had made his life damn near unbearable. What made it more unbearable still was that he didn't know why they were so hostile. It might have been jealousy—here he was, not only on his way up the hierarchy but with a chance at media fame as well—but these weren't ordinarily jealous men. The only other explanation he could think of was a kind of instinctive distaste. Television preaching was for low-rent Protestants, Fundamentalists, and Pentacostals, not the educated army of the Society of Jesus. Maybe they thought he was letting down the side.

He spread the paper out in front of him and read the headline. It would have been impossible not to. It was the biggest type he had ever seen, and so black it looked as if a gallon of ink had been emptied on the page.

"Psychopath," he read. "Psychopath?"

"Open it up," Rodez said.

"Manuel is taking it personally," Jim Barnes said. "He thinks the whole thing is a Protestant plot against Holy Mother Church."

"Open it *up*," Rodez said again.

John Kelly opened it up, to find two black-bordered pictures sitting right below the center crease. The second was of a woman he was sure he had never seen before. The first one, though, was vaguely familiar. He looked down at the caption and read: Margaret Mary McVann.

"McVann," he said. "Didn't I know someone named Mc-Vann?"

"You might have," Borden said. "She ran the soup kitchen for Saint Gabriel's over on the Derby line."

"That's right. She came in asking for money from the diocese. I think we gave it to her."

"She was an ex-nun," Rodez said.

John Kelly said "mmm." He could not imagine leaving the

priesthood himself. The mere idea scared the hell out of him. He left the world of ex-religious strictly alone.

"The thing is," Rodez said, "they were all ex-nuns. All these women."

"All two of them," Keeler pointed out.

"Two is enough. It's a pattern. Even the *Register* thinks it's a pattern."

"A pattern of what?" Barnes asked.

"A pattern of someone going around killing ex-nuns," Rodez said. "And you know what it means if he's killing *ex*-nuns. You have to know what it means."

"What does it mean?" Borden said.

"Traditionalists," Rodez said solemnly. "They've always been unhinged. Now there's one walking around who's absolutely crazy."

Borden threw his hands in the air. "Rodez, for God's sake. You see traditionalists under the bed the way J. Edgar Hoover used to see Communists."

"There's a difference," Rodez said. "The Communists weren't there. The traditionalists are."

"The traditionalists are happy as long as they've got a Tridentine Mass they can go to. Which, in this diocese, they do." Borden looked at the spoon he'd been holding and put it down. It was clean. His plate was clean, too. So were his knife and fork. The only dirty dish at his plate was the cup that had held his single black coffee of the morning. Borden was one of those people who never seemed to eat anything.

He turned to John and said, "I suppose you are going to have to do something about this. God only knows what. The second victim was that Cavello woman who worked at Damien House."

"The second one happened right in the kitchen at Damien House," Rodez said.

Borden ignored him. "I don't think it has anything to do with the Church, but the bishop might. Isn't this the kind of thing you're supposed to handle?"

"I don't think there's ever been this kind of thing before,"

John said, and it was true. He'd heard of priests gone renegade in one way or another—sexual indiscretions; liturgical innovations; theological scandals—but never of a serial murderer in any way connected to the Church. In real life, at any rate. Like many priests, he read William Kienzle's mystery novels faithfully. The first of those had been about a homicidal maniac knocking off the clergy and religious of the city of Detroit.

They were looking at him expectantly, as if he were about to give them the answer to their ultimate questions, the ones they thought about but never asked: what did he do, and why had he been sent here to do it? Since he didn't know the answers himself— the Bishop had said only that New Haven was "becoming an area of great pastoral concern" and that somebody ought to be here— he looked away out the broad dining-room windows at the back lawn.

"I suppose somebody will call the office for a statement," he said. "They do that every time a Catholic butterfly farts. Maybe I ought to make sure what the police think about this thing."

"Maybe you ought to make sure what you think about it," Rodez said. He dumped the newspaper in Kelly's lap. "Take this."

"I will."

"I'm surprised the press haven't got in touch with you already," Borden said. "Your office board should have been swamped."

John Kelly leaned forward and got a big blob of butter to put on his toast. His toast was cold.

2   Actually, his office switchboard could have been swamped all day yesterday. There was no way he could have known. He had spent all of yesterday afternoon with a lawyer—a Protestant lawyer—from one of the large law firms in Hartford. The firm in Hartford had connections to a firm in New York. The firm in New York did a lot of work with television contracts. He couldn't have afforded either of them, but one of the Hartford firm's senior partners was a Good Catholic Layman of the old school.

Francis Quinn's office had been a room the size of a Record World store, with a fifty-thousand-dollar Iranian rug on the floor. Quinn sat behind his desk, tapping the contract Victor Coletti wanted John Kelly to sign. His suit had been custom made at Brooks Brothers. His shirt had been custom made at J. Press. His tie was dark blue with a pattern of tiny embroidered mallards on it. Even his head had looked both custom made and bought. Money and power had erased whatever traces of ethnicity he had been born with.

"This," he had told Kelly, "is a very good contract. Too good."

"How could a contract be too good?"

"It could be too good in a hundred different ways," Quinn said. "I don't know this Victor Coletti. I've never had any dealings with him." The expression on his face said that he never would. People like Francis Quinn didn't have dealings with people who were so obviously—Italian. "I don't know how this Coletti does business. I just know how he ought to do business."

Quinn started tapping the contract again. "He's giving away the store, Your Excellency. He's giving you things for which I'd expect to have to negotiate for months. And even then I wouldn't expect to get them. Not unless you were already Fulton J. Sheen."

"Maybe he's just what he says he is." Kelly wanted to ask Quinn to stop calling him "Your Excellency." Nobody called auxiliary bishops "Your Excellency." It was a title only rarely used for archbishops these days. "Maybe he's a good Catholic layman trying to do the right thing by a priest."

"He owns a television station."

"So?"

"Well, Your Excellency. I'm a good Catholic layman. I always try to do right by priests. But let me tell you, I'd look at the situation differently if you were a lawyer as well as a priest, and you wanted to, for instance, merge your firm into mine. I'd be nervous about setting a precedent."

"A precedent for what?"

"For future contracts." Quinn was exasperated. "Your Excellency, you're not the only one Victor Coletti is going to sign to appear on the air this year. His station is a network affiliate. He's got to have a local news staff if nothing else. That staff is going to have the terms of this contract before you ever put your signature on it. They're going to cause him a lot of trouble."

"But this is the contract he sent me," Kelly pointed out. "He must be willing to live with the trouble."

"The question is why?"

"Does there have to be a reason?"

"Yes," Quinn said. "There most definitely does have to be a reason. Unless the man is a saint, which I really don't believe."

Kelly wanted to say why not?, but he didn't—any more than he had asked Quinn to stop calling him Your Excellency. He had the devil in him, as his mother used to say, in that brief period in his life when she had been able to say anything at all. He didn't like Francis Quinn. Because of that, he was playing the Unworldly Priest well past the point where it made any sense. He'd grown up on the street, for God's sake. He might not have had much experience with men who owned television stations, but he'd had more than enough with thieves. Francis Quinn couldn't tell him anything about Victor Coletti he hadn't already guessed.

But Quinn was a lace curtain Irishman. Like most of his tribe, he was both arrogant and hypocritical.

"I'm going to send you down to a young man we have," he said. "David Murrow. He specializes in things like this."

"Contracts that look too good to be true?"

"Contracts, period. We don't do a lot with television contracts in Hartford, but David was with Burroughs and Barthe in New York. He did a lot of work for media people there."

"Maybe I ought to just sign this thing," Kelly said. "If Victor's got an ulterior motive for giving the store away, at least he'll be giving it away to the Church."

"In the meantime, he might be doing the Church a lot of damage. See David Murrow, Your Excellency."

"I will."

David Murrow was the Protestant lawyer.

The cab pulled up to the curb in front of the building that housed the diocesan offices, and John Kelly got out. Francis Quinn. David Murrow. Victor Coletti. The names swirled around in his brain in no particular order, seeming all of a piece. Victor Coletti was a thief, but Francis Quinn was one, too. David Murrow was a valet to thieves. Something. John Kelly was very tired. Since Victor Coletti had sent him that letter with the offer in it, he had been having trouble getting to sleep.

He pushed through the revolving glass doors into the lobby and headed for the elevators. There was a woman waiting there, a tall woman in a black wool coat and boots with very high heels, but he didn't pay any attention to her. There were doctors and lawyers in this building as well as Diocesan offices. Their clients always seemed to be wandering in and out, looking lost.

He pressed the up button and thought about Dan Murphy, who would now be forever connected in his mind with Victor. They were of a piece, too, although not in so obvious a way as Victor and Quinn.

The elevator was taking forever to come. He unfolded Rodez's newspaper from under his arm and started to read it. He had just gotten to the part about the crazed killer stalking the streets of the city when he felt a hand on his arm.

He looked up, and the woman in the black coat was watching him. She was very pretty but getting old. There was gray at the roots of her hair and a nest of crow's feet at the side of each eye.

"Excuse me," she said. "Are you Bishop John Kelly?"

"That's right," Kelly said. "I am."

She took her hand off his arm and looked away and said, "I'm Catherine Sargent. I need you to listen to something I have to say."

CHAPTER

Two

1 At first, John Kelly thought the woman had come to ask him to help her find a job. Finding jobs for people was a surprisingly large part of his work, a part he'd never considered before coming up here. Down in the diocesan office in Bridgeport, he'd been protected from all that. He'd been assigned to the bishop for "theological investigations." He'd spent his time wading through encyclicals and dispatches from Rome, trying to figure out how to fit them into an American context. He'd come to the decision that, for Rome, there was no American context. The Italians understood as much about the United States as he did about electromagnetism, meaning nothing; Ratzinger was better. The Polish Pope was worse. Sometimes he'd lain awake nights wondering what it would be like to set an Italian cardinal down in Bridgeport for a year, anonymously, and make him live like everyone else. He kept getting visions of nervous breakdowns in working-class bars and psychic breaks over the morning newspaper.

By the time the elevator reached his floor, he had changed his mind. He'd seen a thousand job-seekers, and she didn't have the look—not even the look of someone come to ask for someone else. She stood in the very middle of the car with her high stacked heels close together and her arms hanging motionless at her sides. Her blond hair had been cut to look as if it had been curled into a pageboy. Her black gloves were lined with cashmere. His assessment was reflexive: money but not serious money; a woman who had married a man in law or medicine.

The elevator doors opened onto a wide hall that opened onto the diocesan offices' reception area, and they both stepped out. Through the archway, Kelly could see Marie at her desk, sullen and bleary-eyed, looking off into space with all the mental alertness of a catatonic on Thorazine. Marie was the daughter of one of those Important Catholic Laymen Kelly could never get himself to like. He was stuck with her until she decided to elope again. The last time, she'd eloped with the ex-mental patient who served as the lead singer in her favorite local punk rock band.

Kelly turned to Catherine Sargent. "My office is through there," he said. "I'll have to talk to my secretary—"

"I'm not going to be put off," Catherine Sargent said. "I'll sit in your lobby all morning, but I'm not going to be put off."

"I don't want to put you off," John Kelly said. And it was true. Too many of the people who came looking for jobs had histories that sounded like his own. He could sympathize, but he could never make himself feel comfortable with them. They scared him. Worse, listening to them was like listening to his mother's soul, an ectoplasmic stream of suffering and complaint. Catherine Sargent was something different, if not exactly something friendly.

She was also looking at him as if she didn't believe a word he said. He gave her a little smile and led the way into reception. Marie had straightened up at her desk—she must have heard them in the hall—and was doing her best to look competent and awake. She looked ferocious instead. John Kelly never ceased to be surprised that she had married as many times as she had, three or four at last count. She was as ugly and intractable as a wart.

He took off his coat and hung it on the rack in the corner, one of those homey touches the diocese was convinced would make the Faithful more relaxed. Whether it did or not, Kelly had never been able to tell.

He turned back to find Marie looking suspiciously at Catherine Sargent. Marie hated pretty women, in any shape or form.

"You've got to answer a lot of calls," Marie said. "The bishop even called. Himself."

Kelly doubted this. It would have been one of the bishop's aides who called, Father Blank or Father Dolan, even if the bishop meant to get on later and do the talking. Bridgeport wasn't much of a diocese, but the bishop was meticulous about protocol.

"Dan Murphy called, too," Marie said. "And that man who calls all the time now. Vincent Carlucci."

"Victor Coletti," Kelly said automatically.

"Him."

Kelly kept himself from sighing out loud by force of will. It only made things worse, he knew that from experience. Marie could go from passively to actively hostile in no time at all. He turned to Catherine Sargent, standing in the middle of reception with her coat still on, and said, "This is Mrs.—Ms.—Sargent. She's going to come into my office for a little while. When we're finished, I'll answer the bishop's call."

Marie stared at him for a moment, then stared at Catherine Sargent, then stared at Catherine Sargent's shoes. "The bishop said you were supposed to call him right back. As soon as you got in."

"The bishop has no way of knowing when I get in."

"She doesn't even have an appointment. You've got a page of people set to see you. Your day's all booked up."

"Obviously it's not booked up now, Marie. There's nobody here."

"I think you ought to call the bishop back right away. He said somebody had been murdered."

Catherine Sargent's eyebrows rose practically to her hairline. John Kelly blushed. The bishop must have been paying more attention to the news than he had, and taking it more seriously. Rodez's paper was still in his hands, unread. But none of this was really important. It couldn't be, unless a priest or nun was suspected of being the killer. If that had been the case, Rodez would have said something about it. All this was was a blip on the radar screen, a problem with an almost untraceable connection, an incident that would require a press release. He turned his back to Marie and smiled at Catherine Sargent.

"I don't know if you saw the papers this morning, but there seems to be a serial killer in New Haven."

"I saw the papers."

"He's had two victims, and they both were ex-nuns."

"I'm glad I'm not an ex-nun."

"Yes," John Kelly said, nonplussed. "Yes. I'm glad I'm not one either." He turned back to Marie. "I'm going into my office and have a talk with Ms. Sargent. I don't want to be interrupted by any calls. Not even calls from the bishop."

"I can't lie to the bishop," Marie said.

"You don't have to lie to him. You can tell him the truth."

"He'll be insulted."

"No, he won't."

"I'll bet she isn't even Catholic," Marie said. "She doesn't look Catholic."

Kelly wanted to ask her what Catholic looked like, considering the fact that the Church had nearly seven hundred million members spread without exception across the surface of the earth. Instead, he walked past her desk into the short hall that led to his office, motioning Catherine Sargent to follow.

2 In his office, Catherine Sargent finally took off her coat. She draped it over the back of one of his two visitors' chairs and walked around a little, reading the titles of the books in his bookcase and the caption under the woodcut that hung on his east wall. She was wearing a dress as black as her coat, but with a white collar and cuffs that made her look as if she'd just escaped from a Swiss boarding school. When she reached the statue of Mary she reached out and tapped it lightly. It made Kelly wonder if she was checking to see if it was solid.

She came back to his desk, sat down in the chair she hadn't thrown the coat on, and folded her hands in her lap. "As I told you downstairs," she said, "my name is Catherine Sargent. I take it the 'Sargent' isn't familiar to you."

"No," Kelly said. "It isn't."

"The girl at the desk was right, you know. I'm not Catholic and I never have been. I'm not anything. Religious."

"Most people aren't, these days."

"I suppose you're right. In this country, at least. My husband is the same way. I think he was raised Presbyterian, but I've never known him to go to church. We were married in my parents' house by a justice of the peace."

"All right." What was this about?

Catherine Sargent shifted, just slightly, in her seat. "Three years after we were married, we had a child. A son we named Robert. He was the only child we had. I don't want to get personal here, but I wasn't capable of having any more. The way things turned out, I think I'm just as glad. Robert turned sixteen at the beginning of last October."

"And?"

She shifted in her seat again, then looked away. Her pocketbook, a black shoulder-strap just large enough to hold a wallet and a set of keys, sat at her feet. She stared at that.

"Excuse me," she said finally. "Would you mind if I smoked?"

"Of course not." Kelly was surprised. Women like this didn't usually smoke these days. Smokelessness had become a badge of their class.

She leaned over, got her pocketbook off the floor, got her cigarettes out. Kelly got the ashtray out of the top drawer of his desk and pushed it across to her.

"My husband," Catherine Sargent said, "would tell you Robert has changed. I don't think that's true. When he was small, I used to wonder if he was mildly autistic. He didn't do that rocking thing autistic children are supposed to do, but he—lacked affect. He'd cry when he was physically hurt. Beyond that, if he had any emotions at all, I never saw them."

"That doesn't sound like autism," Kelly said. "With the autistic, there's supposed to be a lot of anger."

Catherine Sargent nodded. "I know. That's what the doctors told me when I took him, and that's what my husband says when I bring this up. My husband thinks Robbie was just—shy."

"What did the doctors think?"

"They thought I was imagining things. Sometimes they thought worse. One of them suggested I go into therapy myself."

"Did you?"

"No." Her cigarette had grown a long column of ash. She tapped it into the ashtray and took another deep drag. Then she looked at it as if she couldn't imagine where it had come from.

"I quit smoking these things nearly ten years ago," she said. "I started up again last month. I was back on two packs a day in under a week." She took another deep drag and shook her head. "When my husband came home and found the living room full of smoke, he thought somebody had died. He thought Robbie had died. He almost had a heart attack right there."

"I take it Robbie hasn't died."

"No. I almost wish he had."

"Because he—lacks affect?"

Catherine Sargent laughed. "Oh, dear," she said. "He doesn't seem to lack affect anymore. He's got more emotions than I knew existed. It's just that none of them make any sense. Do you know a priest named Father Thomas Burne?"

"Yes, of course." Kelly was surprised again. Burne was a saint to street kids and the police department, a demon to the county social workers, an enigma to the Church, but he was not a casually famous man. Where would Catherine Sargent have heard of him? If she'd been Catholic, he could have put it down to the diocesan newsletter or the Catholic Charities mailing list, but she wasn't. In fact, it was hard to tell what she was. It was impossible to tell what she felt.

He watched her stub her cigarette out, get another, and light up again. Her lighter was one of the gunmetal gray Zippos women used when they'd been to private school. In the glare of the flame, her skin looked as thin as paper.

"When Robbie was fourteen," she said, "he started to get very aggressive. If it had been heavy metal rock or punk clothes, I could have understood it. Half my friends have children who look like they've been sleeping on park benches. Robbie went the other way. We had him at the Thorne School. We were talking about sending him to Deerfield. He'd always been bright even if he'd always been—strange. One day we noticed he'd started coming home with—things. Clothes, mostly."

"Clothes," John Kelly repeated. He was doing his best to sound very wise, but he was thoroughly bewildered. He had no idea what this was leading up to.

Catherine Sargent blew a stream of smoke into the air. "My husband and I are well off, but we're not rich. He's an accountant in private practice. We can do what's important to us if we set priorities. We had enough to send Robbie to Deerfield and maybe to the Ivy League if we didn't waste the money on other things. We gave Robbie a reasonable but not generous allowance. When Robbie started coming home with the clothes, designer clothes, expensive clothes, we thought he was stealing them."

"You've changed your mind?"

"I don't know. We found cash. If he was stealing the clothes, he had to have been stealing cash, too, and I don't know where he'd have done that. We don't keep a lot of cash in the house. It couldn't have come from us. And we kept a pretty tight leash on Robbie. He was only fourteen. He wasn't wandering around in the middle of the night sticking up gas stations."

"How much money was involved?"

This time, Catherine Sargent's smile was thin. "Once I went through one of those new blazers of his and came up with a thousand dollars in hundred dollar bills."

John Kelly blinked. A thousand dollars. Where would a fourteen-year-old boy come up with a thousand dollars? He couldn't have come up with a thousand dollars himself, in cash, if his life depended on it. He hazarded the only explanation he could think of, aware all the while that Catherine Sargent's face had frozen into an expression of amusement that was somehow irredeemably horrible.

"Was it dope?" he said.

"I'm pretty sure not," Catherine Sargent said.

"What was it, then?"

She had smoked another cigarette down to the butt. She lit up for a third time, then stood and walked to his window. She kept her back to him and one arm wrapped around her waist.

"Two days after his fifteenth birthday," she said, "Robbie disappeared. He didn't tell us he was running away from home. He didn't leave a note. Things had been tense for a long time—even his father was beginning to see something was seriously wrong—but we hadn't had a fight recently and we hadn't had a confrontation. He was just gone. We went to the police."

"Did they find him?"

"Nobody found him. We didn't hear anything of him for almost a year. I used to worry that he'd gone to New York City. I used to worry, period."

"I don't blame you."

"I should have been more worried than I was. What do I call a bishop, anyway? Your honor?"

"I'm only an auxiliary bishop. You can call me 'Father' if you want to."

"Well, Father, about a month ago Robbie surfaced. According to what he told the district attorney's office—and what the district attorney's office told us; I'm getting this secondhand—he'd been living on the streets of New Haven all the time, eating out of garbage cans. He said his father was abusive and he was afraid to go home."

John Kelly felt his mood shift. You could never tell in abuse cases. Anybody could be lying and anybody could be telling the truth. With this on the table, Catherine Sargent looked a little shabbier to him. Then, suddenly, he was ashamed of himself. He didn't know anything about this, or about her, and the mere suggestion of abuse had started a litany of accusations in his mind. He felt like an Inquisitor.

"Did the district attorney's office send Robbie to Father Burne?"

"They did indeed," Catherine said.

"Did they file abuse charges against your husband?"

Catherine Sargent turned her back to the window. The smoke from her cigarette rose in front of her face like the smoke from an incense stick and curled around her head. The prettiness was gone from her face. In its place was something both cruel and triumphant.

"The district attorney's office hasn't filed charges yet," she said. "Robbie got a lawyer and filed suit all by himself. But he isn't suing us, Father Kelly. He's suing Father Tom Burne. He's saying Father Burne fucked him and Father Burne would only let him stay at Damien House as long as he went on being fucked."

CHAPTER

THREE

1 On the day Dan announced at breakfast that he would be
home for lunch, Susan decided to go down to Damien House
by herself. It was Monday, December 16, and she didn't actually
decide. That would have taken forethought, and there were times
she thought she'd lost all capacity for forethought in the weeks since
she'd left the convent. Sometimes she thought she'd even lost consciousness. In her first days of being out, the holdover habits of
being in had been so slight, and surfaced so erratically, she'd thought
they'd disappear in no time at all and with no effort on her part.
Then, as morning followed morning, she'd begun to catch herself
doing things that would have looked crazy to anyone who didn't
know her history. Swinging her feet out of bed so that they landed
on the floor with a dull but violent slap; praying in Latin before
she had her eyes open; walking against the wall on her way to the
bathroom: what was coming out in her was something old enough
to be ancient, the routine of convent life before the changes of
Vatican II had made themselves felt. Her order had been laggard
in that respect. While all the other nuns in the archdiocese of Hartford were already experimenting with lay dress and lunches at
McDonald's, Susan had still been wearing a wimple, five layers of
underwear, and a veil that reached down her back to her knees. All
that had lasted well into the 1970s, so that Susan had spent her
first five years after tertiary profession looking—as a man who
stopped her on the street had once put it—like a "real nun." If there
was anything she remembered from that period, rather than simply

had fused into her bones, it was the older people who would stop
her, their eyes pleading and desperate, anxious and afraid of hope.
They all had the same question, which was not really the question
they wanted to ask at all. They wanted to know if they would get
their Church back.

Hearing her feet slap the floor that morning, she pulled them
back under her, ran her palms over her face, and shook her head.
It was still dark out, probably before six in the morning. That was
a habit that had lasted all her seventeen years inside, and that she
thought she would never break. She played her fingers through her
hair until her scalp hurt and then stood up.

The only light in the room was coming from one of the
security arcs outside. She went to the window and pulled the curtains shut, realizing as she did that she had left the window open
the night before, in spite of the fact that it was freezing. That was
more nun stuff, as she was beginning to think of it. Back in canonical
year, her novice mistress, old Sister Marie Bonaventure, had believed in fresh air the way the Nazis had believed in the Blitzkrieg.

Susan put on her robe, stopped herself from fastening it too
tightly around her waist, the way she had been taught to do, and
let herself into the hall. With no lights burning, the hall was pitch
dark and eerie, full of imaginary cobwebs. Full of imaginary skel-
etons, too, Susan thought, and let herself into the bathroom. Like
a lot of other things in the house, it had been renovated. There was
ceramic tile on the walls and floor and ceiling and a big oval tub
Dan had told her proudly was a "Jacuzzi for four." Every time she
saw it, Susan wondered: four *what*? She didn't like to imagine Dan
with all those women at once.

She got her toothpaste and her Camay soap out of the little
green bag she had brought to put them in—*more* nun stuff—looked
at herself in the mirror, and sighed.

It didn't matter how hard she tried to block it, to fill her
head with memories and excuses. It didn't matter how hard she
tried to tell herself she was afraid. Theresa Cavello, the Congo, the
faces of children drifting in the street—going back wasn't sensible,

but it was what she kept feeling she had to do. God only knew she was sick and tired of hanging around this place, brooding about herself, brooding about Dan. Brooding wasn't getting anybody anyplace and it wasn't making her less bored.

Or less anxious.

She turned on the tap, threw water on herself, and scrubbed.

2 She was in the hall half an hour later, putting on her boots and fretting about her coat, when she heard a sound on the stairs and, looking up, saw Andy coming toward her. He looked as much of a mess as always, but less alert and less intelligent. She turned her face away from him and thrust her arm into the sleeve of a parka she had bought for herself when she was sixteen years old.

"Where are you going?" he asked her.

"For a walk."

"It's quarter to six in the goddamned morning," he told her.

Susan shrugged and stuffed the other arm into the other sleeve. She was used to getting up at four and getting to work by five—and besides, what did the time have to do with it? The kitchen was behind her and it was a pit of vipers, her private arena for her private disintegration. She went to the front door and pulled it open, letting in the dark.

"I'm going for a walk," she repeated. "I'm feeling antsy."

"I didn't think *antsy* was the kind of word a nun used," Andy said.

"I'm not a nun."

She stepped out onto the porch and looked down Edge Hill Road, at the street lamps, at the dark. Then, thinking she knew what Andy was worried about, she turned back and said, "I'll be home for lunch. You can promise Dan."

CHAPTER

FOUR

1 He was waiting for her when she came out of the house, sitting in the front bushes instead of the trees at the back, knowing she would bolt. That was one of the things he was good at, knowing when people would bolt, what the limits were to their self-control. He had been watching her for a while now and he had her all figured out.

She came down the porch steps and started across the front walk, keeping carefully in the center of it, as if she were *willing* herself to walk in the center of it. She let herself out the front gate onto the street.

If she went down the hill, she would pass directly in front of him. If she went up, she would move away. He closed his eyes and prayed, hard, until he heard the sound of her feet on the rock salt just a few inches from his ear. He thought he knew where she was going—he had been watching her for so long—but he could never be sure.

When he opened his eyes again, she was already halfway down the hill. She moved quickly and with purpose, as if she knew where she were going.

He swiveled his head around just in time to see a man turn off the light in the house's foyer and head up the stairs. Then he looked back at Susan, in her jeans and old sweater and worn coat. She had to be going where he thought she was going. There was no other reason for her to be dressed that way.

He waited a few moments, just to be sure, and then he swung out on the street himself, following her.

2 Sometimes, thinking about his charism, he was afraid. Sometimes it all seemed so nebulous and diffuse, like the nightmares of the junkies who slept in the boxes in the vacant lots that took up so much of the Congo. It was wrong to call it the Congo now, really, even for the worst kind of racist fool. It had sunk now beneath even the tenuous respectability of a ghetto, and most of the people who slept there were white.

He stepped into the street and began walking downhill that way, watching her slipping and sliding down the sidewalk ahead of him. The rock salt hadn't been spread as thickly at the bottom of Edge Hill as at the top. Below a certain economic level, the city of New Haven stopped worrying about your chances of breaking your neck on the ice.

3 She reached the bottom of the hill, turned the corner, and went on walking. He speeded up and kept following, keeping his distance and varying his pace. He had been thinking about not coming out this morning, thinking how tired he was and how it wouldn't matter if he missed a single day. Now he was glad he had listened to that insistent voice of God in his head and come in spite of himself.

Right now, his charism didn't seem nebulous and diffuse. He was omniscient and invulnerable, guided by the light. He was on the cusp of a prophecy.

Two blocks ahead of him, she turned another corner. When he came around that corner himself he found her stopped under a bus sign, her hands in her pockets and her teeth biting against her lips to keep them from hardening in the cold. He had forgotten that the buses to where she wanted to go started running at six.

He gave her a shy little smile, and stepped back.

She paid no attention to him at all.

4   He had to remember: she was the start of it all, the bad seed of faith who had begun the betrayal and caused the rest of it. She was not like Margaret Mary McVann or any of the others. She had to be handled carefully. Everything that happened to her had to be planned.

Then, too, it was harder to kill a general than a soldier. It took practice. It took rehearsal.

He thought she had to be a general because she was his sister. She had to be the explanation of him.

It was getting fuzzy in his head again, but he knew what he meant.

This was his charism: to find the soldiers of Judas Iscariot and lay them down.

PART THREE

1 Catching the bus at the Green, even making the change at the very last minute in a blackened landscape that looked less and less familiar by the minute, Susan had thought it was going to be easy. Certainly she knew how to get where she was going, even after she reached the point where the buses stopped running and she would have to walk. The memory of her trip with Andy was burned indelibly into her brain, like the memory of where she had been when she heard that JFK had been assassinated. Certainly she knew New Haven. She had been born and brought up there. What she hadn't counted on was the peculiar ebb and flow of city life. The city changed from hour to hour, especially in places like Congress Avenue, becoming unrecognizable to itself in transformations that took split seconds and altered everything. When she got off the bus at Congress Avenue it was nothing like she remembered it. The small novelty stores seemed to have disappeared into the dirt and concrete. The people who crowded the street seemed to have come from some Hollywood censor's fantasy of the evils of prostitution. The light was glaring, neon and jerky and never white. An enormous sign that said GIRLS! GIRLS! 25¢! 25¢! 25¢! seemed to take up an entire block. In the Congo it was still night.

She knew she only had to keep walking along the avenue until she found Amora Street, and so she did, pushing against girls in halter tops and thigh-high sarongs who looked younger than her eighth-grade students back at Saint Mary of the Rosary Parish School. Their makeup was inexpert and halfhearted, but the men who stood behind them were intense. Susan was startled to realize how many of those men there were. Somehow, she had always thought of prostitutes as free agents on the street—with their pimps hidden off somewhere, where the customers couldn't see them.

Still, the prostitutes gave her heart. They looked her up and down in disbelief, checking out her jeans and her parka and her clunky L. L. Bean hunting shoes—baggy jeans now, because the one piece of shopping she had done since she got back to New Haven was to replace the tight ones Dan had bought for her. When she was a third of the way up Congress Avenue, one of the girls came up to her and said, "You ought to get out of here. You ought to get out of here now," and Susan wanted to say something just as pertinent, to find a way through the cosmetic shell. It was more nun stuff, and she knew it, but it was nun stuff that seemed necessary. Surely this girl, with her small undeveloped breasts and her skin as smooth and unmarked as an infant's, didn't want to be standing out here in the subzero cold in less clothing than most people wore to lunch at a beach resort, waiting for men. Then the moment passed and was gone. The girl stepped back into the line and functionally disappeared. A moment after she'd stepped away, Susan could no longer have picked her out of the lineup.

Her guilt at that didn't last very long. It was taken over by fear, and then by confusion. She almost missed Amora Street, because in her mind it was a turn off a dead stretch of Congress Avenue. Two hours from now, there might even be a dead stretch of Congress Avenue. Half an hour might be enough to leach the life out of the place. At quarter after six, it was still spurting blood.

Susan never noticed the beginning of the burned-out buildings, because they were hidden behind a road show. A pimp had set his girls out on the sidewalk like the Rockette line at Rockefeller Center. They were kicking and laughing and blowing white breath into the cold, while he sat on the curb picking his teeth with the edge of a matchbook and flexing the tattoo on his arm. In the weird light, Susan couldn't see what the tattoo was of, but the pimp could see her. He spit into the sides of her boots as she passed and said, "Too fucking old."

The turn for Amora Street was right there, and she missed it. She walked into a ring of men huddled around a fire they had built in a garbage can. God only knew where the garbage can had come from—Congress Avenue didn't seem to have any—and God only knew what had been in it. The fire smelled funny. The men had all shot up, or smoked something. Susan didn't know enough about drugs to tell. She just knew they were all falling asleep in spite of their thin clothes, and some of them were giggling.

Once she got beyond them, she found she was in terra incognita. The landscape in front of her was not burned out but wild. If it had ever been part of the city of New Haven, only an urban archeologist could tell. She backed up, spun around, and headed toward where she had come. She even made herself stop paying attention to the people and start paying attention to the signs. She found Amora Street where the Rockettes started up again.

Standing on the corner, looking into the dark, she found the burned-out buildings she had been looking for. They were out there, in the side streets, like gangrenous limbs on an otherwise living body.

"Jesus Christ," one of the Rockettes said, right into her ear, "if it isn't Polly-wally-anna-all-the-day."

That was when she realized the Rockettes were men.

2 Ten minutes later, Susan was pushing the front doorbell at Damien House, looking back at Congress Avenue through the black around her and wondering what she thought she was doing. The place looked as dead as it had on the day she had come to see it with Andy, just when she thought it ought to be jumping, lit up and ready to take in all those children—like the girl who had spoken to her in kindness back on the Avenue—who were desperately looking for a way into a different life. Then she began to feel like the worst kind of fool—a do-gooder fool, with a head full of

nun stuff and naïve certainties about what the People want. Who was she to tell that girl how to live her life? Who was she to assume that that girl didn't already like her life? Who was she—

She might have given up the whole thing, turned and run and fled back to Edge Hill Road, but she had been leaning against the buzzer the whole time. The dim light above her head was joined by two more, turned on by someone inside. Susan jumped at the little click the lights made and turned to see someone behind the door, a tall, spare, middle-aged woman she didn't recognize, in a robe. Obviously she had gotten this poor woman out of bed and, just as obviously, that made it impossible for her to go. Instead, she stepped back and waited while the woman opened the door.

"Excuse me," Susan said. "I didn't realize I'd be waking anyone up. I assumed—"

The middle-aged woman was already waving this away. "I'm supposed to be woken up," she said. "Come in and sit down if you've got a mind to." Then she looked Susan up and down very carefully, nodded thoughtfully to herself, and added, "Sister."

3 Her name was Marietta O'Brien, and the reason Susan hadn't seen her on the day she came down with Andy was that Marietta had been out shopping. "That's what I do," Marietta said, moving around the kitchen, getting coffee for them both. "I shop. I clean. I go out to the mayor's office and pick up forms, or the welfare office for that matter. What do you do, if you're not a Sister, I mean?"

Susan took a drag on her cigarette, put it in the ashtray Marietta had given her, and sighed. She had gone from fear and elation to comfort and confusion. She was no longer entirely sure what she was doing here. Her penance for this state of mental disorganization was Marietta O'Brien.

"I don't do anything at the moment," she said. "I live with my brothers in the house where we grew up. I read a lot. I've started to smoke too much."

"Nobody smokes anymore," Marietta O'Brien said. "What do you want? You gonna come down here and volunteer?"

"I don't know. I don't know anything about volunteering. I don't even know what volunteers do."

"Get themselves killed," Marietta said, "or mugged anyway. I've been mugged half a dozen times since I got here. Once I got mugged on the back porch of this very house, by a boy who ought to have known better. He lived here three years, for the Lord's sake, before he went back out into that."

"Why do you stay?"

Marietta looked surprised. "I have to stay," she said. "Everybody has to stay. Don't you?"

"I don't know what you mean."

"I think you know what I mean," Marietta said. "I think that's the only reason some ex-nun would wind up on our doorstep at six o'clock in the morning."

"Actually," Susan started to say, "it was six-thirty—"

She never got the words out. Marietta had made some coffee and poured Susan a mug of it. The mug was made of thick white ceramic and cracked. Marietta had gotten milk from the refrigerator and sugar from the cabinet, too, and put them down, with a bent spoon, at Susan's elbow. Now, in the middle of Susan's automatic explanation, she stopped in her tracks and stared at the ceiling above her head.

"There," she said, "that's Father Tom. If Father Tom's up, the rest of them will be too, in a minute."

Then she turned and marched out the kitchen door, into the bowels of the house, leaving Susan alone.

Susan wondered if that was going to be the end of it—if she would drink her coffee in solitude, put the things she had used into the sink, and leave by the back door, never talking to anyone at Damien House who could give her any answers.

4 She was still wondering that, ten minutes later—and even deciding it wouldn't be such a bad idea, since she didn't know what questions she wanted to ask—when the kitchen door opened again. The man who came in was small and stiff and very Irish, and still looked as wrong to Susan as he had the first time she had seen him. Susan wanted Father Tom Burne to be charismatic, tall and strong and wide. Looking "straight out of the Baltimore Catechism," as Andy had put it, like Barry Fitzgerald playing some immigrant Irish priest, didn't quite do it.

It was a train of thought so intrinsically embarrassing, it made Susan incapable of looking Father Burne in the face. She stared into her coffee and missed the quick sharp shake of his head, the decisive gesture of recognition, with which he ended his examination of her. She had the feeling he was staring at her, but she didn't look up.

After a while he said, "It's Susan Murphy, isn't it? Dan and Andy Murphy's sister. You were here the other day."

Now Susan did look up. She felt she had to. She was a little startled to see that Father Tom had taken the seat across from her, and somehow acquired a cup of coffee of his own. Had she really been avoiding any notice of him for that long?

She took another drag on her cigarette, put it quickly down into the ashtray, and said, "Yes, yes, that's who I am. I was here the other day. I mean—"

"You were curious the other day."

"Something like that."

"A lot of people are curious." Father Tom shrugged. "Sometimes I wonder what they're curious about. It's not as if this place is exotic."

"It is where I come from."

"Where you come from," Father Tom repeated. "What did somebody tell me? Maybe it was you who told me. Immaculate Heart of Mary nuns?"

"That's right."

"They used to have beautiful habits. Blue. I remember them from when I was first out of the seminary. No wimple cape to clutter up the line."

"We gave them up a long time ago. IHM out in Montecito gave them up in sixty-eight or sixty-nine."

"You weren't at Montecito?"

"Hobb's Point," Susan said. "We never completely gave up habit at all."

"Were your modified habits blue?"

"Yes."

Father Tom nodded. "That's good. I'm always telling the sisters around here, and the ex-sisters, giving up the habit was the stupidest thing the nuns ever did. Bad for recruiting. Bad for the public image. Bad for everything, really. Nuns in makeup. Why did you come out?"

"What?"

"Why did you come out?" Father Tom insisted. "You must have had a reason. You were in for—what?"

"Seventeen years."

"Seventeen years is a lifetime. You don't walk out on that for no reason at all. Are you one of those women who won't be happy unless the Pope lets you be ordained?"

Susan had never given a thought to female ordination—she'd had much more basic things to think about—but for some reason this comment irritated her. It was as if Father Tom Burne thought of women in favor of ordination as a different kind of animal, not-human, not-Catholic. She had half a mind to tell him that yes, she wanted to be ordained, even though the very thought of it appalled her. Being a nun had been bad enough.

She saw that her cigarette had gone out and lit another one. She saw that half her coffee remained undrunk and took a sip. The real problem, she decided, was that this felt like some kind of test.

"I think," she told him, "that the real problem is that I walked in on it for no reason at all."

"None?"

"Let's just say that, back in my senior year in high school, it seemed like a good idea. I'm still not entirely sure why."

"That was something else that was a mistake," Father Tom said. "Asking the girls to wait a year after high school before they entered. Giving them just enough time to be corrupted by the world, and not want to enter at all."

"You don't believe in mature vocations?"

"I don't believe in maturity at all. Maturity is another name for carefulness. There's nothing careful about heeding the call of God."

"There's a mouse up there in the third-floor dormitory and the girls have turned it into a pet," Marietta O'Brien said, coming through the door like a bad wind. "They've tied a ribbon around its neck and made a nest for it in a bureau drawer. If they hadn't left me a present this morning, I'd have murdered them all in their sleep."

"What kind of present?" Father Tom asked.

Marietta put her hand in the pocket of her dress—changing out of the robe must have been one of the things she was doing upstairs, besides finding mice in bureau drawers—and came out with an amber rosary with hard clear beads that glittered even in the dimness of the kitchen light. I've seen a rosary like that, Susan thought, but the memory was unclear and she couldn't get hold of it.

Father Tom was turning the rosary over in his hands, frowning at it. "Where did you get it?" he asked her. "Who gave it to you?"

"It was on my pillow when I went up to change. One of the girls must have left it. That's the only way it could have gotten in there. I must say it was a nice sight to see. It's amazing, the way people stop giving you religious things when you stop being a nun. Even though religious things are what you need most."

"Where were you a nun?" Susan asked her.

"Sacred Heart," Marietta said. "If you can believe that. Me, and all those girls from the best Catholic families."

5 Later, Susan would wonder what had kept her from leaving then—when the house was waking up, when she was in the way, when she was invisible. People kept coming in and out of the kitchen, getting cereal they ate standing up at the sink, crossing themselves with the holy water that was kept in a little basin just under the crucifix on the west wall. People drank half-cups of coffee and left them on the counters for Marietta to clean up. Small children—too small, Susan thought, to ever have been wandering around alone on the streets—were relieved of the coffee they tried to sneak into their milk glasses and provided with the milk instead. Men and women, girls and boys, religious and clergy and lay people all seemed to be jumbled up together, without "defined roles" or "distinct lines of authority," the way her social work course had insisted that all work with "people in need" ought to be. The scene would have reminded her of breakfast in an old-fashioned "fine Catholic family" if the conversation hadn't been so off-handedly and unself-consciously bizarre.

"Jenny McCormick ended up in detox out in Orange," somebody said. "She had a baby and it was all screwed up, so the welfare people just knew she was on crack, and you know what that means."

"Jenny McCormick won't last fifteen minutes with the welfare people," someone else said. "The last time they tried to mess around with her, she bit one."

"This time they've got a commitment order and they're going to lock her up," the first someone said. "I figure she'll end up dead in about a year. You know what those people are like."

"I know better than you do," the second someone said. "I was actually in one, when I got pregnant. The first time I ever got fucked, it was by my foster father, and he told the frigging social worker I'd been porking half of West Haven, and you know who they believed."

"Didn't Jenny McCormick just have a birthday?" a third someone said. "Her pimp gave her a party down in the Congo and I think she was fourteen."

"Why don't they like the welfare people?" Susan asked, but

nobody answered her. Nobody even heard her. She was not only invisible, but functionally mute. Besides, nobody was really talking to anybody, in the ordinary sense of the phrase. They were simply passing information back and forth, like batons in a relay race.

"Jerry Kevchek's disappeared again. Tony Buto says he thinks he's dead because he got picked up by a john one night and then he just wasn't around anymore."

"Donna Brendan's back on the street. She went home to live with her mother but her mother's a drunk and it didn't work out."

"Barney brought in these two little kids last night, look less than five years old, he found them wandering around outside and now he can't get them to talk. You try to get near them and they just burst into tears and won't say anything at all."

"Does Barney know if they can say anything at all? I mean, with little kids, sometimes if their parents are on dope, they don't learn to talk too good."

"They learn to talk by the time they're five, for God's sake."

"Don't bet on it. Steve brought in one a couple of years ago who was nearly eight and he looked four and he couldn't say a word. I mean, nobody had ever talked to him before."

After a while, Susan got up, stationed herself at the sink, and started to wash dishes. Marietta got used to the new arrangement in no time at all and started to hand the dishes over, from counters and tabletops and even chairs, wherever they got put down in the mad rush to Susan didn't know where, or what. It almost didn't matter. She was moving by then just to keep from vomiting. The conversation was bypassing her brain and going straight to her gut, making it roll. Her eyes were stinging and her vision was blurred and she couldn't find the spigot when she needed it.

She was just beginning to think she would have to get out of there after all—she would have to do something, because one more of those overheard conversations and she would collapse—when she felt someone standing much too close to her and looked up to see Father Tom Burne, leaning against the sink at her side. He had an odd look on his face, one she didn't like, but she didn't have the mental strength to analyze it. She just turned away from him and plunged a dish streaked with grape jelly into the water next to her hand.

A moment later, Father Tom tapped her gently on the shoulder, and she made herself turn. He looked resigned and exasperated, and Susan got the feeling that he had been counting on the reality of this place to drive her away. Now that it hadn't, he seemed to feel stuck with her.

"Come with me to my office," he said. "We'll have a nice long talk about the fact that I am me, Damien House is Damien House, and your brother is that paragon of Catholic laymen, the great Daniel Murphy."

CHAPTER

TWO

1 When the call came in on Ellen Burnett, early on the morning of December 16, Pat Mallory answered it. He had to, because he'd told everyone from the chief of police to the clerk typist supervisor in Homicide that he wanted to be in at the scene of any crime that looked like it had ties to the murders of Theresa Cavello and Margaret Mary McVann. Giving that kind of direction was always dangerous—you got called out on dozens of things that had nothing to do with anything whatsoever—and Pat felt as if he'd spent too much time burning rubber from one end of the New Haven city limits to the other, screeching to stops in front of brick walls that could have mashed him into hamburger, leaping out of cars onto ice so slick it threatened to toss him even in hob boots, and all for nothing. It was playing cops and robbers, and Pat didn't like it.

Still, Ellen Burnett was for real, and that made things better—for a while. At least it made Pat feel less like an idiot with an obsession. He wasn't imagining things. There really was a nut out there, and the nut was good—always a nerve-wrecking sign. In spite of all the true-crime books that cluttered up the bookstore on Chapel Street where he bought his monthly copy of *The Atlantic,* Pat knew psychopaths were not often good at what they did. They were almost never any good at getting away with it. Some of them were schizos, pure and simple. They heard voices in their heads or had visions in their breakfast cereal. Those were the easiest to catch, because they weren't operating in Real Time. If they managed to rack up a victim or two, it was mostly by accident. If they didn't get hauled in after their first crime, it was mostly the stranger factor. It was always harder to find a murderer who had no sane connection to his victim than to find one who had—but with the schizos it was a toss-up, really, whether they started by offing innocent by-standers or doing away with their own families. Pat always thought of the schizos as heroes of chance.

As for the others, the minority, they were something else again. Getting out of his car in the alley behind Arlie's Restaurant, Pat was thinking about them, because the murder of Theresa Cavello had been so damned neat. Schizos had no time to be neat, and junkies had no interest—in the past five years or so, with the coming of crack, they'd had a number of what looked like serial murder cases that turned out to be junkie hits.

He had stuffed his gloves into his pockets when he'd gotten into the car—he hated having to drive with them on—and he got them out. It was bitterly cold and windy, with ice rimming the garbage cans someone had put across the alley access to the diner's back patch. The problem with the killer of Margaret Mary McVann and Theresa Cavello was that he didn't add up. The Eucharistic symbol pointed to a schizo. So did the bruises on Margaret Mary's body. But there were no bruises on Theresa's body, and the cuts were so damn neat, so precise, so carefully calculated. Sometimes Pat wondered about the weather. Theresa had been left inside, but in a place she had to be quickly found. Margaret Mary had also been left inside, but in a place where she was not likely to be quickly found—had the broken window been accidental or deliberate? There was no way to tell, but Pat kept thinking that if that window had not been open, the cut on Margaret Mary's forehead would not have survived well enough for them to iden-tify it.

He edged by the garbage cans and into the small open area that led to the diner's back door, to find Ben Deaver standing beside a tall, thin man in a cashmere coat and a J. Press three-piece suit, looking pained. The tall, thin man looked intolerably smug. Pat got the impression that his coat was open mostly for display. The tall, thin man wanted them all to know he could buy his suits at J. Press; and to see the square black Burberry label every time the wind made the edges of his coat flap. Pat caught Ben Deaver's eye and raised a single eyebrow. Ben Deaver shrugged.

There were crowds of technical people stuffed into every nook and cranny in the back patch, photographers setting off flashbulbs in quick bursts that looked like machine-gun fire, bag men picking up scraps from the ground with tweezers, even a man with a sterile vacuum. Pat walked over to the body and looked down at it. It had been propped carefully against a garbage can, sitting up, the Eucharistic symbol etched clearly and precisely into its forehead. Since everybody on the New Haven police force, in Homicide or out, knew better than to move the body before Pat got to it, Pat could only assume the killer had left it this way—which was bizarre. The other two had been left where they fell, moved only as much as had been necessary to cut them. Pat had seen the body of Theresa Cavello. He had read the report on Margaret Mary McVann: "victim found on carpet, head up." He had also seen the pictures.

He stood over the body for a moment, checked out the scene—more garbage pails, cleaner looking, not as often used; pieces of packing crates; wads of filthy frozen fabric that might once have been aprons or tablecloths. The body was not only sitting upright but wedged into all this, so it didn't look slumped. It was impossible to know if that had been the effect intended.

Pat turned away and walked back across the patch toward Ben Deaver and the tall, thin man. The tall, thin man was looking blue around the lips. Pat stopped next to Ben Deaver and said, "Well?"

Deaver looked at the tall, thin man and said, "This is Dr. James MacLure. He's a psychologist."

"Psychiatrist," Dr. James MacLure said.

"Exactly why," Pat asked them, "do we have a psychiatrist

at the crime scene? Especially a psychiatrist who's not a police psychiatrist?"

"The police department doesn't have psychiatrists," Dr. James MacLure said. "They only have psychologists."

"It's an inferior grade of witch doctor," Ben Deaver said.

Dr. James MacLure had his hands in his pockets. He shoved them even more deeply in and frowned. The blue around his lips was now tinged with red. He was, Pat thought, a man who had a hard time controlling his anger.

"I," Dr. MacLure said, "am a specialist consultant in violent manias at the Yale New Haven Medical Center. I was dragged down here, out of a perfectly sound sleep, by Daniel Murphy himself—"

"He sent a car," Ben Deaver said blandly.

"Of course he sent a car," Dr. MacLure said. "I live in Orange, for God's sake. Dan was in a hurry. He should have been in a hurry. You've got a psychopath on your hands."

"Sociopath," Pat said automatically. Then he saw that the man with the sterile vacuum had backed away from the scene and the photographers had gone with him. They were clearing a path for the ambulance men who had been waiting unobtrusively at the far end of the alley. He backed away a little himself and then grabbed Ben Deaver by the arm.

"Come on," he said.

Dr. James MacLure looked startled and infinitely offended. "I don't have the time to stand around here in the cold getting nothing done," he said. "I have a practice. What do you think I do with my time?"

Pat had a hundred answers to that, but not one of them was politic, at least as long as he wasn't winning. He muttered a perfunctory "Excuse me," kept his hand on Ben Deaver's arm, and started moving up the alley to where he'd parked his car.

2 Once he had Ben Deaver in the car, with the doors closed and the windows up and the motor running so the heat could pump, Pat felt he could relax, at least a little. With the coming of the ambulance men the scene had gone crazy. There was no longer any need for extraordinary caution, and people—professionals and amateurs both—had begun milling around aimlessly, giving in to their need for gossip and their rattling nerves. Pat saw a bag lady materialize out of nowhere and take a seat in a pile of garbage at the very edge of the alley. He wondered what she expected to find when the crowd dispersed.

It wasn't the kind of thing that bore thinking about. He turned to Ben Deaver and said, "Well? What was all that about?"

Deaver shrugged. "How am I supposed to know? He showed up on his own in a city car. He said he came from Dan. I checked with Dan's office and they confirmed."

"What does he want?"

"Publicity, I guess. What do Dan Murphy and his people ever want? He was providing me with a psychological profile of the killer."

"Right there, on the spot?"

"Right there. Jesus, Pat, it was more bogus than that. All he knows about any of it is that this is the third. He's exactly one jump ahead of the New Haven *Register* and it's not a very big jump."

"Did you listen to him? About his psychological profile?"

"Every time he got started, I told him he'd have to wait for you."

Pat nodded and looked through the window next to his arm, up the alley again. Dr. James MacLure had collared one of the uniforms and was lecturing. The uniform was either too cowed, or too polite, to object. Pat turned away again.

"Never mind Dr. James MacLure for the moment," he said. "I can deal with him later. Tell me what's really been going on over there."

"Guy who owns the diner found the body this morning,"

Ben said. "He came out here to dump some crates and there she was. Our techies say she might have been out there two, three days. She's damn near frozen solid."

"What about last night? Didn't he throw out his garbage?"

"Yeah, he did, but he says it was dark and it was late and it was cold, and all he did was open the back door and toss. They only use that place in the back there for big stuff, crates and junk that has to be carted away special. They've got garbage cans back there but they're just for overflow, if they're needed. I looked at them. I don't think they ever have been needed."

Pat thought about it. "He didn't see *anything* strange there last night? Or the night before? Or the day before?"

Ben shook his head. "He really couldn't have, Pat, not if he did what he said. You can't see that place she was left from the back door. I checked. There's a big pile of crates blocking the view and there's a bend in the wall there anyway."

"A bend?"

"A corner, for God's sake. But it's worse than you think, Pat, a lot worse. It's nuts."

"Why?"

"Because as far as anybody knows, the last time anyone saw her was last Friday morning, early. That was three days ago."

Out in the east, the sun was beginning to rise, as much as it was going to. It was threaded with thin dirty streaks of clouds that looked like cotton soaked in mud.

"Look," Pat said, "let's start from the beginning. Who was this woman?"

"Ellen Burnett."

"And who was Ellen Burnett?"

"I don't have the answer to that the way you want it, not yet. All I'm sure of is that she was a waitress in that diner over there."

"Her boss doesn't know anything about her?"

"Not much. They go to the same parish church, Saint Malachy's. She'd been going through a bad time and some people at the church were trying to help her find a job. He needed a waitress so he took her on."

Pat nodded. "Okay. She was a waitress on the breakfast shift?"

"Yes. And lunch, too, sometimes. She took over for other people a lot when they were out sick or needed a substitute. The way this guy talked, Ellen Burnett was looking for as much work as she could get."

"Admirable," Pat said dryly. "Was she on for breakfast shift Friday morning?"

"She was not only on, she opened."

"Fine. And then what?"

"Nobody knows. She was here right through the heavy-duty traffic, between seven and eight. He wasn't," Ben jerked his head back toward the diner, "but one of the other girls who was on yesterday morning is here today, and she said Ellen was right where she belonged, doing her usual thing, until at least, say, ten or five of seven."

"How can she be so sure?"

"Between six and six thirty it was busier than usual. 'Hell on wheels' is how she put it. They had to do a reset at twenty to seven."

"What's a reset?"

"Putting out more sugar, more ketchup, that kind of thing. The lady says it takes about ten to fifteen minutes to do a reset and Ellen did it by herself, because she—this lady—was 'really tied up.'"

"Did you get this lady's name?"

"Not yet."

"Get it."

Ben nodded. He really hadn't had to be told. "Anyway," he said, "this lady went back to the kitchen for something—with the old guy out they were all doing their own cooking—and when she came back Ellen Burnett was gone. And she stayed gone."

"Was it near the time she was supposed to leave? Could she just have gotten pissed off and walked out?"

"She was supposed to stay for lunch."

"Fine," Pat said. He put his head back against the car seat and closed his eyes. Even with the heater going full blast the car felt cold. The whole world felt cold. "What about this lady of yours," he asked. "When does she say she came back out from the kitchen?"

"About a quarter after seven."

"Fine," Pat said again. "So. Sometime between twenty of and quarter after, give or take ten or fifteen minutes on the assumption that your assessment of the lady as a sea slug is correct, Ellen Burnett walked out back of this diner and got herself killed. Why?"

"Why did she get herself killed?" Ben was surprised.

"No, why did she walk out back of this diner? Did you find any bruises on her?"

"It'll have to wait for the med reports. I didn't see any except the usual. You know, on her neck. And the cut."

"On her neck and the cut. Like Theresa Cavello. Not like Margaret Mary McVann, no bruises, no contusions, no struggle."

"I don't get it," Ben Deaver said.

Pat didn't get it either, but he was willing to explain. He pulled himself forward off the seat and opened his eyes, trying to put the pieces together in a sequence: Theresa Cavello and Margaret Mary McVann; bruises and the lack of them; care with the body and the lack of it—it was a *progression*. Margaret Mary McVann had been roughed up. Theresa Cavello had been taken care of. At first glance, this one looked as if she had been taken care of, too.

"Mallory 2-11," the dispatcher said, in that nasal monotone all dispatchers seemed to have. "Mallory 2-11 Klemmer. Mallory 2-11."

Pat and Ben stared at the radio in amazement. "Jesus Christ," Ben said, "2-11, from *Klemmer*? What's he got down there, Lazarus raised in glory?"

"I don't know." Pat picked up, gave the answer that indicated merely that he'd heard, and put down again. Then he turned to Ben and said, "Get out of here. I'm going to answer this. Maybe he does have Lazarus raised in glory."

"What am I supposed to do about Dr. James MacLure?"

Pat looked back at the man, at the cashmere coat. He had a grip on the uniform he had been lecturing and was yammering away.

"Shoot him," Pat said. "Then skin him, stuff him, and donate him to the police museum."

THREE

1   When Pat got back on the road, it was rush hour. The streets were clogged in every direction and the built-up slush and hardened mud of weeks of bad weather didn't help. He thought about putting his siren on and decided against it. It wouldn't do him much good. Even the drivers who wanted to get out of the way wouldn't have anywhere to go, and there would always be those others, down dirty furious at being asked to put anybody else's interests above their own, who would be deliberately obstructive. He put on his light alone and kept his fingers crossed.

He had better luck than he'd expected to have. He made his lights, one after the other.

All the way, he was thinking about getting a 2-11 from Klemmer, about how absurd it was. A 2-11 was a life-and-death call: a shoot-out in progress, a live bomb, the spiritual descendants of the Symbionese Liberation Army in possession of the mayor's office. Pat supposed some of those things could apply to Anton— certainly there could be a bomb in the morgue—but if they had, his 2-11 would have gone out to a wider audience than Pat Mallory alone. Nothing else Pat could think of would require a 2-11. Another body in the Ellen Burnett–Margaret Mary McVann–Theresa Cavello mode could wait until Pat had the time to drop in. Any body could. Anton had clients who were never in a hurry.

Pat eased himself into a right turn that brought him on to Dordon Street. It was a straight shot now from where he was to the morgue. If he had been doing anything but what he had been doing—if he had not been faced with James MacLure, waiting to be primed and petted and made to feel essential—he knew he would have called in before hightailing it out here, 2-11 or no 2-11. He tried again to think of what Anton could possibly be involved in, and failed. Then he decided it was a grace, like the nuns used to talk about back in parochial school. Anton was pulling some kind of joke, and God had let him pull it at the precise moment when Pat needed to be rescued.

He had just about convinced himself of the truth of that—just about given himself permission to go back to thinking of Ellen Burnett, and of the progression, when he reached the corner the morgue was on and happened to look left, down the side street that crossed in front of the morgue's back door. In his shock, he hit the brake and came to a dead stop. He felt the car behind him plow into his rear and come to a stop itself. He bounced against the strap of his shoulder belt and back again without noticing.

To his left, the side street was crammed full of vehicles: medical vehicles mostly, ambulances and cars with M.D. plates and emergency units and 911 vans. There was only one police vehicle, and that was a patrol car. It was parked on the sidewalk thirty feet from the morgue's back entry and it was empty. Pat snapped his seatbelt off, kicked his door open, and jumped out.

Behind him, the driver of the other car had also gotten out. He was big and red-faced and angry and Pat could see him coming, striding out across the street like a Trojan on his way to war. The regulations clicked through Pat's head, perfectly formed but without effect: procedures, responsibilities, oversights, repudiations.

On the side street, a pair of men in overalls were pulling oxygen tanks out of a van and handing them to another pair of men. They had an old-time fire brigade of oxygen tanks set up at the morgue's back door.

Pat gave one last glance at the angry older man still chasing along behind him, and then he started to run.

2 There was a patrolman stationed at the door, but all the patrolmen knew Pat Mallory, and he wasn't stopped. Once inside the long corridor that led to the cold boxes, Pat stopped himself. His legs were aching and his chest was shot through with needle pains. He had been breathing in great gulps of air without compensating for the cold at all. He leaned against the nearest wall and forced himself to correct for it, forced himself to slow down, forced his heart to stop beating so hard. It was difficult, because the scene around him was chaos. The corridor was full of morgue personnel—attendants, clerks, lab technicians, assistant examiners—who hadn't seen a scrap of excitement for years, except maybe on movie screens. They were all over the place now, milling and agitated. Some of the women were crying, and one of the men was being sick in a wastebasket. The emergency people were better organized but nowhere near calm. They kept striding back and forth, in and out of rooms, carrying heavy pieces of equipment that left Pat completely bewildered. The scene would have made a kind of crazy sense if it was being played out in a hospital emergency room. It made no sense at all here.

As soon as he was sure he had his breath back—and his heart, and his lungs—Pat pushed himself away from the wall and headed down the corridor. He had to thread his way through tighter and tighter knots of people as he went along. From somewhere far away, he could hear a man shouting, angry but controlled, "Clamp, God damn you, give me a clamp set up that blood get that tube in here you motherfucking idiot get me that clamp *now*."

He passed a woman he recognized vaguely as being "someone from Anton's office" and grabbed her by the arm, spinning her around. She looked like she was in a state of shock and barely registered what he had done.

"Anton," he screamed into her face. "Where's Anton?"

She came to, barely, and said, "Anton?"

Somebody behind him tapped Pat on the shoulder and said, "Dr. Klemmer's in the file room?"—just like that, with a question mark at the end of it, as if he were giving an answer in a quiz where he wasn't even sure of the questions.

Pat did an about face and headed for the corridor he knew would bring him to the file room, but he never got there. A hand came out and jerked his head around, away from the scene he had been staring at, until he was looking into the eyes of Dr. Anton Klemmer instead. The Anton Klemmer he knew was a man of great wit and great serenity. This Anton Klemmer was as tight as a cat in heat.

"Listen," he said. "Pat, listen to me. I've got one."

"Got one what?"

"One of the boys. The prostitutes. From the executions."

Pat's brain tried and failed, tried and failed, tried and failed to make the switch—and then finally made the connection. The boy prostitutes. The gangland-style executions. Edge Hill Road.

"Pat," Anton said, "I've got one and I've got him alive."

"What?"

Anton Klemmer looked around, found the closest door, opened it and looked inside. Then he nodded and pushed Pat toward whatever was kept in that dark and now deserted place.

"Go," he said, "go and I'll tell you all about it."

3 The room turned out to be an ordinary office, two green metal desks pushed up against each other and a small collection of filing cabinets along one wall. Pat had no idea what it was an office for, and was sure Anton had no idea either. The desks were neat and the desk blotters looked unused. The walls were devoid of windows. The only light there was came from a bank of fluorescents in the ceiling. Pat looked at the walls—cinderblock painted pale green, like the walls outside—and saw that they were sweating.

Anton had taken a seat on the edge of one of the desks, and the white deadness of his face had begun to mellow into something pale, but at least recognizably human. The sounds of what was going on out in the corridor were audible, but muted—and that made all the difference. It was making all the difference for Pat, too. Not being in the middle of it made it easier to think.

Anton took a handkerchief out of his pocket and wiped his face. In spite of the cold—and it was cold, Pat realized, it was freezing down here—he had been sweating. He forced a weak imitation of his old smile across his face and said, "It's been years since I've been part of an emergency. I seem to have lost my knack for it."

Pat looked back at the door to the corridor. "Is it an emergency?" he asked. "What's going on out there?"

"What's going on out there is that a team from the Yale New Haven Hospital is doing their best to make a temporary miracle permanent. I hope they succeed. He is very young. I would say no more than eight."

"The boy," Pat said.

"The boy." Anton nodded. "I've never put out a 2-11 call before, Pat. If the circumstances had been different, I might have been amused."

"I thought you were amusing yourself. I thought it was some kind of joke."

"I almost wish it were."

Anton got off the desk, fumbled around for a chair, found one and sat down. He looked too tired to stand and too shocked to meet Pat's eyes.

"It started this morning, you know, very early this morning, just after five o'clock. God only knows what would have happened if I hadn't come in."

"Why did you come in?"

"Woman trouble." Anton shrugged. "Woman trouble and the great void. I seem to be going through one of my periods of existential angst. If you don't believe in God, there are only two cures for those, and the woman wasn't cooperating, so I decided to work."

"And?"

"Well," Anton shook his head. "I came in at four thirty. I

did my files. I did my files again. I worked on a paper I'm presenting in Toronto next month. I puttered and told myself I was being productive. Then, at about five after five, we got a van call. Three bodies in the water, out by the New Haven railroad station."

"Three," Pat said.

"Don't look so surprised. When they come up from the water, they come up in singles, pairs, triples, anything. The triples usually come in the spring. I don't know. Maybe it was odd for winter."

"This call of yours come from cops?" Pat asked.

"Of course it did."

"Did you examine them?"

"Well, I didn't go out on the van call, obviously. When the announcement came over the speakers that the van was in, I went down, yes. I looked them over. Two old men and this boy. I would have sworn all three of them were dead."

"The boys who have been executed had the backs of their heads shot off. What about that?"

"What about it? The three of them were all covered with weeds and dirt. I didn't do a formal examination, Pat. I—just looked them over. And had another attack of angst. When I get really worked up, I can sound like Young Werther with no trouble at all."

"When you get really worked up in the other direction, you can drink like a fish. What did you do then?"

Anton rubbed his hands against his face. "I went back to my office," he said. "I puttered around. I tried to pretend I had something to do. The patrolmen were still down here, all that time. They must have been, because I passed them later when I came down again—"

"Why did you come down?"

"I told you. I was pretending to be useful. There was some nit-picky point in one of the examinations I'd done yesterday that I didn't like the look of, so I decided to come down and check."

"What time was this?"

"It was—quarter after six by then, I think. At any rate, when

I got down to this floor, the patrolmen were still here, looking absolutely livid. The guy on watch here at night isn't too bright. He makes up for it by being painfully careful about procedure. He was putting them through the wash, making them fill out every form in the Western world, asking them questions they couldn't possibly answer—you know what those forms are like. Thought up by some fool with a Ph.D. in the commissioner's office, all the legal points neatly outlined in black and white and absolutely useless in the real world. Anyway, I saw them standing there and I remember thinking I ought to stop and get them out of it—but I didn't."

Pat smiled. "What's the matter, Anton? Your empathy wearing thin?"

"It's not my empathy I'm worried about. Sometimes I think all women are crazy. Anyway—again anyway. I went into the cold storage. The body I wanted was in the back, in one of the drawers with the green tags on them that let the attendants know they're available for release. The three new bodies were on tables in the middle of the room. They should have been stored when they came in, but we only have that one man on duty nights, except for weekends, and he was too involved with his papers. So I had to walk by these three bodies lying out to get to the drawer I wanted, and as I was going past—"

"What?"

"What do you think? He moved, for God's sake. He picked up his hand and he God damned *waved* at me. I spun around and stared at him, but he was still, and then I thought, well, it's impossible, but you ought to check, you have to check. So I did."

Up to then, Pat had been standing, shifting back and forth on his feet in a halfhearted attempt to stay warm. Now he sat down on the edge of the desk Anton had vacated and put his hands in his pockets, so that he didn't have to watch them shake.

"Then what?" he asked, and his voice sounded tight and high. "*Then* what?"

Anton smiled. "From Edgar Allan Poe to Stephen King. The boy opened his eyes, looked straight into mine, and said, 'Father.'"

"Oh, dear sweet Jesus Christ."

Anton bolted out of his chair. "Listen," he said, "it's bad, but it may be better than you think. If they can keep him alive long enough to get him to the hospital—if they can stabilize him here— I think he's going to live. And not just live, Pat. *Think.* I checked him out while I was waiting for the emergency crews. They shot off a lot of hair and a lot of skin but practically no skull. They didn't get his brain at all. He may still die—from the shock and the exposure, all that time in the ice and water—but if he survives he's not just going to be alive. He's going to be *functioning*."

CHAPTER
FOUR

1 By the time Susan got home, it was late—later than she'd promised to be—and the weather had gone from miserable to apocalyptic. Getting off the bus on Chapel Street, walking across the Green toward Prospect Street and Edge Hill Road, she kept wondering why she had been so reluctant to ride back to a sensible stop. Down on Congress Avenue she had told herself she was in a hurry. She'd left Damien House just after eleven, full daylight as daylight went in weather like this, and the surrounding neighborhood had gone eerie. She'd almost wished for a return of the Rockettes and the young girls in sarongs. Walking down the long stretch between Amora Street and that part of Congress Avenue that was still what Dan would call "economically viable," she was looking for the boogeyman. Boogeywoman. Her final conversation with Father Tom Burne—the one after the one about Dan, which hadn't quite made sense—was dancing in her head.

"Do you know where they get most of these kids?" he'd said. "The eight- and nine-year-olds they use for prostitutes?"

"No."

"Foster homes. State-approved, state-paid, state-regulated foster homes. There's more child abuse, especially child sexual abuse, in foster homes in this state than in all the other family venues combined."

"But if the real parents—"

"If the real parent—and it's usually only one—if the real parent is an abuser, he ought to be locked up. Child abuse is the only crime we have where we punish the victim instead of the offender, by law. Do you know what we do here, Miss Murphy?"

"I think I do."

"I think you don't. We provide an escape hatch. Most of these kids will do anything—and I do mean anything, including selling their butts on the street—to stay away from the social welfare people. We give them an alternative. We fight their battles with the departments. We help them avoid the depredations of the helping professions. And we get royally and eternally hassled."

"I—"

"You have to go home, Miss Murphy. You have to come back when you've made up your mind."

Up on Prospect Street, she couldn't even make up her mind to go home, although she knew she had to. The street was full of Yalies and girls from Albertus Magnus, pale biology majors of both sexes weighed down under book bags, nice Catholic girls in nylons and long coats with their hair pinned up under red-and-green snow hats. It wasn't snowing but it looked like it ought to be.

Near the Gesell Institute, she stopped, picked up a rock, and looked at it. A pair of students passed her talking about Kent, and then another pair talking about "the practically irradicable phallocentrism of Western society." She put the rock in her pocket—God only knew why—and headed toward home.

One way or another, it all reminded her of the day she had left home for the convent. She was striding ahead, giving the best imaginable impression of purpose and determination, while all the time she was simply going the only place she could think of to go.

2   "Listen," Andy said to her, as soon as she walked in the door, "where have you been? There's a frigging sit-down lunch laid out in the dining room."

Sit-down lunch. Susan looked at the parka in her hands and frowned. She had known all along that Dan was coming home for lunch. She'd even known he expected her to be here.

She put the parka on a hanger in the foyer closet and sat

down on the small bench next to the front door to take off her boots. Overhead the chandelier was blazing, its light coming clear, and she realized someone must have polished it. In fact, someone must have polished it today. She'd turned it on last night and gotten only a muddy smear of half-illumination. Even the bulbs up there had been caked with dust.

She got one boot off and kicked it into the closet. "I don't understand why you're so anxious," she said. "It's just Dan. It's just lunch."

"He's in one of those moods." Andy looked off toward the center of the house. "Did you go down to that place? To Damien House?"

"Yes, I did."

"And?"

"I don't know."

"I don't think you ought to tell Dan you were there. I don't think you ought to tell him we were there. I don't think he'd like it."

"I'm not sure I care what Dan would like."

"You ought to."

The other boot was loose. Susan kicked it into the closet after the first one and sat up. Andy was still staring off toward the center of the house and he was sweating.

Once, in her senior novitiate year, Susan had passed a mirror and seen her face looking just like Andy's did now. It had been the day before a scheduled Chapter of Faults and she had had a fault to proclaim, a very serious fault, because she had broken a mirror, failed to report it, and let another sister take the blame. After hearing about eight-year-old prostitutes and twelve-year-old porn queens and children who died of cocaine overdoses at the age of ten, it seemed like a little thing, but it hadn't then. What was worse, she had made it worse by becoming petrified of what would happen to her if anyone found out. Every time she tried to imagine confessing it, even to a priest, she got visions of her life ending in fire.

Right now, Andy looked like his life was going to end in

something much worse than fire, end by the hand of whatever it was he expected to come through that damned door. The problem was that Susan couldn't figure out what it was he thought he was going to see.

"I can take care of myself," she said, thinking that wasn't what he was up to at all. He wasn't worried about her. "You don't have to run interference with Dan for me."

"I know I don't."

"Then what's wrong?"

Andy forced his eyes away from the back foyer door. Sounds were coming from back there, clankings and rattlings, the music Susan remembered as the overture for a Really Formal Lunch.

"They're all crazy about him," Andy said. "The housekeeper and those people, I mean. They think he walks on water."

"Dan's good at making people think he walks on water. It can be useful, sometimes."

"Dan always makes himself useful."

"I mean useful to us." Susan hesitated. "It was once, wasn't it? When we needed it most?"

This time, Andy turned his back to the foyer door. It was an effort. Dan was bounding through the door, literally, like Ben Vereen playing the leopard on "Zoobilee Zoo." His arms were waving in the air. His lips were stretched across his face like a rubber band pulled to the breaking point. His teeth shone.

"Susan," he was shouting. "Susan, Susan. Hurry up, you're almost late."

"Hurry up for what?" Susan said.

There was no more time for explanations than there had been for conversation. Dan threw his arms around her waist, picked her up, and charged off toward the dining room and the back of the house.

3 Susan had forgotten how intense Dan could be, how wild, how blind to the fact that other people might not be as excited for him as he was for himself. She let him carry her because it was easier than struggling. His grip was too soft to make her feel secure, and she kept imagining them tumbling over, tumbling down, breaking bones against the living-room furniture they had to weave their way through to get to the dining room. When he stuffed her in the armed captain's chair at the foot of the table she breathed a sigh of relief, and when he thrust a glass of wine into her hand she drank it, even though she never drank wine. Andy came in behind them, dropped into a side chair, and smiled weakly.

"Christ," he said, "I thought you were going to kill her."

"I'm going to kill everybody," Dan said happily. "I'm going to explode the biggest bomb the City of New Haven has ever seen. I'm going to end up governor in two years and the fucking president of the United States in six."

"My heart bleeds for the destruction of my country," Andy said, but his heart wasn't in it. His voice was flat.

Dan was at the head of the table now, fiddling with a big black box that Susan suddenly recognized as the kind of radio usually called a ghetto blaster. Between them was the long, dark mahogany table, set with lace-trimmed Irish linen place mats. All the place mats had been set for lunch, even though they weren't having guests. There was something weird about all those fans of heavy sterling silver, all those ranks of leaded Waterford crystal, all those arrangements of Royal Doulton plates, offered up to nobody and nothing at all.

"You got out all of mother's things," Susan said.

Dan fiddled with the radio dial. "Mrs. Menninger got them out. She always does when I come home for lunch. I told her it wasn't necessary, but she likes to do it."

"You never told her it wasn't necessary," Andy said.

"I don't see any reason for hurting her feelings. It's not like she leaves the stuff around and makes me clean it up."

The radio finally hooked into a clear station. From the look on Dan's face, it was even the right clear station. A tinny voice shot into the room, half perky puppy and half whine, saying, "This is WNHC two minutes before the hour, coming up with news."

"Two minutes." Dan dropped into his chair. "I hate radio stations. Armageddon could be going on right in the middle of the Green, and they'd still wait two minutes to get to the news."

"Radio stations sell advertising time," Andy said, "that's how they make their money."

"Radio stations ought to be publicly financed," Dan said, "then they'd learn to develop some concern for the public interest."

"Of course, you mean some concern for you."

Dan ignored him. It wasn't hot, but he was jumpy, so he stood up, took off the jacket of his suit, and hung it on the back of his chair. Then he unbuttoned his vest and rolled up the sleeves. Sitting down again, he reminded Susan of the pictures of him that appeared in the *Register* at the start of a case. Once he got to court he was always photographed in full Brooks Brothers splendor, but just after he'd announced his intention to go to the Grand Jury he liked to appear workmanlike. At the head of the table, what he really appeared was much too thin.

"The problem with most district attorneys," he said, pacing back and forth in front of the radio, "is that they're afraid to take on high-visibility cases. They're afraid of the downside."

"I thought district attorneys liked high-visibility cases," Susan said, "I thought they were good for their careers."

"They are if you win them." Dan patted the radio, like a child, on the head. "The problem is, it's so easy not to win them, especially if the case is notable because the people in it have a lot of power. I mean real power. Not just a title and a weekly check from the state."

"I take it you're not about to arrest our esteemed state senator," Andy said. "Who are you about to arrest?"

"The problem with power is that it really is very diffuse," Dan said. "It's not so much what you control and who you control. It's image. You get what I mean?"

"No," Susan said.

"Well, think about it. How much power do you assume Mother Teresa has?"

"Mother *Teresa?*" Susan blinked.

"Good God," Andy said, going white again. "I can't believe it. I can't believe you think you're going to get away with it."

"Get away with what?" Susan said. "He can't arrest Mother Teresa. She's in Calcutta."

"The problem with people like Mother Teresa," Dan said, "is that they appeal to the emotional in people. They get everyone all gushy and mushy. They totally circumvent all common sense."

"If you mean it's not common sense to spend your life doing good for the untouchables in India, I agree with you," Susan said. "Fortunately, not everyone is all that wedded to common sense."

"They ought to be. Mother Teresa is a very dangerous woman. People like Mother Teresa are dangerous people. They— wait."

Dan stared at the radio, which was sending out a little jingle about a used-car place in North Branford. The song was soprano-sharp and unoriginal, and he frowned at it.

"I wouldn't go there," he said. "I know the guy who runs it. I would go to Stephen's World of Wheels out in Bristol."

"Stephen's World of Wheels sells new cars," Andy said.

"You're a fool to buy a used car anyway. Not that you ever buy cars."

The jingle stopped and was replaced by a gong, a contralto sequence dangerously close to the one NBC used to use in the early days of television. Dan grabbed the radio and turned it first toward him and then away, toward them, as if it were a defective loudspeaker and they needed to have it pointed directly at their ears to hear anything at all. The gong stopped ringing and the tinny, perky, whiny voice from two minutes before came back, saying,

"It's one P.M., and this is WNHC at the top of the hour with the news."

"*There*," Dan said, and then he sat down, abruptly, like a sitcom drunk collapsing into his chair.

Susan found herself reaching for her cigarettes automatically, lighting up without looking to see if there was an ashtray on the table. The room was suddenly very tense, with Andy wound up tight and Dan oddly deflated. Susan thought Dan was like a small child who had waited all week for a party, only to begin being disappointed as soon as the party got under way. Andy was something else again. There was too much going on for her to be able to think about Andy.

The tinny announcer had been replaced by the basso voice of an actor pretending to be a newsman. "At the top of the news this hour," the actor was saying, "sources close to the top of District Attorney Dan Murphy's office report that the New Haven prosecutor has ordered a hush-hush investigation of Father Thomas Burne, founder of New Haven's Damien House, on charges of child abuse . . ."

"*Child* abuse," Andy burst out. Then he picked up his wine glass, broke it off at the stem, and said, "Son of a bitch."

CHAPTER
FIVE

1 From the beginning, there was one thing he had always been careful about, and that was drugs. He had seen too many people flying to believe in them. The high never lasted very long and it never solved anything. When the crash came you were just where you had started out to be, except that you were sick. Even so, it had been hard to stay away from them. Five years ago, crack had been practically a medium of exchange on Congress Avenue. Young boys who sold themselves to chickenhawks almost had to be junkies, because they had no pimps to negotiate for them and the johns expected to pay off in dope. He thought it was wrong of all those clean and shiny people to be so outraged about the pimps. The pimps served a purpose—the way lawyers and tax accountants served a purpose on Prospect Street and Edge Hill Road.

It was getting late in the day now and he was tired. He was cold, too, but he thought he was going to be cold for a while. It was better to pretend that he was warm than to try to do anything about it. There were a thousand different ways of surviving on the street and he knew them all, but he wasn't really good at any of them except shoplifting. He'd already picked up enough to eat so that he wasn't hungry, and there wasn't any point in going looking for anything else. All the best places to steal would be getting ready to close.

He was in a part of town he didn't know very well, just walking. The streets were lined with dry cleaners and delis and religious-articles stores, stuffed into the ground floors of six-story buildings. Above him the sky seemed to be composed of plate-glass picture windows, lit up, tortured into odd shapes by the curtains that hung at their sides. Every once in a while he would see a woman—always a woman—carrying a vase of flowers or a glass of something to drink.

Not knowing what else to do, he turned right at the next intersection and kept going. He wanted to see if he could get himself lost.

2   Twenty minutes later, he was still walking, now on streets too well-kept to be abandoned but too dark to be inhabited. The people who lived in the houses around him were Catholic, but probably Hispanic Catholic. There were stained-glass window-hangings of the Blessed Virgin and the Sacred Heart in the windows, but there were also a lot of those rainbow-colored roosters. He didn't know what the roosters were supposed to represent, but he did know they had something to do with being Catholic, at least for people from Latin America. Someone—maybe Theresa Cavello—had tried to explain it to him once.

When he got to the next intersection, he stopped. In heavily Catholic neighborhoods there were heavily Catholic churches, often churches that were open all night. If he could find the one that belonged to these people, he could go in there and think. He had a lot to think about. All day the street had been full of stories about Stevie Marks. His first name hadn't really been Stevie and his last name hadn't really been Marks, but it didn't matter much.

He'd heard first about Stevie Marks while he was standing on the corner of Congress and Strove, long after he'd followed her down from Edge Hill Road and realized she was going to disappear into Damien House for hours. He'd gone back to Congress Avenue to decide what to do, and one of the girls had come up to him and told him. Like most of the girls, she got paid in money, but she doped to take her mind off her life. She was supposed to stay clean on the street, but she hadn't. When she came up to him her eyes were small and hard and bright.

"It was dumb," she'd said, after she'd told him the story. "It's the stupidest thing in the world, coming back from the dead."

He had wanted to tell her about resurrection, but he hadn't. She wouldn't have understood and it wouldn't have done him good. His charism was like the fine soft skin on a fashion model, a gift of God that had to be carefully taken care of, a grace that could too easily be lost.

Now he walked another block and looked down another intersection, into blackness, into nothing, and wondered how long it would take for him before he found what he was looking for.

A church.

And a chance.

3 It was called Saint Mary of the Pines, and its name was written, in Spanish as well as English, on a square little painted sign on the street-end of the lawn out front. He read the Spanish words in the light streaming out of the church's open front door—*Santa María de los Pinos*—and decided that, Hispanic or not, this was a better neighborhood than Margaret Mary McVann's. In Margaret Mary McVann's, no one would have considered leaving the church doors open at night.

He walked to the bottom of the steps, looked in through the door, and saw nothing. Then he walked up the steps and looked in from the porch. Not only the front doors, but the vestibule doors were open. He could see straight up the center aisle to the altar. The altar had been covered with a cloth, and there was a monstrance on it with the host exposed in a circle of gold. There was one old woman leaning just inside the aisle rail of the left front pew. He dipped his fingers in the holy water and blessed himself and went inside, genuflecting automatically. The consecrated Host was the real body and blood of Jesus Christ, made present, and he knew he ought to be in awe of it. In fact, he had never been able to make himself take it seriously at all. The knife, in the right pocket of his jacket again, just the way it had been the day he went to Margaret Mary McVann, felt more real.

He backed all the way out into the vestibule again, and there she was, a small dark girl in a long blue skirt and a white blouse. She was wearing a Miraculous Medal around her neck. It was one of the ones with a blue glass covering that was supposed to look like sapphire.

"You," she said, and then went off in a stream of Spanish, incomprehensible but musical, an alto chant.

He shook his head.

She looked disgusted. "Of course not," she said. "You're not here for the Forty Hours Devotion."

"Is that what that is?"

"Twice a year. What are you here for?"

"I was walking around."

"In the cold?"

He shrugged.

She went up to the vestibule door, looked inside, and shook her head. "I've got a list here, all these old ladies. That's all who ever volunteers. Sister Annacita says it's a scandal."

"Who's Sister Annacita?"

"She's my history nun. She's a hag, really, a woman without blood. That's what my mother says. She's not really Annacita."

"What is she?"

The girl made a face. "Anne. An Anglo. They come down here and they're so proud of themselves, lifting us up from poverty. We lift ourselves up from poverty as long as we stay away from them. You're an Anglo. You don't look proud of yourself."

"I'm just tired."

"I'm tired, too, but I have to be here all night. I have to do the baking. Then when the old ladies come in I have to check them off on a list, and if they don't come in I have to call up and find out what's happened to them. Not that that's going to do any good. Most of them don't have phones. If somebody doesn't come in I'll just go next door to the convent and get one of the nuns. They ought to be here. Letting old ladies ruin their health in this cold kneeling all night in front of the Blessed Sacrament."

"You don't like nuns," he said.

The girl shrugged. "Nuns are nuns. None of them has any blood and none of them makes any sense."

She turned away from him and looked off toward the right, where there was a door he hadn't noticed before. The door was open and a faint shaft of light was spilling out of it.

"I've got to go down there," she told him. "I've got to take calls and I've got to pretend I'm being alert. You can come with me if you want."

He was going to tell her he didn't want, but she didn't give him time. She went for the door in a run, pulled it open, and rushed through. She reminded him of the street girls just after they'd taken a hit of speed, except that she hadn't taken anything.

When she was gone, he put his hand in his pocket and felt along the blade of the knife. It was knicking him the way it had the last three times he'd brought it with him, the sharp tip stabbing into his flesh over and over again like an angry wasp. He pulled it halfway out and wrapped his hand around it, squeezing it until the blade cut into the flesh under his knuckles. When he felt blood he began to feel dizzy.

He also began to change his mind.

4 The Holy Spirit was a bird, a dove, and birds sang. The Holy Spirit sang out His charisms and poured His music out over the men and women who listened to the Word of God. The Holy Spirit gave the gift and gave the power and you could hear about it any night you wanted to on television. Somewhere in this place filled with Hispanic people and Anglo nuns there was someone he was looking for and all he had to do was listen to the music, listen to the music, feel himself fill up with the Holy Spirit and then start to fly.

5   When he looked down the front of his jeans were soaked with blood. His hand was a mess and his knuckles ached. Everything hurt and all he could think of was crucifixion. He'd been nailed to a cross once, but the cross was upside down and that had been another life.

Besides, this was a charism, too.

When she saw him bleeding she would take care of him.

Taking care of him, she would tell him what he had to know.

PART FOUR

CHAPTER

ONE

1 Thirty years ago, Father John Kelly's job would have been very straightforward: take care of the Knights of Columbus, and make sure none of them, in the local chapters or the national office, got upset. Thirty years ago, New Haven was not only the world headquarters of the Knights, but the most fiercely loyal Catholic city in the world. Unlike the Catholic cities of Europe, like Dublin and Paris and Rome, it had never developed a hard strain of anticlericalism, a visceral suspicion of priests. Unlike the Catholic pockets of New York and Chicago and Boston, it had never had its feelings hurt by the Vatican. Even that old fart of a papal legate who had served under Pius XII, whose personality had acted like sandpaper on a raw wound on every other collection of prelates and laymen in America, had managed to be charming here. John could remember the building of the world headquarters in the late sixties, how impressed and shocked everyone had been. The Church was falling down around their ears. Nuns and priests were defecting en masse. Every product of a parochial school over the age of twenty-one was writing a book on how terrible it had been to be raised Catholic in the days before birth control was a sacrament—and the Knights had calmly collected a few million dollars, put up a building the size of a New York City flagship hotel, and dedicated the project to the Mother of God. Maybe, Father John Kelly thought, that was why his job hadn't *existed* thirty years ago.

At the moment, it existed with a job description that did not match its duties, because no one—least of all the bishop—wanted to admit in public that the Catholic church in New Haven now needed a referee. What Father John Kelly was supposed to do was simple: keep the liberals on one side of the fence and the conservatives on the other, and make sure they didn't beat each other to death in front of a dozen television cameras. It wasn't easy. As an order priest, locked away for the most part on college campuses where "dissent" meant desperately sincere, studiously intense discussions of the possible connections between the theology of the Trinity and sexism, he had had no idea how bad it had gotten. On his desk at this moment, at eight o'clock in the morning, there was a pile of message slips an inch and a half thick. Twenty or thirty of them would be from Saint Michael's Parish out on the Milford border, where the bishop had made the mistake of assigning a sweet old priest, close to retirement, to what John Kelly considered a nest of sharks. Every time the old man gave a homily that so much as mentioned the word *sin,* the whole parish council called in, demanding to be assigned a priest who wasn't so "negative." Father John Kelly thought the parish council at Saint Michael's could have found negativity in the Resurrection if they'd really tried—and if they'd had it preached to them by a priest who insisted on upholding Rome's ban on altar girls. Then there would be the calls from Saint Rita's, which was close to being an inner-city parish, but not quite. The "not quite" meant that the place was full of charismatic Hispanics threatening schism, and being badly served by a nice young man from the local seminary who thought speaking in tongues was the province of Protestant holy rollers. Parishioners at Saint Rita's got up in the middle of Mass and went into religious ecstasies. Their priest, forbidden by the bishop to throw them out, was near to a nervous breakdown. Somehow or the other, John was supposed to calm them all down and make sure none of them, or few of them, left the Church. He was beginning to wonder why the bishop wanted him to bother. In these days of democratic governments and religious pluralism, the Catholic Church was a voluntary organization. If you didn't want to belong to Her, you ought to be allowed to leave in peace.

He picked up the stack of message slips, turned it over, and put it down again. He listened for sounds in the outer office and heard nothing at all. Marie wasn't due in until nine and wouldn't arrive until half past. Most of the rest of the world wouldn't think it was polite to bother him until after ten. He had never told anyone how early he sometimes came to work, not even the bishop. His office was his refuge from the other Jesuits in his house and the problems of his job. The woman at the switchboard—the one who had taken the messages—knew enough not to put any calls through unless they were from the bishop himself.

As a matter of fact, he was expecting the bishop to call and was a little surprised that he hadn't. He had given the bishop all the information necessary for one of his patented rampages—all the news on Father Tom Burne, Dan Murphy, and the three women who had died with the Eucharistic symbol carved into their foreheads. Now that the third one had been found, the papers had stopped asking "Is there a Catholic connection?" and started screaming instead. The subhead on the second lead story in the *Register* John had picked up on his way in had used the term *religious mania* in a way that made him feel distinctly queasy. The lead story had been worse: FATHER BURNE, DAMIEN HOUSE, SUBJECT OF SEX ABUSE PROBE. It was like the sixties, only worse, because this time the enemy wasn't made up of discontented parishioners itching to be part of the *Playboy* generation or long-haired radicals who didn't really believe in God at all. This time the enemy was the City of New Haven.

John Kelly got up, went to his door, and opened it carefully. Just in case Marie had come in early—an event as probable as a visit from little green men from Mars—he didn't want to startle her. The outer office was empty. He went back to his desk and looked at his clock: 8:06. The digital underline said: December 17.

Father Tom Burne was six minutes late.

2 In the end, Father Tom Burne was twenty minutes late. He came bounding through John Kelly's door at 8:20:04 without apology or explanation—and without warning, either. It was the lack of warning that got John so upset. By then, he had half convinced himself that Tom Burne wasn't going to show up, that he'd cut his throat and made a run for it, that the whole situation was going to turn out to be nothing more than another wearying scandal to be handled by his best efforts at damage control. His mind had swerved off on other things, like the fact that he was due in the studio to tape the first of his broadcasts at four thirty-five today. He kept trying to picture himself on television and failing. When he closed his eyes, the face he saw staring out at him from the screen always belonged to Fulton Sheen.

He was trying to banish this ghost when Father Tom Burne came in and threw himself unceremoniously in a chair. He was carrying a Styrofoam cup with a plastic lid on it in one hand, and it was steaming.

"Too hot," he said, putting it down on John Kelly's desk. "Everything in my life these days is either too hot or too cold."

John Kelly was still all tangled up with Fulton Sheen. He cleared his throat, looked out the window, looked at his hands, looked at his feet. Finally, he looked at Tom Burne, but it didn't help. "Yes," he said. "Well."

Tom had taken the plastic top off the cup. He sniffed at the coffee and grimaced. "If you want to know why I wasn't here when I was supposed to be, I was out looking for Marietta."

"Marietta?"

"Marietta O'Brien. Older woman. She's been working as our housekeeper for—I don't know. Years."

"And she's missing?" John Kelly looked down at his paper, folded on the corner of his desk. He had folded it carefully, so that he could see nothing of the stories that upset him, but he could feel them there.

Tom Burne looked at the paper, too. "That's what I was

trying to get across. With—everything that's going on, I don't like not being able to find her. It's not right."

"Did she—does she live at Damien House?"

"Oh, yes. Up on the third floor with the girls."

"Ahh," John Kelly said.

Tom Burne stood up and began to pace—reminding John Kelly that he always paced, that he was one of those people who could never sit still.

"The problem is, the whole thing's so weird. She's in her sixties, at least. She makes a big show of how well she gets around, but she doesn't really. We've been talking about finding a different place in the house for her to stay, trying to figure out a way to keep her downstairs without getting her offended. She'd never just go wandering around in the middle of the night on her own, even in a better neighborhood."

"How do you know she went wandering around in the middle of the night?"

"I saw her just before I went to bed. She came downstairs for hot milk. Actually, she came downstairs for a painkiller. She's got wicked arthritis. Her legs kill her."

John Kelly rubbed the side of his nose. "What are you going to do about it? What can you do?"

"What I did do. I got Pat Mallory out of bed and asked him to go down to Damien House. Personally."

"Will he?"

Tom Burne stopped pacing, caught John Kelly's eye and held it. He wasn't smiling, but John felt there was a smile there and it made him uneasy. It was as if emotion were a climate and the weather had changed.

Tom Burne grabbed the chair he had been sitting in, pulled it back, and sat down in it again. Then he put his elbows on his knees and rested his head on his hands.

"The police," he said carefully, "as far as I can figure it, seem to believe that I am going to be crucified, in all my innocence, by the political ambitions of one Daniel Murphy."

3 The problem with talking to Father Tom Burne, John Kelly decided as the morning went on, was that he wasn't quite human. At least, he wasn't quite human as priests were supposed to be human. His words never meant what you expected them to mean, and his emotions were—out of whack. John Kelly could have understood a Father Tom Burne who was afraid, or close to cracking under pressure, or overcome by remorse. He could even have understood a Father Tom Burne who was working very hard to keep his courage up. What he couldn't understand was this—distance, this utter calm, as if nothing very surprising had happened at all. What was worse, it was the same distance, the same calm, that Tom Burne always wore. John Kelly amended his initial analysis. With Tom Burne, it wasn't as if nothing surprising had happened, but as if *nothing* had happened.

They went around it once or twice, but there was only one place to settle, only one real topic of conversation—unless Tom Burne could be made to think about damage control, which John Kelly didn't think he could.

"What worries me," he told Tom, even though it wasn't what worried him at all, "isn't so much the accusations themselves. You've built up a lot of emotional capital in this town—"

"Is that what it is, emotional capital?"

"Public support," John Kelly said, flushing, feeling he'd said the wrong thing again. "If these were financial accusations, I wouldn't be worried in the least. But child abuse—"

"Yes, John? What about child abuse?"

"Well. Oh, for God's sake, Tom, what do you think? Don't you remember Bruce Ritter?"

"Of course I remember Bruce Ritter. He was the one who managed to end up getting lynched by his own Church."

"Oh, for God's *sake*." John Kelly shot up and started pacing himself, even though he hated to pace. "Will you please see reason? What the hell else was the Church supposed to do? What if—?"

"What if Father Ritter actually did the things he was accused of doing? Maybe he did. We'll never know."

"But Tom—"

"Three investigations, all done internally by Church authorities. A report whose presentation of evidence was damn near nonexistent. A lot of government investigations suddenly dropped—"

"That's better than what could have happened. The government investigations could have kept going. Why can't you see it's much better like this? There's no—no record—no—"

"No trial?"

"A trial—" John Kelly felt as if he were choking. No, he knew he was choking. He was suffocating.

"I think you'd better understand something, Father. If it comes to me, I will demand a trial. I will demand it publicly. You're right when you say I've built up a lot of public support. Some of that support is with the media. We can talk about this all you want. I will talk about this all you want, but you'd better understand this: I will not put up with being treated as Bruce Ritter was treated. I will not retire to a monastery. I will not keep my mouth shut when reporters come around. I will not cooperate in internal investigations which issue reports full of bland declarations that supposedly discovered 'evidence' that would not hold up in any court of law—"

"That's not true," John put in desperately. "They didn't do that. The child abuse thing is—"

"What?" Tom Burne said. "Entirely different?"

"The rules are different." John settled sullenly into his chair. "You must know that by now, Tom. Even the Supreme Court says—"

"Yes," Tom said softly, "I know what the Supreme Court says. We can tear up the Constitution, deny a defendant the right to discovery, deny a defendant the right to confront his accusers, turn the whole damn legal system into a career mill for men like Daniel Murphy—because child abuse is different. Trust me, John, I know child abuse is different."

"I don't know what you want me to do," John said. "I don't

know what you want anybody to do. What the hell good is it going to do you to go to trial?"

"It depends on what I go to trial for." Tom had settled back, the distance once more in evidence, the calm like a ghost's shroud covering him from hair to shoes. John Kelly found himself once again shifting uneasily in his chair. He didn't understand a man who could get so worked up over abstractions—constitutional law, for God's sake, at a time like this—and remain so unaffected by hard reality.

"I still don't know what you want me to do," he said. "I still don't understand what you think you're getting at."

"I don't suppose you do." Tom Burne nodded. "The thing is, John, I don't think Dan Murphy is going to try to stick me with child abuse."

"You don't?"

"There are too many problems with it. Too many people still feel as if Bruce Ritter was jobbed—too many people didn't like the way that whole thing was handled. Too many people out there are susceptible to conspiracy theories."

"I don't understand what you mean."

"Whatever else Bruce Ritter may or may not have done, he was one of the most effective campaigners against the kiddie porn industry this country has ever seen. There are a lot of people who think that maybe what happened to him was that mob-connected types decided they didn't like the way he was interfering in their business—"

"That's not—"

"True?" Tom Burne said. "No, you're right, most likely it's not true. But if I'm right, and if what Dan Murphy is after here is a shot at the governor's mansion, it doesn't matter if the same thing is not true here. The mere suspicion of it is a taint."

"So?"

"So."

Tom Burne moved forward and took the paper off the desk. John thought he was going to go to the story about himself, maybe point out a paragraph that John had naturally missed, since he hadn't read the thing. Instead, he flipped through the front section to an interior page, folded the paper into a neat thick quarter, and handed it back.

"Upper-left-hand side," he said. "Tell me what you think of that."

The small headline on the upper lefthand side said, BOY FOUND IN RIVER EXPECTED TO LIVE. John Kelly stared at it in confusion.

"I don't understand," he said. And then he felt he'd said that so often, it ought to end up engraved on his tombstone.

Tom Burne took the paper back. "The boy in question is named Stevie Marks. Not his real name, by the way. You never know their real names. Stevie Marks is ten years old. He's a prostitute."

"What?"

"He's a prostitute," Tom Burne repeated. "Maybe I should say he was. A very well-kept prostitute, by the way. One of the boys who gets used by the upper-income types for kicks. He's the third they've found."

"In the river?"

"Shot. In the back of the head. According to Pat Mallory, the other two boys died of what looks on the surface to be gangland-style execution shootings. With this one, whoever it was got sloppy. The shot didn't go right. The kid lived."

"What has this got to do with you?"

"I don't know. That's one of the things I want you to do for me. Check around. Talk to Dan Murphy. Find out if he put his sister up to volunteering at Damien House."

"*What?*"

Father Tom Burne, John Kelly decided, had a smile like a snake. He always looked so damned pleased to watch you fold.

Two

1 For Pat Mallory, the woman who answered the door at Damien House that morning of December 17 was a mixed blessing. He had met her before, right here in the Damien House living room, when she was visiting with one of her brothers. He had liked her, in a not very focused way, and thought she was attractive. The truth of it was, she was very attractive, in spite of all those years locked up in what was a very conservative order of nuns. Some women coming out of the convent were oddly flat. Their hair didn't work right. Their makeup ended up looking like paint. Even women who belonged to orders that allowed them to live in lay clothes never seemed to get the hang of looking like civilians. Except for her silence and her reserve, this one might never have been a nun at all. He didn't know if that was a good sign.

The problem, of course, was that she had another brother, not the Andy she had come down here with—and that brother was Dan Murphy.

He looked her over anyway, automatically, because men did that to women. They learned it in high school and never were able to shake the habit. Then he held his breath and waited for the blasting sermon on sexism he got from so many ex-nuns. It didn't come.

He was standing under the porch light in the cold, with the wind whipping across his bare neck and his knuckles feeling frozen inside his gloves. She stepped back and let him inside, one arm crossed over the bulky sweater that covered her from shoulders to knees. He looked down and saw that she was in socks but without shoes.

"Splinters," he said, pointing down.

She smiled. "I'm not worried about splinters. I've been trying not to scratch these floors any more than they've been scratched. They're made of what's really beautiful old wood."

"I don't think anybody has the time to notice."

"Maybe not. You're Patrick Mallory, aren't you? I met you here a couple of weeks ago. I'm Susan Murphy."

"I remember."

"You remember because of my brother Dan. Father Tom isn't here, you know. I'm not sure where I'm supposed to put you."

They both looked from side to side, then up and down. Living room, door to kitchen. Stairs and floor. Crucifix and mirror. The whole house was lit up, but this part of it was oddly empty. Pat could hear sounds coming from the back, where the kitchen and the two small bathrooms were. He thought there were also bathrooms upstairs, but he wasn't sure.

"Well," he said. "I suppose we should go to the kitchen. I could use a cup of coffee. I could use a few people to talk to, too."

Susan looked toward the kitchen and bit her lip. "A lot of people don't know she's gone yet. I mean, they know she's not around. They can see that. But they don't know she's gone. Father Tom felt, with all the murders, people would jump to conclusions."

"They're probably jumping to conclusions anyway."

"Maybe. But some of the kids are only six or seven years old. I know they've seen a lot, but still—"

"How come *you* know?" he asked her. "You can't have been around long enough to make it into Father Tom's inner circle."

She had been looking everywhere but at him—deliberately, Pat thought—and now she took a pack of cigarettes out of her jeans and bent her head over her preparations to smoke. She had her blue Bic lighter turned up too high. The flame shot out of it, a long stream of fire in the air, nearly singeing her nose. She got the cigarette lit anyway, dragged on it, and blew out a stream of smoke.

Pat Mallory found himself wondering why so many of the ex-nuns he knew got addicted to nicotine.

"The thing is," Susan Murphy said, "I had to know. I mean, I was sharing a room with her last night."

"Upstairs?"

"That's right. It was a kind of test, I think. I'm never sure what Father Tom is up to. I was here yesterday morning."

"All right."

"I don't know why I came, yesterday morning, I mean. I was just here. Then I went home for lunch, and Dan was there—my brother is—"

"I know who your brother is, Miss Murphy. I think we went through this the last time."

"Yes. Anyway, the news came over the radio about the investigation of Father Burne, and I came back."

"Just like that?"

"Just like that. I think I got a little crazy and refused to leave."

"You think?"

Another drag. Another stream of smoke. Blue eyes and black hair. "Do you know they have mini-retreats here, the way we used to give in the convent schools? Four or five hours of praying and edification and then a night under discipline of silence. I used to think that was strange even in the old days."

"You did that here, last night?"

Inhale, exhale, tap ash. "I remember wondering if it had been Marietta's idea. If she wanted a little peace and quiet for once. They've—we've—got fourteen girls up there. Most of the time it's probably like a nonstop pajama party."

"Did Marietta leave before the silence started, or after?"

"Before. We were just starting a rosary. She left that for me to do. She didn't really trust me to do much of anything else."

"So she came downstairs while the girls were saying a rosary. She didn't come back up again."

Susan Murphy shook her head. "No, she didn't. I suppose I

should have raised the alarm—I've been kicking myself all morning for not raising the alarm—but I didn't think anything of it. Last night at dinner, Father Tom was saying how when a kid came to the door, whoever let him in was supposed to stop everything to take care of him. Everything. You weren't even supposed to go to the bathroom. I just thought—"

"A kid had come to the door." Pat Mallory nodded. For all he knew, a kid had come to the door. He had been working in New Haven too long to believe in the innocence of street children.

The smoke from Susan Murphy's cigarette was curling up through her great mass of hair, creating a fog that he didn't find unpleasant. Usually, some atavistic part of him rebelled at the sight of women who smoked. For some reason, he actually liked it on her. He just wished she would relax, instead of twitching and looking away. He was in and out of Damien House all the time. Half the police force was, because Damien House was the best place to bring the kids they found sleeping on the Green and under the stairways of abandoned buildings all winter long. He wasn't used to having to be nervous here.

"Look," he said, "there must be someone around who knows something, someone I could talk to. I can't do anything to help unless I get more information."

"Father Burne—"

"Father Burne went to see the auxiliary bishop," he said patiently. "He told me he was going to on the phone. Under the circumstances, that could take hours."

"I know," Susan said, "but—"

"Look," Pat said again, "what about Francesca? Francesca's usually around somewhere—"

"I know where Francesca is," Susan said. She looked around the foyer, as if she expected the older woman to materialize, and then seemed to make up her mind about something. "You go into the living room," she told Pat. "I'll get her and send her out to you. As long as I don't bring you into the kitchen, no one can accuse me of not thinking about the children. That's where most of them are this hour of the morning."

"But—"

She shook her head at him and walked away, moving like a nun.

2 "The problem," Francesca said, after she had scooped him out of the living room, deposited him at the kitchen table in spite of Susan's Father Tom–inspired worries about traumatizing the children, and handed him a cup of coffee, "is that there's just so many places we can search. I don't mean there's just so many places she could be. You could hide a townful of bodies out there in those vacant lots. But searching—"

"It wouldn't make much sense to find Marietta just to get yourself killed."

"Mugged, anyway," Francesca said. "According to the kids, some new drug hit the street about four days ago. I didn't need them to tell me. There's been a rash of robberies from one end of the Congo to the other and we had our Virgin stolen again. I hate it when our Virgin gets stolen. The lady who gives them to us gets absolutely infuriated, and she always takes it out on Father Tom."

As far as Pat Mallory was concerned, everybody took everything out on Father Tom, as a matter of principle. He thought about Dan Murphy's investigation and flushed.

"Tell me what happened last night," he said, "as far as you can figure. Tell me about Susan Murphy."

Francesca's eyes went to the door. Susan had gone out to dump some trash. He and Francesca seemed to be the only people who noticed her absence. The kitchen was full of kids eating breakfast standing up, but they not only had no time for Susan Murphy, they had no time for Francesca and Pat.

Francesca poured herself half a cup of coffee, and filled the other half with nondairy creamer. "Oh, Susan," she said. "Well, she's here. She showed up yesterday afternoon—"

"I thought it was morning."

"I heard something about morning. Don't ask me that. You know how I am about mornings. All I know for sure is, she showed up yesterday afternoon, right after the news came out, and she was very upset. Whether it was real or fake, I couldn't tell you."

"What did it look like?"

"Real. But Father Tom thought it was fake."

"Why?"

"Well, she's Dan Murphy's sister, isn't she? And let me tell you, whatever that man is doing, it's stranger than it looks on the surface. I know what child sexual abuse cases look like, Pat, I was a social worker. This is—"

"What?"

Francesca shrugged. "Father Tom says it's because the boy is so much older than accusers usually are in these cases. Did you know Dan's office had a boy?"

"No, I didn't," Pat said. He turned it over in his head a few times. It didn't make sense. "How could he have? Do you mean one of the boys from Damien House walked over to Dan Murphy's office, or some police station—"

"No, that's exactly what I don't mean. Do you remember what happened to Bruce Ritter?"

"Oh, yes."

"Everybody does, I suppose. Well, if you ask me, what's fishy about all of this is that it's happening in exactly the same way. This boy is grown now, or nearly. Theoretically—and notice I said theoretically—he went to Dan and said that, I don't know, years ago, Father Tom molested him. Then his mother showed up in John Kelly's office and said it was all a crock—just like with that boy who accused Bruce Ritter and his own father said he was an habitual liar."

"Maybe the kid read the reports in the papers on the Ritter case. Maybe he thought that's the way things were supposed to be done."

"Crap," Francesca said. "That's utter trash and you know it. Most of these kids can barely read, and that one—I remember that one. I've been here forever. What most of us think around here is, *Dan* read the newspaper reports on the Ritter case, and Dan set it up."

"Why?"

"I don't know." Francesca's coffee cup was empty again. This time, so was the thermos she had brought to the table. Pat watched her get up and walk to the counter where another pot was brewing, pour her cup half full, fill the thermos. She was moving slowly and painfully, showing her age for the first time Pat could remember.

"I can't help feeling it's all connected," she said, coming to sit down again. She filled the rest of her cup with nondairy creamer again and stirred. "Not just Dan and this boy who's accusing Tom, but these women who are being murdered and then these boys—"

"Francesca, where do you get your information?"

"About the boys I get it from the papers, same as everybody else," she said. "About Dan Murphy—let's just say there's someone in that office with a *very* close connection to Damien House."

Pat Mallory sighed. "I thought there might be. But it's not a very safe thing to do, Francesca. There isn't a cop in this city who trusts Dan Murphy as far as he can throw him. There's no reason to trust him."

"We don't trust him. Why do you think we spy?"

"It would be better to leave him alone."

"Why? He won't leave us alone. He's out to shut this place down for reasons that are beyond my power to comprehend."

"Francesca—"

"Never mind," Francesca said. "You came here to talk about Marietta, not the Machiavellian machinations of Dan Murphy. I should take you outside and show you how it went."

3   She did take him outside, but not, as Pat had suspected, to show him how it went. There was no "how it went." The small square yard at the back of Damien House was clean and empty. There was not only no body, but nowhere to hide one. Somebody

had already emptied the garbage cans and taken the garbage away. Since trash removal service was nonexistent on Amora Street, that meant someone had stuffed the back of a car full of plastic bags and hauled them out to the nearest public dump, somewhere in the suburbs. Pat thought it was a good thing most public dumps had no system for identifying the people legally allowed to use them. If they had, the garbage would have been piling up around Damien House for years, until it ate the building whole.

"I wonder where Susan went," Francesca said as they came outside. The garbage cans were bright silver and clean, in need of being stuffed with plastic bags. "Timmy's already gone to the dump. She didn't come back inside."

"Maybe she went to the dump with Timmy."

"There's never any room in the car for anything but Timmy and the trash." Francesca walked over to the garbage cans, looked deeply into one, and shook her head. "That's the first thing we thought, you know, when Marietta wasn't in the kitchen this morning. That she'd come out here to dump some trash—there's always so much trash—anyway, that she'd come out and then had a heart attack or collapsed. She's really not well, you know. Then we looked out here, of course, and she wasn't anywhere in sight, and then Susan came down and said that Marietta hadn't been in bed all night, and then—"

"Did you see her last night?" Pat asked. "Did you talk to her?"

"Just to say hello. She was coming downstairs for her milk and her pills."

"You didn't see her go outside?"

"No, I didn't."

"Did anyone? Father Tom?"

"He said he didn't," Francesca said. "Pat, if you think she might be somewhere in the house, don't. We looked."

"Hard?"

"Very hard."

"Including in the basement? And the attic?"

"We have a cellar, not a basement. We don't have an attic at all. That's the infants' dorm now. And yes, we looked."

"What about the doorbell?" Pat asked. "You're up most of the night, aren't you? Did you hear the doorbell ring?"

"No, I didn't. And I would have heard. Those ringers are right outside my door. I'm the emergency squad of last resort around here."

"Mmmph," Pat said. He looked at the garbage cans again, at the ground, at the low wall that blocked Damien House off from the vacant lot behind it. The wall was new, built by a couple of volunteers after a rash of robberies a few years ago, totally ineffective. From where he stood, he could see piles of cardboard cartons shivering in the wind. They were probably full of junkies freezing to death.

"Sometimes," he said, "I want to come down here and torch the whole Congo."

"If you do, you'll torch us with it," Francesca told him.

Somewhere much too close at hand, someone was screaming.

CHAPTER
THREE

1 Father John Kelly didn't know what he was going to do if
Dan Murphy was at the studio when he came in for rehearsal.
He didn't know why he hadn't thought about it before, if not last
night, when his head was still full of the press coverage of the
possible investigation, then this morning, when Tom Burne was in
his office. The truth was, he was having a hard time thinking about
anything at all. He had been aware for a while now that something
was wrong, not with the world but with himself. Little things he
had always been able to handle had begun to feel beyond him. He
had even found himself sympathizing with the people some of the
other priests down in the chancery had called "The Tridentine
Cheerleading Squad." It was a priest joke unlikely to make any sense
to outsiders. It had to do with the reams of people—there seemed
to be more of them all the time—who had never really gotten used
to Vatican II. The Tridentine was the old Mass, the one most of
the new priests considered stuffy, pompous, and excruciatingly
"negative." It was supposed to represent everything that had been
wrong with the pre-Council Church, from weekly confession to
rosary novenas. Father John Kelly was beginning to realize he
missed it.

He waited until Father Tom Burne was safely out of the
office—thumb on the intercom button so that he could hear into
the outer office; Marie's voice coming in at him, even more nasal
over the wire than in person, telling Father Tom to have a good
day—and then he picked up his phone and made a call on his own.

He had always had a suspicion that Marie listened in when he called the chancery. The last thing he wanted now was to be overheard.

Far away—in Bridgeport or Fairfield or wherever the damned residence was these days—the phone rang and rang. It was barely nine o'clock in the morning, and John had a vision of the priests out there, still in bed, ears plugged up with pillows. It wasn't fair. He'd been a priest out there himself not long ago, and he knew the residence got up early. The bishop liked being able to say that he said Mass, read his Breviary, had breakfast, and started work before seven.

The phone was picked up, and a low voice that sounded half-irritated and half-asleep said, "Our Lady of Peace Rectory."

John Kelly couldn't remember when they'd renamed the residence Our Lady of Peace. He only remembered when he'd started hating it.

"Stephen?" he said.

"Oh, crap." There was a hacking cough, the sound of phlegm being cleared from a throat, a snort. "It's you. What the hell is going on down there, anyway? We've been up all night over here and all we know is it's all your fault."

"I've been up all night, too." That wasn't true, not quite, but he didn't want to go into it. He just wanted to get Stephen off the phone. There was something in him that didn't like priests who swore too casually—something not as strong as but related to the thing that didn't like priests who made fun of solemnity in the Mass. Sometimes he thought he was turning into an old fogey much too young.

"Look," he said, "is Riley around? I've got to talk to him."

"Oh, Riley's *around*," Stephen said. "At least, he's around for *you*. The rest of the world could be destroyed in a nuclear holocaust in the next three minutes, he'd been unavailable, but he's around for *you*."

"Stephen—"

"Never mind," Stephen said.

There was a *thunk* on the other end of the line, the phone

going down on the telephone table in the hall. John Kelly could picture it, right to the muddy red light thrown out by dim sunlight coming through the stained-glass windows that flanked the door. He got his secret stash of cigarettes out of the center drawer of his desk and lit up.

A few minutes later, he heard the wheezing wind of what he knew must be Monaghan Riley coming down the stairs to the phone—Monaghan Riley, who had his mother's maiden name as a first name like a Protestant, and who had had to pick a new first name when he was ordained, because that was in the days when the Church insisted that Her children be called after saints. Maybe She still did.

The phone was picked up and wheezed into. A voice tinged with brogue said, "John? Is that you? I've been waiting to hear from you all night." It was sometimes hard to remember that Monaghan Riley, now officially David Monaghan Riley, had been born in Waterbury, Connecticut.

John took another drag of his cigarette, put it down on the edge of the desk, and said, "Yes, Your Grace. Good morning. I didn't call you last night because I didn't have anything to say."

"Don't call me 'Your Grace.'" Riley coughed. "They said in *Connecticut* magazine I missed the days when people went around kissing my ring. They were lying."

"Yes, Yo—yes."

"Well?"

John picked up his cigarette again. The ash on the end of it was huge. He tapped it into the wastebasket and watched the pieces fall.

"Well," he said, "I've had Tom in here this morning. I suppose you knew I was going to do that."

"I expected it. You had to."

"I know I had to. I wish I hadn't had to. It was a mess."

"Tom wasn't being cooperative?"

Another drag on the cigarette got rid of his irritation. As much as he tried to hide it—assuming he tried at all—Riley admired

Tom Burne for not "being cooperative." "Being cooperative" was Riley's code for what he called in private "those masters of conformity, the Spirit of Vatican II priests."

"I think," John said carefully, "that we're going to have to accept from the beginning that Tom isn't going to let us clean this up quietly. To tell you the truth, Father, that's an understatement. He wants a full-blown media exhibition."

"You couldn't talk him into any kind of compromise."

"I could hardly get a word in edgeways. What kind of compromise could there be anyway? Either there's going to be an ecclesiastical investigation and we'll have control of it, or there's going to be a civil investigation and we won't."

"Have you heard from your friend Dan Murphy? Has there been any hint that he'd do a deal—go away and pretend that none of it's real as long as we issue reports about internal investigations and get Tom out of there?"

"No." The cigarette was burned down to the butt. John opened the center desk drawer again, rummaged around inside, and came up with a small ashtray. "No," he said again. "I know what you're thinking. It was the first thing I thought of, too. You ever been down to Congress Avenue?"

"Of course I have. I go every year. You've been there with me."

"Mmm." It was true, of course. The bishop went not only to Congress Avenue, but to all the other first-class awful neighborhoods in New Haven—and the first-class awful neighborhoods in Bridgeport and Danbury, too. It was part of the new "pastoral orientation" that was the rage everywhere, even with men like Monaghan Riley, who ought to know better. To be fair, Riley knew it was all a crock. He didn't fool himself into believing he did some good by marching through the trash cans and the ruined buildings, or that he saw much of reality while he was doing it, either. He did it because he was expected to and then went home and got down to serious business.

"The thing is," John said, "that march down there, it's like the Empress Catherine and the Potemkin Villages. They clean the place up for you and you know it. I take it you've never been down there when nobody knew you were coming."

"Not since it got bad, John, no. I used to go down there when I was a kid, in the forties. It was different then."

"Everything was different then." John lit another cigarette. "Right now, what you've got down there is a lot of prostitution. On the side streets, you've got a lot of child prostitution—"

"On Tom's side street? On Amora?"

"No. Father, on Amora there isn't much of anything but Damien House. The place is abandoned. I'm talking farther up, closer to civilization. If you go up there and off to the side, you find a lot of girls, eight and ten years old, walking the streets. You also find a lot of movie houses, little hole-in-the-wall places, with discreet little signs—"

"Kiddie porn?"

"Yes, of course. Do you know a man named Pat Mallory?"

There was a pause on the other end of the line, cough, wheeze, rumble. The rumble was half a laugh.

"Big man," Riley said, "really massive. Shaggy hair. Very Irish in the face. Has an attitude."

"He's chief of Homicide for the City of New Haven."

"Good Lord."

"He's been very helpful to us here on one or two occasions, Father. There always seems to be someone up here with a son in trouble or a daughter on drugs. Of course we don't get much homicide among the parishioners—"

"—Of course not—" Dry.

"—but he has influence and he uses it for us when he can. A couple of months ago he took me out to dinner."

"Did you ask him if he still goes to Mass?"

"No, Father, I didn't." John took another drag on his cigarette, put it down in the ashtray, rubbed his forehead. Did Riley really expect him to have asked something like that? It was hard to tell. "Actually, Father, the conversation was on somewhat more mundane matters. The police had just recovered a missing person for us—for a parishioner out in Dellford Heights, to be exact. It was his daughter—the parishioner's, I mean. She was nine. They found her on one of those side streets I was telling you about, off Congress. She was—"

"I can guess."

"They found her fast, Father. Fortunately they found her before much damage could be done. Unfortunately, since it was before much damage could be done, the girl didn't really know anything about the operations down there. And when Mr. Mallory bought me dinner, he said something—something I kept thinking about the whole time Tom was here this morning—and—"

"What?"

"It's hard to put into words." Actually, it wasn't hard to put into words at all. It was hard to think about. John took another drag, tapped another ash, walked over to his window, and looked outside. The sky was darker now than it had been when he first came in, and there was something coming down out of it, neither rain nor snow. He turned his back to the glass and sat down on the windowsill.

"According to Pat Mallory," he said carefully, "there's a ring operating in this city, selling very young boys to rich older men for sex—"

"Boys?"

"That's what I said, yes. Apparently girls aren't that big a draw—I'm sorry about this, Father, but I'm trying to repeat what I heard as accurately as I can. Anyway, the big money is in boys, specifically boys between the ages of eight and twelve. Somewhere in this city, somebody has an entire stable of them, a kind of kiddie call-boy service, specifically for establishment types with thick wallets. Every once in a while the police would find one of these boys, all dressed up in designer clothes, usually dead of a drug overdose. They have always been white. They have more often than not been blond. They have always been—delicate."

"Did Tom Burne find a few of these boys, too?"

"No, Father, he didn't. According to Pat Mallory, Father, whoever's operating this service must have connections somewhere, in City Hall, at Yale, somewhere, because no matter what has surfaced, no matter what evidence we find, no matter what bodies show up, we never get close to the people who are running it, and we never get any real publicity. It's not only been very quiet, it's been invulnerable."

"All right."

"Well, Father, a couple of weeks ago, something very strange began to happen. A number of these boys began to turn up dead, not from drug overdoses but from gunshot wounds to the back of the head—Tom Burne called them 'gangland-execution' style killings. He said that the word out on the street, what his kids have been telling him, is that these executions were warnings. What he's heard is that there's a boy out there, named Charlie Burton, who used to be part of this stable—"

"Used to be?"

"Yes, Father. Used to be. That's the point. What ordinarily happens in this situation is that, when a boy reaches the end of his usefulness—"

"Oh, Lord Jesus *Christ*."

"Yes, Father, I know. It's hard. But you have to listen to this. When a boy reaches the end of his usefulness, he's gotten rid of—another drug overdose, a nice jump in the river—"

"They kill them *all?*"

"Tom says they have to. The boys know—things. Who sold them, for one thing. Who bought them, for another. So the boys are gotten rid of. But this one wasn't. He just—disappeared."

"Right," Riley said. "So. These killings are supposed to—what?"

"Warn him off telling anyone what happened to him. And especially who did it to him."

"Right," Riley said again. His wheeze now was mostly indignation. John found himself thinking how odd it was that Riley's emphysema could almost always be cured, momentarily, by the rites of righteousness. He got off the windowsill, went back to his desk, and sat down again. His cigarettes were still lying right out there in the open, but he didn't take one. He was suddenly feeling much more relaxed. Whatever other problems he had, at least he didn't have a problem with his bishop. Monaghan Riley wasn't one of those new clerics who "understood" everything and everyone, who only half believed in sin, if that. Monaghan Riley knew sin when he saw it and knew he didn't like it. He would have made an excellent fire-and-brimstone preacher.

"Listen," John said, into Riley's wheeze. "The thing is, these killings have not been quiet. They couldn't be. They were—"

"Supposed to be public service announcements, so to speak."

"Exactly. They haven't got the play you'd have expected, because we've had other things going on—"

"Women being killed."

"Yes, women being killed. But then there's the problem that the boys are prostitutes. The papers shy away from it. Lower-class crime. Still, they haven't been quiet and they have been murders of children. Tom Burne says the case is going to have to be solved one way or the other, or Dan Murphy's going to end up looking bad. And if Dan Murphy ends up looking bad, he's the kind of man who'd make sure to make the police department look worse."

"So?"

"So Tom thinks that's what this is all about. Not an investigation into possible child abuse at Damien House, but an attempt to set him up to take the fall for the boys—"

"For the *killings?* Tom *Burne?*"

"Father, please, listen. You remember I told you about that missing person case, and about Pat Mallory taking me to dinner?"

"Yes. Yes, of course I do."

"Well, that's the thing, you see. When Pat took me to dinner, he said something I forgot about for a long time, but when Tom was here I remembered it. Pat said that they found her too easily—

the girl, I mean. They found her too fast. They should have had to make a search. Instead, they just found her wandering around. It was as if whoever took her had been made to feel they'd made a mistake, and she'd been dumped where she could be found. And Pat said there was only one way that could have happened, and that was if these people had someone inside the police department, or someone connected to the police department, who was connected seriously with—"

"Stop," Riley said. The wheeze was entirely gone. John listened carefully but could detect no sign of it. With the wheeze gone, Monaghan Riley sounded like a much younger man.

"Pat Mallory," Riley said, "is the man working on these murders, right now?"

"Yes, Father. He's the man working on the murders of the women, too. He works on everything, you know, because he's—"

"Chief of Homicide. You told me. I want to talk to him. Do you think you could set it up?"

"I—"

"Of course you can set it up. You have to set it up. I'll be in New Haven at six. Have Mallory at Queen of Heaven rectory at six thirty. I'll feed him."

"Father—"

"Make the call now, John. I have to get moving."

John Kelly knew he ought to say, "Yes, Father," but he didn't feel like it, and he didn't do it. He just said good-bye.

2   Half an hour later, having left messages for Pat Mallory from one end of New Haven to the other, having found no trace of the man at all, John Kelly went back to smoking cigarettes. In his desk, he had the text of the sermon he was supposed to rehearse for television this afternoon. He took it out, looked at it, and decided he would never be able to read it. The letters seemed to be fluid, living things, like small fish, that darted from one edge of the page to the other.

The real problem was, if the bishop was going to be at Queen of Heaven rectory at six, he was going to have to be there, too, and he didn't want to be. All of a sudden, he wanted not a single thing more to do with this mess. It was bad and it was only going to get worse, and that was not what he had signed on for when he became a priest.

CHAPTER
FOUR

1 Susan Murphy had never seen a splatter movie, but she had heard about them. Mostly she had heard about them from students. Knives and guns, blood and skin and bone, *The Texas Chain Saw Massacre*. She was standing against the low stone wall at the north end of the Damien House lot, looking out over the rubble and the raw sewage, not looking down. Down was an abyss, even with all these people around her, the people who had come when she had screamed. Out was a lunar landscape, nowhere on earth at all. She was in space. That was why she was so cold.

She felt a hand on her arm and turned to find Pat Mallory beside her, holding out a pack of cigarettes, her own. There was something coming down on her hair and face, something half-frozen and wet, and she realized she wasn't really wearing much in the way of clothes, not for this weather. Jeans and a turtleneck and sweater and knee socks, that was fine, but instead of shoes on her feet she had a pair of clogs that belonged to one of the girls upstairs and didn't quite fit her, and she had no coat at all. She had been standing around in the kitchen, listening to Pat Mallory and Francesca talk, and she had felt so useless—so damned wrong. Kids had been coming in and out for breakfast, paying no attention to her. Even the girls she had gone through the mini-retreat with the night before had been behaving as if she were invisible. Cold, cold, cold, she thought now, the word for all of this is cold. Inside of Damien House or out, she was always cold.

On the other side of the low stone wall, more than half buried

209

under a pile of rotting lumber that might once have been the side
of a house, was the body of Marietta O'Brien. Susan could see one
short fat leg sticking into the wind, the ankle oddly twisted and the
foot swollen. The foot was bare and there wasn't a shoe in sight.

Pat Mallory touched her on the shoulder again, held something out to her again, nodded slightly. Susan made her eyes focus
and saw that it wasn't the pack of cigarettes she was being offered
this time, but a single cigarette, lit. She took it and sucked on it,
using it for anesthetic.

"Dear sweet Christ," she said.

Pat Mallory nodded again. "Everybody else is back in the
house. I can't go until the cars get here. Stay and talk to me."

"Here?"

"We could go back against the other wall."

The other wall was the one lined with garbage cans. The cans
looked too shiny to be real, and the day looked too gray. Susan
tried to drag herself back to some semblance of self-discipline and
found that it was impossible. She had lost hold on time. She remembered being alone out here and screaming. She remembered
being surrounded by people. She could see she was alone now with
only Pat Mallory at her side. She would have sworn she had been
out here less than a single minute.

"Dear sweet Jesus Christ," she said. "I must have been looking
at it for ten minutes—that foot—and I didn't even know what it
was."

2 It got better. For some reason, she had expected him to
interrogate her immediately—for *some* reason?—but he only
pushed her down against the opposite wall and walked away. She
watched him go back to where she had been and stand looking
down at what she had been trying so hard not to see again, but
without any of her paralysis, mental or physical. He paced back and
forth against the short stretch of wall that had helped to hide the
body of Marietta O'Brien, stopping every once in a while to lean

over a little farther or to stand back and cock his head. After a while, she realized he was talking to himself, too. The wind would whip around and bring a word or two of it back to her, intriguing words that were somehow just as cold as everything else. "Position," he said to himself, and then "progression," "angle," "neck." It ought to have repelled her, being clinical, but it didn't.

Once, soon after she had told Reverend Mother everything about what had happened on Edge Hill Road, she had requested permission to see one of those priest-psychologists who had become all the vogue after Vatican II. She had seen him twice, just long enough for him to tell her she was desperately in search of a father figure. At the time, she had simply thought he was being snotty and cynical about both her faith and her vocation—which he might have been. That was the time when the professional heretics were coming out of the woodwork, the priests who didn't believe in God, the bishops who didn't believe in the Resurrection, the moral theologians who didn't believe in sin. In those days she had been very devout and very committed to her order. The order was engaged in what amounted to a war against the wholesale laicization of religious women. The first time she walked into the priest-psychologist's office he had stared at her in surprise and said, "You're still in habit. We'll have to make sure you get out of it."

She had finished her cigarette. She seemed to remember something she had read once, in a detective story, about how bad it was to leave innocent butts lying around the scene of a crime, so she put it out with a pinch of snow and put the butt in the pocket of her jeans. Then she lit up again. She hated to admit it, but the priest-psychologist may have been right—without knowing it and without having had enough time with her to give him just cause for what he was saying. She probably was desperately in search of a father figure. A father figure was what she was turning Pat Mallory into, right this minute, by taking comfort in the size of him and in the way he walked, so purposeful and sure, so quickly and without hesitation. God only knew, she had never felt this way about Reverend Mother, who had been just as purposeful and just as sure.

Out at the other end of the lot, Pat Mallory seemed to come to some sort of conclusion. Instead of pacing or looking or leaning, he backed up. Then he pivoted on his heel and started walking back to her. Susan watched him come, the way his legs moved inside his jeans, the way his shoulders moved inside the heavy padding of his open jacket, and wondered why he wasn't in uniform.

He came up beside her and said, "What did you do with the butt from the other cigarette? That can't be the same one."

"I put it in my pocket."

"Good girl." He sat down next to her on the wall and stretched his legs. "I don't know if you can hear it yet, but I can. Sirens. Help is on the way."

"I hope it's fast. It doesn't seem right to me, having her lying out there like that."

"How do you know it's her?"

"Maybe I don't. I didn't move anything, if that's what you want to know. It was just the leg. Like her leg. She had—such a strangely shaped body."

"Had."

"I don't know what you want me to say," Susan said, suddenly near tears. "I don't know what you want me to do. I don't know anything. I just came out here to get away from all that—all that in the kitchen—and I was walking around and then I stopped, I don't know why, I was cold and then—"

"He took the trouble to hide her."

"What?"

Pat Mallory shook his head and stood up again. Now Susan could hear the sirens. They were everywhere, all around her, not only in the air but in the ground. It was as if all other life and sound had stopped to make room for them. She looked automatically toward the road and then away again, feeling foolish. Of course she wouldn't be able to see anyone coming from here. The view to

Congress Avenue was blocked off by what was left of the few other standing structures between here and there. The view in the other direction went nowhere, to a place where nothing could be coming from.

"If it's her, he took the trouble to hide her," Pat Mallory said, repeating himself. "You might not know about that. It isn't classified information, though. It's been in the papers. He never took the trouble to hide any of the others before this."

"Is that supposed to mean something?"

"I don't know."

"I should think he'd want to hide them, all of them. So that people didn't—didn't catch on, if you see what I mean."

"You're making the assumption that his primary purpose in life is not to get caught."

"Nobody wants to get caught."

"He doesn't think he can get caught—no, that's not true." Pat Mallory stood up and stretched. "That's what I used to think, when these things started. I used to think I had an ordinary psychopath, religious mania—"

"Does *everything* have to be *religious* mania?" Susan asked, resentful—and that, she thought, was a good sign. Now that she could get angry again she would be back to normal in no time. "You'd think people would have other kinds of manias sometimes, secular humanist manias, evolutionist manias—"

Pat Mallory looked amused. "Holy Mother Church is not opposed to all aspects of the theory of evolution. And he is killing ex-nuns. Marietta was an ex-nun."

"Yes, she was," Susan admitted.

"So were the other three. The other three we know about. It's not all that easy to find ex-nuns if you're not looking for them. I say four out of four would be too much of a coincidence."

"Maybe you're right."

"Do you know exactly what it is I could do for you that would make you happy?"

"Take me to bed."

She said the words and he heard them. They were out in the air before she even knew she was thinking them, palpable, like the rings of Saturn, like a million pieces of ice caught in orbit by centrifugal force. In the meantime, the wind had gotten higher and more violent and the sirens had come closer. Cars were pulling to screeching stops not very far away. "Where the hell do you think the goddamn body is?" someone shouted. Then car doors began to slam and feet began to pound on icy pavement. Somebody fell and used a word that made Susan blush.

Nothing should make me blush, Susan thought. After that, absolutely nothing should make me blush ever again.

Pat Mallory hadn't left his place on the low wall beside her. He hadn't spoken and he hadn't moved. Susan couldn't imagine what he was thinking and didn't want to ask. God only knew she didn't want to look at his face.

The door to the kitchen opened and a uniformed patrolman came out of it. The door to the back lawn opened and another uniformed patrolman came through that. Susan jumped up and went running back to Damien House, alone.

3   Ten minutes later, Pat Mallory, surrounded by uniformed cops, medical technicians, ambulance men, police photographers, evidence experts and no fewer than four reporters from four different media—newspaper, magazine, television, and radio—finally let himself think about it. It had started to snow in earnest by then. The temperature had dropped, the ground was being rapidly covered by a fall that had never been white, and the scene was a mess—a much bigger mess than the scene at the death of Theresa Cavello had been. It was so much easier on everybody when the bastards left their victims in nice safe buildings. Nice safe buildings could be secured against the ravages of curiosity and greed. They could be secured against the uninvited intrusions of the district attorney's office, too. Pat was expecting such intrusions any minute now. They always showed up when a crime made the news.

He left the med tech he'd been talking to—position of cut, shape of cut, smoothness of cut, snow in cut—and walked over to Ben Deaver, who had been cornered by a pair of reporters who had started out looking exasperated and were now near explosion. Ben had a positive talent for looking like a media patsy but not being one, and a kind of antitalent for getting rid of jerks. Pat grabbed him by the arm and pulled him away bodily, without apology, because by now there was no way else it could be done.

"Well?" he said, when he got him far enough away for form's sake. There was no such thing, in this small backyard, as far enough away not to be heard.

"Well, what?" Deaver asked him. "You want it like a litany? Cut on the forehead exactly the same. Knife used probably the same. Neck broken, almost certainly the same—"

"Okay."

"My point. What's the matter with you?"

Pat shrugged. He was standing very near the kitchen window, and the light was on inside, which made it easy for him to see into the house. Unfortunately the kitchen was empty and there was no sign that it was going to be full again soon. There was certainly no sign of *her*.

"Are you married?" he asked Ben Deaver.

"What?"

"Nothing. I was just thinking about something Anton said the other day, about cops and women and work and existential angst."

"'Existential angst,'" Deaver repeated. "I think Klemmer ought to lay off the dead bodies for a while. Existential fucking angst. Are you sure you're all right?"

"I'm fine. I'm going to go call in."

"You do that. It'll keep you from worrying too much about your existential angst."

Pat left Deaver where he'd dragged him to, right in front of the kitchen window. He thought about going out to his car through the house and decided against it. He thought it would be too damn obvious, and that was nuts.

He had enough dead bodies to worry about to make him the head of an army med-vac in a hot war, and instead he was wandering around worrying about *this*.

Worrying, to be precise, that she'd be too embarrassed about what she'd said to ever actually talk to him again.

CHAPTER

FIVE

1 It was Tuesday, and because it was Tuesday there was going to be a party down at The Apartment. Actually, since it was ten o'clock, there was probably already a party down at The Apartment. Parties there started early and went late, especially in winter, even more especially near Thanksgiving and Christmas, when businesses were supposed to be particularly busy. That was the excuse these men gave to their bosses and their wives, the midday excuse of clients met for lunch and the midnight excuse of clients out on the town after dinner—the excuse nobody ever believed. What he really wondered about, when he wondered at all, was what they told themselves about what they were doing. He knew there were men out there who had made a philosophy out of it—the Man-Boy Love Association, and all that kind of thing—but those weren't the men who came to The Apartment. The Man-Boy Love Association was what had convinced him that Sister Mathilde had been absolutely wrong about Freedom of Speech. He didn't care what those old farts who had started the country had thought they were doing. He certainly didn't care what Sister Mathilde had thought they were doing—although he did realize, by now, that Sister Mathilde had taken the whole thing a little far. When he had first left The Apartment and gone out on his own, he had spent a great deal of time in the Public Library on Elm Street. It was an old building and there were places to hide in it, which wouldn't have been true in one of the newer places out in Branford and Orange. On school days, he could sneak out and get books to read. On weekends he

could sit in the reading rooms and work his way through volume after volume in public. At night, he could come out of hiding and rummage through the small refrigerator in the office where the librarians kept their lunches. There was always something left over to eat and a big cooler of water to drink. When the restrooms were empty, it wasn't even all that hard to work up a bath. Sometimes he thought about the library with fondness, because he had been warm and dry and safe there. He never thought about The Apartment with fondness, because although he had never imagined that there was luxury like that in the universe—and never expected to see anything like it again—he had been anything but safe. Every day he had spent in that place had brought him twenty-four hours closer to being dead.

Now he looked out over the rubble and the dying grass of the vacant lot that lay between the ruined building where he sat and the backyard at Damien House, watching the police and the medical people and all the rest of them digging Marietta out of the woodpile. They had been there for hours and so had he. They had done a hundred things over there that he didn't understand, and only now were getting around to what he had expected from the beginning. He was relieved to see it. He was sitting up on a third floor that was only half a third floor. What was left of the attic above his head was even less than that. The whole building listed to one side and swayed in every strong wind. Once it had been a triple decker, three floor-through apartments one on top of the other, home to good Catholic families with mothers at home and fathers with jobs at Sikorsky and Rumbold. Now it was just one more pile of pick-up sticks threatening to fall down. More than once today, he had been sure it was going to fall down on him.

Over at Damien House, two broad men wearing jackets with sheepskin collars were climbing over the wall from the place where Marietta was. They stopped just on the Damien House side of the wall and leaned back over to help two other men get Marietta's feet in the air. He could hear them grunting and groaning, cursing and laughing, as they got the feet over the wall and made the body follow after it. He leaned forward and tried to see Marietta's face, with the carving on her forehead and the dead eyes open and staring at the sky. He didn't feel sorry about Marietta. She had left her order, changed sides, come over to them. It didn't matter that she had still been at Damien House, pretending to be one of us. He felt himself leaning too far out—there was no glass in this window, no glass anywhere on Amora Street anymore except at Damien House and in shards on the ground—and pulled himself back in, thinking that they would have closed her eyes anyway. It was something he believed the police always did.

Every once in a while, he turned his attention to the windows at Damien House, lit up and warm in the bad-weather darkness, and remembered other lit windows in another house in another place he'd thought he'd forgotten about. That other place had been bubbling to the surface of him for days. Now it seemed to have surfaced permanently, to be sitting in the middle of his brain like one of those bullets They had visited on Billy Hare. This place was a small brick ranch house in the middle of a small square of lawn in a town called Oxford, Connecticut. It had a heavy painted-black door right in the middle in front. If you went through that door and on back down the hall, past the living room, through the dining room, you would come to a kitchen with a big smooth table in the middle of it. Sitting at that table, in a chair covered with something shiny and green, there would be a woman in a yellow dress with her hair pinned up on top of her head, drinking coffee from a white ceramic mug.

His mother.

He leaned out the window again, looked out over the yard at Damien House again, pulled himself back in again. The men had Marietta in the yard. They had the ambulance wedged into the alley with the doors open, waiting for her, an ambulance even though she was dead. He wondered what they had done for Billy Hare and the rest of them, what they were doing now for the one who had lived, the one who had been just like him. They—the They with a capital *T*, not the they that was the police officers and doctors and medical technicians—They always said your mother wouldn't want you anymore, once she knew what you had been doing. It was one of the gifts of the Holy Spirit, part of his charism, that he now knew that wasn't true.

The wind was rising all around him and whatever had been falling from the sky all morning had finally solidified into snow. His jacket wasn't warm enough and he hadn't had anything to eat since the night before, when that Spanish girl had taken him to the basement of her church and filled him full of strange spicy things wrapped up in tortillas. That was before she had told him what he needed to know and he had gone off to do the last thing he had to do before he finished this project completely. The next to the last thing. He was supposed to finish with Marietta first, but it hadn't worked out that way.

Back home, in parochial school at Saint Bridget's, Sister Mathilde was always saying you had to do the will of God the way God wanted you to do it, or you weren't doing the will of God at all. That problem was in figuring out what the will of God really was. Back in parochial school at Saint Bridget's, Sister Mathilde had told him she thought he had a vocation to be a priest.

He left the room by pushing himself backward on his ass. He didn't stand up until he got to the staircase, out in the hall, because he wasn't really sure the building was strong enough to handle it. In the stairwell, he could hear the junkies snoring in the basement, moaning in their sleep sometimes, as if they were in pain. He didn't know what junkies felt and he didn't want to. He was hungry and tired and cold, and before he went up to The Apartment he wanted to go to Church.

2   This is what had happened to him, what he could remember now that he had been out on his own long enough so that his mind was clear:

It had been a cold day in late October, and he had been in the third grade at Saint Bridget's School. It was a Tuesday, the day Father Moore came to teach religion, replacing Sister Mathilde.

The lesson had been about the Holy Spirit. In the morning, Sister Mathilde had asked them all to draw doves. When they were finished she had put the doves in a line on the wall opposite the windows, where there was a thin strip of cork especially for tacking things up. After lunch, Father Moore had come down and told them all about how the Holy Spirit came to each and every person and told them what God wanted them to do with their lives. He had said that this call from God was what was meant by a vocation and that there were many kinds. "Most of you," he had said, "will be called to be mothers and fathers." "Some of you," he had said, "will be called to be priests, sisters and brothers, religious in the world for Christ. All of you," he had said, "should start thinking about your vocation now, and listening to the voice of God, and trying to figure out what He wants you to do."

He had been listening very hard for the voice of God that afternoon when he left school, carrying his dove picture in one hand, bundled up against the cold in a blue down parka his mother had saved from her grocery money to buy him. The schoolyard had been full of children in lines, and nuns. Yellow school buses had been lined up just outside the gates with their red stop signs popped out to let the cars behind them know it was not all right for them to pass. He had stood for a while next to a friend of his in one of the lines, talking about Sister Mathilde and whether or not they would ask to join the altar boys. Then his friend's bus had started loading and his friend had gone away, and he had been left alone among a lot of strange older children. He lived only two or three hundred yards from the school and no bus would take him so short a way. He usually walked home with a little girl named Donna Bannagan who lived next door to him, but she was out sick. Nobody else lived out his way. When he had realized there was nobody left in the yard who knew him except the nuns—nobody at all except a line of bigger kids going out to one of the older subdivisions on the Seymour line—he had turned toward the back of the yard and headed for the hole in the fence that was his shortcut home. That was all he had really wanted that day: to be home.

The road he had had to walk was lined with trees, but not much else. The first building on it, after the school, was his own house. Through the thick red leaves he was not able to see it, and that had made him uneasy. It always did, even when he had Donna for company. Alone, it was almost as bad as being by himself in the dark. He had been afraid of cars, then, so he had stayed well onto the grass, as far from the road as he dared to get—but he had been afraid of trees, too, so that hadn't been too far. All the trees on that stretch of road were big and old and gnarled. They had faces in their trunks, like the faces in the trunks of trees in *The Wizard of Oz*. Above them, a strong sun had tried to force its way through to the road, and succeeded only in creating shadows.

He had gone half the distance to his house when he heard the sound of a car on the road behind him. He had drawn back instinctively, because he had heard a hundred stories about children being hit, and crushed, and dying in hospital rooms. He was at a stage when the mere sound of a car engine made him imagine his bones were breaking. The car passed him at a fair clip, safely, and he started to mutter a prayer Sister Mathilde had taught him, thanking both God and his guardian angel. In the middle of it, the car had come to a quick and rather noisy stop. It idled for a while and then began to back up.

Later he would know that it had not been an accident. They didn't go wandering around in cars, looking for stray boys on the road. They picked a boy and watched him for weeks, sometimes for months, working out his schedule and getting their timing right. At the time he had just been confused. The car had backed all the way up to him and stopped. The woman in the front passenger seat had rolled down her window and stuck her head out and smiled at him. He had known immediately that he did not like her at all.

"Hello," she had said, showing her teeth, with the line of red lipstick across them and the yellowness in back. Her voice was funny, not like a woman's voice at all, too low and too rough. Her face—too close now, she was leaning so far out of the car—was a mess. It was pocked and picked at and seemed to be growing a beard, even though he knew that was impossible. He wasn't too clear then on the differences between boys and girls, men and women, but he did know this: women did not grow beards.

"Hello," the woman had said again, and that was when he felt it, one of the only two things he remembered feeling all the rest of that day. The driver must have gotten out of the car when he wasn't paying attention. The air was suddenly full of the smell of mothballs and his mouth was suddenly full of cloth, wet cloth. It covered not only his mouth but his nose, his cheeks, his chin, everything but his eyes. He dropped his picture of the dove that was the Holy Spirit. He jerked his head back, trying to get away, and managed only to see the trees above his head and a crow sitting in one of them, pecking away at nothing, making no noise. There was no noise anywhere and he couldn't make any. He was choking. He was heaving. He was kicking out at air. The passenger door had popped open and the woman had gotten out, all done up in very high heels and a tight skirt of shiny red like a woman on television. "Jesus Christ," she had said, "what are you doing with him? How much of that stuff did you use?"

Then there was nothing at all, because he had fainted.

Sometime later, he was in the back of the car and the woman was there with him. His hands had been tied behind his back and his legs had been fastened to two ends of a long piece of wood, forced apart. He didn't know what had happened to his pants. There were curtains on the windows in the back of the car. Maybe they had been there all along. He was scared to death and he was crying.

"Come to finally," the woman had said, except that he could see up her skirt now and he didn't know what to think. She had nothing on under there and she had a boy thing, a huge boy thing swollen up and red, jabbing against the inside of her skirt.

"Make him tractable," the man in the driver's seat had said, "make him tractable fast, for God's sake. We need him to be all right for tonight."

"That's your own damn bad planning," the woman had said. Then she had turned to him, smiling through those teeth, and flicked up the end of her skirt. Her boy thing was in the air and pulsing, pulsing right into his face. That was when he'd first realized he still had something over his mouth, something tight and thick, because what he wanted to do was bite that thing she was pushing at him right off, but he couldn't. She grabbed him, turned him over and threw him back on the seat, face down. With the way he was tied, his bottom shot into the air and the joints in his legs began to ache, to scream really, and he had begun to cry again.

"Listen," she'd said to him, just before she started something that would be the worst pain he had ever felt, the worst pain he would ever feel, not even that time later after he had run away and They had cut him, "listen. This is going to be better than a spanking."

3 Now it was noon and years later, years and years, and he was free. Marietta was behind him. He had left her and the people who were attending to her back on Amora Street. The Spanish woman who had once been a nun was behind him, too, although nobody had found her yet as far as he knew. He had gotten to her in her own apartment after the Spanish girl at the church had told him what he needed to know. He was free and out on the street and even a little safe, because they would never expect to find him where he was about to go.

Coming up Church Street he brushed by an older man in a suit with his topcoat open. He lifted the man's wallet—it was easiest with the ones who wanted to think they were too tough to really need a coat—and trusted that to give him the money he needed for lunch. Then he started walking up the steep hills that led to Prospect Avenue and Edge Hill Road.

If there was one thing he had figured out, after all the time he had spent in The Apartment, it was that to do what had been done to him you had to be not only bad, but rich.

PART FIVE

CHAPTER

ONE

1 For Susan Murphy, coming back to Edge Hill Road was disorienting. It reminded her of the first time she had come back to the Motherhouse after three years on mission, teaching in a parish school in the very worst part of the city of Detroit. She had been in Detroit for so long without a break, she had begun to think of her life there as normal. Small rooms, bad plumbing, mostly inoperative heating systems were the most she could expect. The Motherhouse, with its stone and stained glass and marble, had felt at first like a fairy tale and then like a prison. She could not make it make sense or make herself relax there. Walking up Edge Hill from the bus stop after two days of Damien House felt the same way. The houses all looked thyroidal. The fairy lanterns and colored tinsel that lined the walk to the O'Mara place—decorations for the open house they were holding that night, coy signposts to show the way to a party everybody knew their way to anyway—looked insane. She stopped for a moment at the O'Maras' walk and fingered the soft metallic wings of an angel that had been taped to the lamppost there. Nobody took the injunction against decorations in Advent seriously anymore, she knew that, but the angel offended her anyway. There was something so damned blatant about it. Like coming back to Edge Hill Road had reminded her of coming back to the Motherhouse, the angel reminded her of the signs on the side streets off Congress Avenue. TENDER LOVE. YOUNG LOVE. INNOCENCE. They might as well have put up a blazing board of neon and said it straight out: CHILDREN FOR SALE.

She walked slowly up the rest of the way to her own walk, then down her walk to her door, and let herself inside. The foyer was empty. The house was quiet. She kicked her shoes into the foyer closet, took off her coat and threw it on the stair rail. She didn't feel like caring if the house looked a mess. Someone had turned the heat up and left it up. The foyer was close to steaming. Susan pushed up the sleeves of her sweater and her turtleneck both. Then she stood still and listened hard, for the sound of someone or something in the house. She got nothing.

She had a new pack of cigarettes, bought on Congress Avenue after she had left Damien House. She took it out, opened it up, and dropped the torn cellophane on the floor. Then she got a cigarette out, lit up with a match from the matchbook she had picked up at the diner where she had tried to have lunch, and dropped the spent match on the floor. Then she gave up, because nothing she could do, short of going to work with an ax, could make the foyer really look ragged. It was too big and too solidly built. Instead of trying, she headed for the back, where the kitchen was, and where she could be reasonably sure of finding some whiskey to put into her tea. She needed a drink and she needed a smoke and she needed somebody to scream at, preferably Dan. She thought two out of three might not be all that bad.

On her way to the kitchen, she passed the portrait of her grandmother her mother had always hated, hanging now in the back hall. Her grandmother had been a great enthusiast of social causes and a great advocate of political reform, as political reform had been defined in the days of Franklin Delano Roosevelt. Susan remembered her as a nasty old lady with an even nastier temper, always talking about the deserving and the undeserving poor. She had used her own peculiar vision of Science as a weapon. It had been a weapon that cut.

Susan stopped in front of the portrait, ran her fingers through the dust that had collected on the top of the frame, and then turned the damn thing to the wall.

2 She had been alone in the kitchen for half an hour, drinking cups of tea half full of Benedictine, by the time Dan came in—the same Dan whom she had thought, only a few hours before, she was ready to kill on sight. The Benedictine had mellowed her. She had lost the energy she needed to do much of anything, and most of the urgency she needed to do it with conviction. She was still angry, but not on the warpath. Dan must have been coming in from work. He had his overcoat on and his shoes were wet. He smiled when he saw her sitting at the table and headed for the cupboards near the sink, where the coffee things were.

"It's too damn bad you're so damn into tea," he said. "I thought for a while there that with you home I'd be spared the taste of brother Andy's coffee."

Susan picked up her cigarette, took a drag, put it down in the ashtray again. She had lit it just a few moments before Dan had come into the kitchen, so it was still long and almost ashless. She blew smoke into the air and watched Dan through it, putting down a cup and saucer, putting water on to boil, measuring instant out of a green-labeled jar, hunting through the sugar bowls for the one that was actually full of sugar.

"If anybody calls tonight, you've got to tell them I'm not in," Dan said. "I brought a shit load of work home with me and I've got to get it done. That's why I'm so early."

Susan was still watching his back. It looked narrower than she remembered it. Dan looked smaller.

"I don't know that I'm going to be home tonight," she said.

"What?" He turned around and raised an eyebrow at her, that old Murphy trick their father had once used so well. "Don't tell me you have a date."

"No, I don't have a date."

"The O'Maras then? We were invited. I've got too much work to go, but Andy's going. Is Andy going to take you to the O'Maras?"

"I always hated Denny O'Mara," Susan said. "He was so damn full of himself he gave me a headache."

"He's married to Margaret Mary Beshnik."

"She's not somebody I know."

Dan picked up the sugar bowl and spooned sugar into his coffee. For Susan it would have been too much sugar. For the old Dan, it would have been a sacrilege. She didn't know what the tastes of the new Dan were. She didn't know anything about him at all.

"Look," he said, "I take it you're pissed off at me for some reason or the other, and I take it I'm going to have to listen to the reason whether I want to or not. Why don't you just get started?"

"Why don't you take off your coat and sit down?"

"All right, I will."

Dan brought his coffee to the kitchen table and put it down. He took off his coat, one sleeve at a time, elaborately careful, and laid it over the seat of a chair. He pulled out the chair directly under his coffee cup and sat down in it.

"All right," he said again. "I have taken off my coat. I am sitting down. Now what?"

Susan crossed her arms and rested her elbows on the table. Dan was tight, very tight, and she didn't blame him. In his place, she would have been very tight herself. What she hadn't expected were lines around his eyes and the tightness under his jaw—the face he wore when he went to battle against his enemies. She hadn't made up her mind about him, not entirely, but he had made up his mind about her. It felt like the death of something.

"What I want," she said slowly, "are the answers to a few questions. Will you give them to me?"

"Yes," he said.

"Just yes? Just like that?"

"I don't see why not. If I don't, you'll probably hound me into the nuthouse."

"I never hound, Dan, and you know it. Do you know where I slept last night?"

"Of course I do. Damien House."

"And?"

"And what?" Dan shrugged. "Christ, Susan, if you want to run off and play Mother Teresa, it's your own damn business. I don't have anything against Damien House. It was my idea Andy go there in the first place."

"I know it was. Now you're prosecuting Tom Burne."

"I'm prosecuting Tom Burne because I have a case."

"Dan, that's bull manure, and you know it. I was down on Sedger Street today. They do everything but post pictures of those children in their plate-glass windows with the prices underneath. You have a case."

"I only have a case if the cops bring me one."

"Is that what you want me to think? The cops don't bust those bastards on Sedger Street?"

"They don't."

"They don't dare," Susan said. "While I was sitting around at Damien House this morning I had a few talks with a few people. Cops. People who work at Damien House. Kids—"

"There was another murder down there this morning," Dan said abruptly, "another murder of an ex-nun. I wish to Christ you'd realize, Susan—"

"That I'm an ex-nun? Oh, I realize it, Dan. I realize there was a murder, too. I ought to. I found the damned body. I'm not interested in that right now."

"You ought to be."

"Don't you dare tell me what I ought to be. According to one of the cops I talked to, they don't bust those places on Sedger Street because it's too good a way of putting their careers in a sling."

"You'd have to talk to their sergeants about that."

"Not according to this cop. According to this cop, I'd have to talk to you."

"What the fuck is that supposed to mean?"

Her cigarette had managed to burn halfway to the butt in peace. It was lying in the ashtray looking like a worm turned to cinders. She spun it to get the ash off, picked it up, and took another drag. This time, when she blew the smoke out, she blew it directly into Dan's face.

"Do you remember a case about two years ago, guy picked up down on Sedger for running a strip show with eight-year-old girls? He had a bar called Eden Rising."

"Yes, I remember it."

"According to the cop I talked to, the police department closed the Eden Rising down and handed the kids over to social services. Three weeks later, the kids had vanished into thin air—"

"That happens all the time," Dan said quickly. "Why the hell would you think I had anything to do with that? Do you know what the foster parent system is *like*?"

"I'm beginning to get a fair idea, Dan, yes. And I've had chapter and verse from Francesca about how pimps come and steal their stables back when social services actually manages to get anything done. But this time the pimp was in jail."

"I know where he was, Susan. I ought to. I put him there."

"You also let him out. According to this cop—"

"Oh, crap," Dan said. "What the hell do you think you're playing at, anyway? Some cop hands you a cop legend and you swallow it whole. One walk down Sedger Street and you're out to save the universe. One case gone sour and suddenly I'm the devil himself in horns and a tail—"

"The cop who busted the man who owned the Eden Rising ended up getting busted off the force three months later—"

"—For stealing two pounds of cocaine from the evidence room," Dan exploded. "My God, Susan, what the hell do you think you're doing? Are you even listening to yourself? You even *sound* like a cop. You sound like one of those fool women on television shows with the badges and the bad language and the—what the hell did you do in that damn convent of yours, anyway, read detective stories and fantasize about being on foot patrol?"

"The cop I talked to said you set that other cop up."

"The cop you talked to had his reasons. A commitment to veracity wasn't one of them."

"The cop I talked to said it was common knowledge in the police department that you've been taking bribes from those people on Sedger Street—"

"Oh, Jesus," Dan said, "bribes. Bribes. Susan, what in the name of shit fuck would I want to take bribes for? Have you got the faintest idea how much money Daddy left me?"

"After you killed him?"

Dan reared back in his chair, white and stiff and wired as an electrified corpse. "Oh, that's fine, Susan," he said, "that's wonderful. First I'm a pimp for the pimps of children and now I'm a goddamned murderer."

"I always thought of it as a kind of euthanasia," Susan said softly, "an act of corporal charity for the sake of Andy and me."

"It might have been an act of corporal charity, Susan, but if it was, it wasn't one committed by me."

The Benedictine was making swirls like oil slick in her tea. Susan tilted the cup first one way and then the other. Then she drank what was left of it down and stood up. The sink was too far away, across the room, impossible to get to. She headed for it anyway, moving slowly, feeling drunk.

"Dan," she said, once she was far enough past him so that she could no longer see his face, "I'm not Pat Mallory. I'm not a cop or a newspaper reporter or one of those people from the mayor's office you have meetings with at seven o'clock in the morning. I'm your sister and I can tell when something is not quite real with you. Now you know and I know that Father Tom Burne is the only person down in the Congo making any headway at all against those people on Sedger Street. And you know and I know that Father Tom Burne has not molested any of the children at Damien House—"

"—Bruce Ritter—"

"No matter what Father Bruce Ritter may or may not have done," Susan said. "We're not talking about Bruce Ritter here. We're talking about Tom Burne. You have built your reputation in this state on fighting cases of child abuse. Now you're doing your best to knock out of commission the greatest force against child pornography and child prostitution this state has ever seen. You've started an investigation on the unsubstantiated word of a boy who is, from all reports, both an habitual liar and a borderline psychopath. You had the fact of that investigation leaked to the press and you were very proud of yourself for doing it—and don't lie about that, Dan, because I was here to see it. No matter what you believe, I am not a naïve little nun who believes anything anybody tells her. I am perfectly willing to believe that that cop I talked to this morning had it all wrong. But, Dan, I'm going to find it very hard not to believe that cop if you won't tell me why you've started this insane holy war against Father Tom Burne."

"Jesus fucking Christ," Dan said. "Jesus fucking Christ, Susan, I have told you and I have told you and I will tell you again. I am investigating Tom Burne *because I have to*."

"Right."

Susan dropped her cup into the sink. It landed with a thud, but didn't break. She turned away from it and headed for the kitchen door.

"Where are you going?" Dan asked her.

"Out."

"Out where?"

"I don't know."

That was a lie. Susan hadn't thought she would care, but she did. She cared more that Dan not know where she was going.

Out in the foyer again, she looked up the stairs, expecting to see Andy sitting on them, and got blackness and absence instead. She wondered vaguely where he was and then went into the closet for her things.

It was a long trek out to the Yale–New Haven Hospital, and she was already very tired.

CHAPTER

Two

1 The offices and studios of WNHY-TV were on Orange Street
at the very edge of the commercial district, on the third,
fourth, and fifth floors of a six-story building with a dry cleaner
and a sex aids shop on the street level. Walking up to the building,
Father John Kelly found himself resenting his life—his real life—
for the first time. It was strange. Even if he hadn't had a vocation—
and he had, you had to to accept celibacy with any kind of equan-
imity; it was just that with everything else that was going on, with
his head full of fears and confusions left over from a childhood
horror story, it was hard to remember it—even if he hadn't had a
vocation, he might still have wanted to be a priest. There were so
many advantages to it. In fact, unless you were some kind of sex
fiend, there were nothing but advantages. The Jesuits had given
him an education the like of which could not be had anywhere in
the world outside the Church. They had sent him to London and
Paris and Rome and taken care to see that he read half a dozen
languages, ancient and modern, just in case he needed them. He
knew more about the economy of Central America than the radical
nuns who lived in the base communities of Nicaragua. He knew
more about the theology of the patristic Church than the schismatic
traditionalists who surrounded Marcel Lefebvre. He knew more
about English literature than most Oxford dons who taught the
subject and more about French philosophy than most of the exis-
tentialists who had preached Sartre at the Sorbonne—and it was
all side knowledge, what the Jesuits considered necessary back-

ground for his serious education. That had been in theology, and as far as he could figure out, he knew more about that than the Pope and almost as much as Cardinal Ratzinger.

Then there were the living conditions. Over a period of years, he had lived in every possible kind of place, from a palazzo in Venice to a hut in the Mojave desert, but most of the time he lived in ordinary Jesuit rectories. Ordinary Jesuit rectories were not luxurious, at least not most of the time, but they were comfortable. They were certainly much more comfortable than any of the places he had been allowed to occupy as a child. They offered good food and good books and good conversation. They offered refuge from the craziness of the rest of the world. They offered a kind of automatic acceptance of the intellectual life that left him free to work and to think without being under pressure to also be "normal."

Most of all—and John Kelly knew this—the Church had given him a community of merit, a world working overtime to ensure that oldest and most startling of Western ideals, the absolute equality of every soul under God. When he told people that they argued with him. They brought up dozens of things that had nothing to do with anything. Weren't women barred from the priesthood? Wasn't the Church a hierarchy? It was all true and all beside the point, only credible to people who had spent four years of college hearing that all that mattered was gender, race, and class. In the world John Kelly had entered on the day of his ordination, gender, race, and class were not supposed to matter at all. Every man and woman was a descendant of Adam and Eve. They were brothers in blood as well as in metaphor. Every man and woman, rich and poor, black and white and red, was stained with the same Original Sin and charged with the same mission: to work out his own salvation and give glory to God. What the Church was trying to be was what the rest of the Western world had always considered itself to be, inaccurately and unreflectively: a world where advancement was won by *merit only* and sanctity was a gift that could not be boasted of because it could never be deserved.

Just why he was standing on Orange Street thinking about

these things, he was not sure. It was passive thinking anyway. What little active thinking he was doing was all about nonsense. Dan Murphy, Victor Coletti, Tom Burne: the fact was, he was afraid to go inside, and he didn't want to be. He was a little embarrassed by the homily he'd written, too, but that was something else. He looked up Orange Street and found it empty. There was a girls' school up there, run by the same nuns who ran Albertus Magnus College, a good one. The order was a good one, too, or had been before Vatican II.

He checked out the curious display in the plate-glass window of the sex aids shop—it was called A Marriage Made in Heaven, and all it had for decoration was a lot of Valentine hearts edged in paper lace; if it hadn't been for the discreet sign on the door, PRACTICAL HELP FOR THE HO-HUM RELATIONSHIP, he wouldn't have known what was going on in there—and then forced his way through the glass doors. The small lobby inside was empty and cold and floored in stale linoleum.

What he should have done with his homily was to make it the first in a series, the start of a course in the Catholic religion, the kind of course no one ever taught anymore in America but that he had been trained to put together when he was in the seminary. Either that, or he should have prepared a statement on the plight of Father Tom Burne. Anything would have been better than what he had done, which was to put together half an hour of platitudes and abstractions on the Trinity.

He let himself into the elevator, pressed the button for the second floor, and sighed.

2 "The recording studios are up on three," the receptionist said, when he had presented himself at her desk. "That's where we'll be going, Father. If you want to smoke, you have to wait in the green room. Fire regulations don't permit smoking in the studios and common sense doesn't permit it in the technical rooms— I don't know if you realize, but the lens on a single one of our cameras, just the lens, costs over fifteen thousand dollars."

The receptionist was a tall woman in middle age, very thin and very well put together, wearing a gold crucifix on a chain around her neck. John Kelly had tagged her immediately as being the kind of cradle Catholic who prided herself on having "her own opinions." There were more and more of those running around every day, and the opinions they prided themselves on having were usually heretical. It made him a little nuts. A Catholic who did not believe that the Consecration changed the bread and wine into the true Body and true Blood of Christ Jesus was a Protestant, and so was a Catholic who thought Rome had too much to say in the affairs of the American Church. The receptionist had gone back to the elevator and pressed the call button, and John found himself holding back, reluctant to follow her.

The elevator came to a stop in front of them and the doors popped open. The receptionist held one of them open with her hand and shooed him in.

"Dan Murphy has told us all about you," she said as she followed him. "We've been very excited. Most men don't have the kind of commitment to his faith community that Dan does, don't you think?"

"Mmm," John Kelly said. He was biting his lip, trying not to wince. "Faith community." Dear God in Heaven.

The receptionist punched the button for three. "I know everybody talks a lot about community these days," she said, "but they don't really do anything about it. You work in the bishop's office, not in a parish, don't you?"

"That's right. Actually I'm not at the chancery at the moment, I have my own—"

"You really wouldn't believe what it's like in the parishes. You wouldn't. We held a sleep-in for the homeless in my parish only last week—"

"A sleep-in?"

"It was a gesture of solidarity. My parish priest—Father Reynolds, out in Branford, at Saint Thomas Aquinas—Father Reynolds has a really inspiring passion for social justice, a real sense of empathy for the poor. It was his idea. We were all—the whole church, except tiny children and sick people and like that—we were all supposed to bring sleeping bags and spend a night in the basement of the church to show our solidarity with the homeless—"

"Oh."

"—and practically nobody came!" The receptionist looked triumphant. "Can you believe that? Nine o'clock on the night, a Friday night, nobody has to work on Saturday morning, and still there were only six of us there. It's Ronald Reagan, that's what I think. He turned the entire country into a pit of mindless greed."

"Mmm," John Kelly said again. They were walking through windowless winding corridors. John thought that the floor must have been gutted and reconstructed to accommodate the studios, or actually built for the studios. He couldn't imagine any other kind of business that would need this kind of arrangement. After a while, the windowlessness ended, but what windows there were didn't look out on the street. They looked in at rooms, full of couches or equipment, lit by dim fluorescent lights. In the rooms with the couches, men in jeans and sneakers and flannel shirts were smoking cigarettes. In the rooms with the equipment, they were fooling with dials.

"Are you going to want to smoke?" the receptionist asked him.

"What?"

"Smoke," the receptionist said patiently. They had stopped before a door with a window in it, looking in on the shabbiest carpet and the shabbiest couches John had seen yet. The receptionist was frowning at him sternly, maybe because she had tagged him just as surely as he had tagged her. He was a lump with his consciousness unraised.

"Smoke," she said for a third time. "It's the way I told you downstairs, the only place you can smoke—as a visitor, I mean; people can smoke in their own offices—the only place you can smoke is in the green room. This is the green room."

"It is a green room," John said, "yes."

"It would be called the green room even if it wasn't. That's just the name for it. I don't know why. If you don't want to smoke, you can go directly to Studio Four."

"I do want to smoke."

"That's all right. A lot of people do, their first time on television. They get intimidated." She popped open the door of the green room and looked around. "It's really a mess, isn't it? Everybody thinks commercial stations are practically minting money, but it doesn't seem to be that way around here. We are going to get this room redecorated, though. Dan Murphy arranged it."

"Why?"

"What do you mean, why?"

"Well," John said, "as I understand it, it's a man named Victor Coletti who owns this station, not Dan Murphy. Why would Dan Murphy want to get the green room redecorated."

"Victor Coletti?" the receptionist said. "I don't know, Father. You must be mistaken. I've never even heard of anyone named Victor Coletti."

She put her hand on his arm, pushed him into the room, and closed the door behind him.

3   Half an hour later, after he had read through his first issue of *Hustler* in growing alarm and smoked enough cigarettes to make his throat ache, someone came for him. He was relieved beyond measure to see that it was not the receptionist, but a young girl dressed in much the same way the men he had seen were dressed, in jeans and sneakers and a flannel shirt. She had her hair pulled to the back of her head in a rubber band and a wedding ring on her left hand. She introduced herself as, "Tracey, you know, the story editor on your series."

"Story editor?"

"Don't worry about it, Father. In your case, all I do is make sure the art people get your name straight on the intro board and work with your title."

"I don't have a title."

"Let me have your script while you're in makeup. I'll read it and we'll come up with a title."

He had the "script"—which he thought of as a "paper"—in a folder in his briefcase. He took it out and handed it over and then let Tracey lead him out of the room and back into the hall. They were going deeper and deeper into the building, past more and more rooms with windows on the corridor. It was an alien place, and for a while he let himself drift with it. Consoles and cameras and lights on tripods. People moving either too quickly or not at all. Silence. The whole floor seemed to be soundproofed.

Tracey led him down a corridor even narrower than the others, past doors marked MEN and WOMEN, and finally into a warren of cubbyholes that looked like miniature dentists' offices. All but one of them was empty. The one that was not was occupied by a short blond girl with straight bangs that fell into her eyes.

"Debra," Tracey said, "I've brought you Father Kelly. He's got to look like he's not made up."

"They all have to look like they're not made up," Debra said. She looked like she was made up. Her lips were a deep purple with white hearts painted into the centers of them. She gestured to her dentist's chair without looking John Kelly in the face and turned away to get her makeup box. "I just had a woman in here, fifty if she was a day, and what she wanted was pink. Can you imagine that? Pink."

John Kelly didn't know what was wrong with pink. He put his briefcase on the floor, sat down in the dentist's chair, and folded his hands over his stomach.

"Can I ask you two something, just as a point of information?"

"Ask away," Tracey said.

"I never really know the answer to anything," Debra said.

"Have either of you ever heard of a man named Victor Coletti?"

"Victor Coletti?" Tracey looked at Debra. Debra looked at Tracey. They both shrugged. "Who's Victor Coletti?" Tracey said.

"You've never heard the name before?"

"No," Debra said. "Should we have? Is this Victor Coletti in television?"

CHAPTER

THREE

1 Pat Mallory could think of a lot of things he would like to do with his evening, and not one of them was dancing attendance on Bishop Monaghan Riley. There was a row of women's pictures across the top of the corkboard in his office, just like the row of women's pictures that was going to appear, no matter what he tried to do about it, on the front page of the New Haven *Register* tomorrow morning. There was a stack of files on the deaths of boys lying on his desk, just like the duplicate stack of files on dead boys Anton Klemmer kept at the morgue. There was what he had come to think of as the Problem of Susan Murphy, which had to be worked out, one way or the other, before he ran into her again. On that score, he was a little surprised at himself. He didn't subscribe to Anton's analysis of existential angst. If existential angst was what Pat Mallory had on those days when he felt too tired to get out of his chair to go to the bathroom and couldn't remember what it was life was supposed to be for, then women had never cured it for him. Only work had ever made him really free. He had enough work now to be free as a bird indefinitely.

Still, Bishop Monaghan Riley was Bishop Monaghan Riley. He was not only visible and effective guardian of Pat's soul for as long as Pat lived in the diocese of Bridgeport, he was a politically important man in the State of Connecticut. He was not as important as Archbishop Whealan of Hartford, but then archbishops were always more important than bishops, or almost always.

Queen of Heaven Rectory was in one of the nicer parts of

New Haven, way up on Prospect Street past Albertus Magnus, near the Jesuit rectory. Pat got there by car, for once unworried about where he was going to park. As chief of Homicide, he was technically allowed to park anywhere he wanted to on public property as long as he was on duty, but he didn't like to. It tended to get the ordinary civilians pissed off, and he didn't blame them. Queen of Heaven Rectory had its own private parking lot, however, and it was next to a big church that had a private parking lot, too. The parking lots were around the back so that they didn't mar the pristine loveliness of upper Prospect Avenue.

On the street, he hesitated between the rectory and the church parking lots. The rectory lot was closer, but narrow and harder to get in and out of. He chose it anyway, because it had started to half-drizzle, half-sleet again. Pulling into the space beside the big black car that had probably brought the bishop up from Bridgeport, he looked for Father John Kelly's car and didn't find it.

He did find John Kelly. As soon as Pat got out of the car he saw him, standing on the small back porch. The porch light was on above his head. The rectory's back door was open. He looked tired and a little odd, wearing one of those old Jesuit cassocks nobody bothered with anymore.

"Father Kelly?" Pat said. "Is that you?"

"Yes, Pat. It's me. Hurry up and get inside. It's lousy out here."

Pat never knew what to do with comments about the weather. About this one, he did nothing, just jogged a little as he crossed the lot. By the time Pat got to the porch, Father John Kelly was already back inside.

"The bishop's been here since four o'clock," he told Pat, "two hours early, which is par for the course, and now he's roaring. I hope you're in a tractable mood this evening."

"I don't have anything to be tractable about," Pat said. "I hope the bishop's in a brief mood this evening. I've got a lot of work to do."

"We've all got a lot of work to do. Never mind me. I like the old man. I always have. I've just had a very tiring day."

"I can bet."

"The bishop thinks you're staying for dinner. If you're not, don't tell him until after you talk. Otherwise he'll spend half an hour making you change your mind."

"He couldn't make me change my mind."

"Yes, he could."

Father John Kelly had stopped them at the bottom of the stairs. He looked up the long green runner to the landing and shook his head slightly. He looked like a man with something going seriously wrong in his life. Pat supposed that it was just the bishop.

"You going to take me up or let me go myself?" Pat asked him.

"I'll let you go yourself. It's the first room at the top of the stairs, the one with the double doors. Father Dolan's study."

"Is he alone?"

"I think so, yes." John Kelly hesitated, pressing his hands together the way Pat had noticed Jesuits did, as if they were taught how in seminary. "Pat," he said, "by any chance, have you ever heard of a man named Victor Coletti?"

"*Victor* Coletti? I know a *Louis* Coletti."

"Could he have a brother or an uncle or something somewhere named Victor?"

"I wouldn't know, Father. That's not my department. That's organized crime downstairs."

"Oh, *fine.*"

"What's the matter?" Pat said. "Are you involved somehow with this Coletti person? Does he want something from you? A lot of these guys throw a lot of money at the Church. It usually ends up in bad publicity."

"I know."

"So?"

"I *don't* know."

245

"I don't get it."

Father John Kelly sighed. "Never mind," he said. "It's too complicated to explain right now with the bishop upstairs waiting and everything else that's going on. Maybe you could do me a favor, or get someone in your office to do me a favor, as soon as you get the time."

"Like what?"

"Like find out who this Victor Coletti is, for one thing. And then find out who owns WNHY-TV."

"WNHY-TV," Pat repeated.

Father John Kelly was turning away, expecting him to go upstairs and do his business with the bishop. In John Kelly's mind, business with the bishop probably took precedence over any and all other business, except business with the Pope.

Pat Mallory was about to make his way upstairs, when he realized that Father John Kelly had turned back to him and was staring. He paused politely and waited.

"You know," John Kelly said, "what really bothers me about all this is, I had him checked out before, at the beginning. I'm not a complete fool."

"The check didn't turn up anything?" Pat asked him.

"Not a thing."

"Maybe there wasn't anything to turn up."

John Kelly shook his head vigorously. "If there wasn't, I'll eat this cassock. Go upstairs and talk to the bishop, Pat. I'm ready to drop and I still have a million things to do."

Instead, Pat Mallory stood where he was, minute after minute, until the sound of Father John Kelly's footsteps had died into the silence of the rectory.

2 "So you see," the bishop was saying half an hour later, "John isn't the best person to have in the face of a conspiracy, but he isn't the worst, either. He's very good at reading the public pulse. He's absolutely right about what Dan Murphy can and can't do to Father Burne. Molestation charges—John's right about that, too.

Charging Bruce Ritter with molesting the children at Covenant House didn't do anybody any good politically in the Manhattan D.A.'s office or anywhere else. That kind of thing backfires. We may bend the Constitution to get those cases into the courts and get some convictions, but it's a lot harder to bend the mind of the man in the street, especially when you don't have anything he'd consider proof. And you know what the evidence is like in sexual child abuse cases."

"Either really good or nonexistent," Pat said cheerfully.

"The man in the street," the bishop said, "tends to feel that if the evidence is nonexistent, the crime has not been committed. As a philosophy of law, it has more merit than we give it credit for."

Father Dolan's study was a large room with windows looking out on Prospect Street. The ceilings were high and the boards on the floor were thick and old. In one corner there was an ancient desk neither Pat nor the bishop had been interested in sitting at. In the other there was a filing cabinet. The middle of the room was occupied by a pair of loveseats facing each other across a small coffee table. Pat and the bishop were sitting on those.

So far, Pat thought, the meeting had been less onerous than he had expected—although it had been long-winded, because Monaghan Riley was a long-winded man. At least he had come to the point immediately and only then gone on to elaborate. Some men started with the elaborations and let you stew interminably before they let you know what they were talking about. The bishop's point had been simple, emphatic, and illuminating. He was here to ask Pat Mallory to investigate the possibility that someone—possibly Dan Murphy himself—was set on framing Father Tom Burne for the murders of four boy prostitutes.

It was not a theory Pat Mallory would have thought up on his own. Like most cops, he didn't really believe in frames—even though he'd seen a few. In most cases, the guilty party was so obviously guilty it was hard to understand how he'd ever thought he was going to get away with it. That was why Pat Mallory generally supported capital punishment for purposes of retribution, but never for purposes of deterrence. If a grown man couldn't be deterred from passing bad checks by the fact that there was going to be sixteen security cameras photographing him doing it, he couldn't be deterred by anything.

On the other hand, he was a man who liked Tom Burne and didn't like Dan Murphy. He did, however, think he understood Dan Murphy, and, in the light of what he understood, the investigation of Tom Burne had made no more sense to him than it had to Father John Kelly. Not only did Pat not think Tom Burne had molested any of the boys at Damien House, he thought Father Kelly and the bishop were right on the money in their analysis of the situation. The Bruce Ritter investigation had done nothing but harm to the people who started it. The odd way it had been dropped by the public authorities and seemingly shoved under the rug by the ecclesiastical ones had made most people feel that Ritter had been jobbed. The whole mess had done nothing but leave a bad taste all around.

On the matter of the murders, Pat wasn't so sure. He could see how it would work—brilliantly—but not that it was working. He'd been on the case now for weeks and there was no hint of anything of the kind.

"The thing is," he told the bishop, "in order to run a frame, you have to plant evidence. I can tell you right now that no evidence against Father Tom Burne has been found at the scene of any of these murders."

"Yet," the bishop said, "what about the other thing John brought up, that the murders were being committed for a warning?"

"Less farfetched than you might think."

"What about the possibility that the people who run this ring have someone in the police department?"

"It wouldn't have to be the police department," Pat said. "It could be the D.A.'s office or the mayor's office or even social services. But, yes, I do think there's some connection, if you want to know the truth. Everybody does. We've thought it for years."

"There is such a ring?" the bishop asked. "A high-class call service that provides—uh—that provides—"

"Very young boys to establishment males for the purposes of prostitution?" Pat smiled wanly. "Yes, Your Grace—"

"—Don't call me 'Your Grace.'"

"—there is, not only in New Haven, but in almost every city in the country, major and not quite major, including Bridgeport, from what I hear from people I know down there. This is a growth industry, Bishop Riley, the biggest growth industry in vice in the country. This is what happens to about one of every twenty of the children who are kidnapped—"

"—One out of *twenty?*"

"I get so damned sick and tired listening to social workers talk about how the family is the most dangerous place for children," Pat said, "I want to scream. The family is not the most dangerous place for children. The street is the most dangerous place for children, and there are millions of them out there. And the foster system—dear Lord Jesus Christ. We managed to put a couple away about a year ago, took in a foster child who'd been removed from a home some asshole social worker had labeled 'abusive.' These two foster-parent saints said the child, it was a girl, said she'd run away. Turned out they'd sold her to a pimp in the Congo—and I do mean sold. They got three thousand dollars for her, tax free."

"But there are abusive homes, Mr. Mallory. There was the Lisa Steinberg case."

"Lisa Steinberg was not Joel Steinberg's natural daughter. She was a product of child protective services herself. And where the child protective system gets to the point where it will remove a child from the custody of its parents for abuse that consists of refusing to let that child watch television, you're going to have a lot of cops on the street who stop believing that those bitches over there are protecting anybody but themselves."

"This," the bishop said, "is off the subject."

"No, it isn't," Pat said. "I know you think we—the police—are being held back from investigating these things because of pressure from criminal groups, because of official involvement in child prostitution, because of—because of a lot of things—and it might even be true. I'll check all this out to see if Father Kelly was right about what Dan Murphy is doing to Tom Burne. I wouldn't put it past Murphy, at any rate. But most of the pressure we get not to investigate these people, not to make a big deal about any of this, not to rock the boat—that's right out front and it comes from the juvenile authorities."

"Mr. Mallory, that is *insane*."

"Is it? There are thousands of people sitting over there at juvenile. They've got social work degrees from tenth-rate colleges. They're overworked and they're underpaid—but they're paid a million times better than they would be waitressing or hairdressing or any of the other things most of them would have been stuck with if it hadn't been for the great bureaucracy in the sky. They have a vested damn interest in making sure the public doesn't find out that the most dangerous home a child can be in is a foster home. They have a vested damn interest in making sure that the public doesn't find out that the result of the billions of dollars that this country has poured into child abuse management over the last ten years has made matters worse and not better. Do you know there are poor parents in this city who will not take their children to hospital emergency rooms for any reason whatsoever short of death, for fear that those children will be taken away from them summarily by a bunch of people who do not have to *prove* anything, who just have to have a *suspicion,* to whisk a child away into a never-never land his parents may never recover him from? And of course these people always have suspicions, Your Grace. These are middle-class white people come down to give the gospel of therapeutic living to poor black people and the poor black people just absolutely refuse to listen."

"Don't call me 'Your Grace,'" the bishop said.

Pat Mallory stared at the bishop's cigar and wished he smoked. He delivered that lecture of his only once a year, and it always made him suicidal.

CHAPTER

FOUR

1 All Susan Murphy really knew about him was that he was in the Yale–New Haven Hospital, which was a little like knowing he was in Detroit. If she had only read about him in the papers or heard about him on the evening news, she would never have gone looking for him. She would have realized how impossible it was. Everybody still called it the Yale–New Haven Hospital, but it wasn't that, not really, and hadn't been for years. It was a medical complex, part hospital, part research center, part medical school. It wasn't even in New Haven anymore. Parts of it were, but most of it was strung out across the countryside in the small towns that had once been considered New Haven's suburbs and were now known to be its hemophilia, housed in a series of ultramodern, underwindowed buildings that looked like spaceships that had taken root. Susan had forgotten about all that because of what the cops had been saying at Damien House. They had been talking to each other, not to her. She didn't even think they realized she was within hearing distance. She'd sidled up to them because she hoped to get some information on the death of Marietta O'Brien. What she'd gotten instead was the saga of this boy, who was in the Yale–New Haven Hospital and who was not dead.

If it had been an adult she'd gone looking for, she would never have found him. There were too many wards, too many specialties, too many intensive care units, too many subclassifications she didn't even know the names of. Looking through the Directory under "Yale–New Haven" in the phonebook was like reading a litany of disease. Fortunately, the categories that applied to children—ranged neatly under a subhead that said PEDIATRIC MEDICINE—were less complex. There was *Pediatric Center,* which was not what she was looking for. There was *Congenital Disease,* which was not what she was looking for either. Beyond that, there were only two possibilities: *Pediatrics* proper and *PICU.* To Susan's mind, PICU was the only possible place. Anyone who'd had the back of his head assaulted by a gun and the rest of his body assaulted by a winter river had to be in an intensive care unit.

There should have been something else to worry about— meaning the police guard that would surely be around this boy's room—but heading out to YNH, Susan didn't think about it. She was doing something that might have been enormously naïve or enormously sophisticated, depending on how she was going about it. She wasn't aware enough of anything to pick between the two. Going out in the cab she was only startled to discover that she was as "centered" as she had ever been in her life, when her novice mistress had once despaired of getting her ever to "center" at all. "You're not going to get any use from divine contemplation," Sister Marie Bonaventure had said, fretting, and it had been true, until now. Now Susan could feel herself anchored in a world of visions. The visions were all of a small damaged child whose hands reached out to her, looking for something simple, like candy.

By the time the cab let her off, her vision had dragged itself around her imagination and come to rest not in a hospital, but back at the Motherhouse, so that she kept seeing a small boy sitting in the big yellow wing chair in the front parlor, drinking hot chocolate. It was insane and she felt dizzy. She paid the driver and tipped him too much and got out of the cab. She told herself that if her life ever got sane again she would consider going back.

She didn't think she had anyplace else to go.

2   Fortunately or unfortunately, the cop on duty outside PICU was someone Susan had met. The other three, ranged around the observation room like sentries in a toy castle, were complete strangers. The observation room was called that because of the big window behind the receptionist's desk. It looked in on a line of beds full of sleeping children. Susan was reminded of the nurseries on hospital maternity wards, except that she was sure the nurses here wouldn't hold the children in the air for the contemplation of fond relatives. Most of the children here were tied down to their mattresses anyway—if not by the thin gauze restraints used to keep children still after surgery, then by wires and tubes and intravenous systems for glucose and blood. The receptionist was missing from her desk, so Susan went to the window and pressed her face against it. There was no way to tell which of the children he was, or if he was any of them. Through the glass, she could dimly see the back of the PICU. There were other children there, in muslin-curtained cubicles like convent cells. He might have been one of those. Susan wanted to ask the cop she'd met, but knew it wouldn't be a good idea. The entire New Haven Police Department was probably waiting for some jerk to show up in this place to finish the kid off.

Dan was right. She was beginning to think like a television cop show.

There was a little girl at the left front edge of the window, blue around the eyes but peaceful. There was a small boy—too small to be *the* boy?—who was smiling in his sleep. Susan wondered if the receptionist was on a break or gone for the night.

She was just backing up, deciding to go home, deciding she had been an idiot to come, deciding that she should stop running off to do things when she hadn't even nailed down what it was she was running off to do, when she felt a hand on her shoulder. She turned, expecting to find a cop, and found instead a wan woman, makeup-less and tired, who should have been young. Under the lines of fatigue and worry she was young, certainly younger than thirty, maybe younger than twenty-eight. Her hair was blond and thick without a trace of gray in it, and without that telltale shadow at the roots. Susan hadn't noticed it at first because it was pulled back so tightly into its bun.

"Excuse me," the woman said, and then blushed, as if it embarrassed her just to be talking. "Excuse me—you're—you're a nun, aren't you?"

"No." It was Susan's turn to be embarrassed. "No, I'm not a nun."

"Oh." The woman looked back at the plate-glass window and bit her lip. "I'm sorry. I'm—I'm very tired. I've been here, it seems like forever, days, it hasn't been that long, you know, but it feels that way and my husband—my husband—"

"Actually," Susan said, "I used to be a nun. I left my order—"

"So many people do that these days," the woman said. "All my friends who joined the convent after high school—there weren't so many of them—three or four—but none of them stayed—"

"My mother superior was always giving lectures on how in the old days everybody used to stay." Susan smiled. "I stayed for seventeen years. Maybe I at least gave them their money's worth."

"My husband went down to talk to that doctor again," the woman said. "He's always going down to talk to that doctor. I don't know why. There isn't anything more to say. That doctor doesn't like talking to people, I can tell. He only puts up with Ken because—because—well because he has to. He just has to."

"Why?"

The woman looked surprised. "Because the reporters would notice," she said. "There's a reporter downstairs right now, right in front of that doctor's office. They're here all the time. Waiting for Denny to wake up. If you're not a nun anymore, are you a reporter?"

"I'm Susan Murphy. The district attorney is my brother. I haven't not been a nun long enough to be anything else yet."

"I hate reporters," the woman said. "I hate everybody but Ken and Denny and the police. They had to throw the reporters out of here this afternoon. They were—the reporters were—they were causing a fuss and getting all the children upset. You can't upset children in an intensive care ward."

"No, no you can't."

"I thought you went on talking to me because you knew who I was. I'm not making much sense. I know that."

"I think you're making perfect sense."

"Denny is the one in the middle." She walked over to the window and looked down at him. He was, Susan realized, the one who looked the least sick. There was an IV in his arm but nothing else. The other children must all have come down from surgery recently, or been on some kind of maintenance.

"I look at him and he looks just the same," the woman said. "It's been so long and yet he looks just the same. I can't understand it. And then Ken starts talking about God and I—I—what are you doing?"

"Doing?" Susan said. She was standing in the middle of the room. She was trying not to move.

The woman had turned away from the window. "Now," she said. "What are you doing now? Do you have a little time?"

"I have all the time in the world."

"I can't leave here, you see," the woman said. "He might wake up. I want to be here when he wakes up. But I don't know where Ken is and I don't know where that receptionist is and the nurses are all busy—"

"What do you need?" Susan asked gently.

The woman blushed again. "Food," she said. "I forget to eat. There's a cafeteria downstairs, I know that, but I don't want to go there. Usually Ken brings me something, but he's gone and I don't know when he's going to be back. And I'm dizzy."

"Do you remember the last time you had something to eat?"

"No."

"Could you tell me what you like to eat?"

The woman shrugged. She was looking through the plate-glass window again, pressing her face against it just as Susan had.

Her shoulders were squared and her spine was as straight as a pre-Vatican II mother superior's, but her head was sagging.

"Food," she said again. "I don't really care. I'm allergic to strawberries."

"That's all?"

"Yes."

"I'll be right back," Susan said.

The woman swayed a little, put her hands on the edge of the window, and steadied herself. "It's not just that I don't want to leave here," she said. "It's that I hate it down there. I went there once and I hate it. They're all over the place down there, the people who ask questions. They won't leave me alone."

3 If they were all over the place down there, the people who asked questions, Susan didn't see them—or didn't recognize them, which was the same thing. She picked up a tray and a pile of silverware at the beginning of the cafeteria line: two forks, three spoons, a knife. It was a collection with very little rationale, because she hadn't the faintest idea what she was going to buy. What she imagined herself buying was "everything," meaning everything that didn't have to be cooked to order. It was the first time in her life she could remember being a Murphy of Edge Hill Road being any use to her. The one thing she didn't have to worry about was money. Her wallet was stuffed with it, residue of the ridiculous "allowance" Dan insisted on giving her and that she never spent. What in the name of God he thought she was going to do with two hundred and fifty dollars a week was beyond her comprehension.

She picked up a chef's salad, a large bowl of clam chowder, and another large bowl of French onion soup, four rolls and twenty pats of butter. Butter was supposed to be bad for you because of the cholesterol but good for you because of the tryptophan, which was a natural tranquilizer. Or something. Her last health course had been in junior high school. She picked up a plate of macaroni and cheese, a plate of Swedish meatballs on egg noodles, and a plate of chicken à la king on rice. The tray was full, but the line behind was blessedly empty. She went back to the trays and got another one. A pair of very young men in white coats came up behind her and got trays, too. They were both wearing black plastic tags above the breast pockets of their coats, imprinted in white with their names and the designation, "M.D." They both looked twelve years old.

"The problem with your ordinary kitchen stabbing," one of them was saying, "is that these women always use serrated knives. It's crazy. It just rips the shit out of everything in there, shreds it, you know, and then you're standing down in emergency and—"

"What I don't like is the cocktail cases," the other one said. "They come in, they're showing symptoms of sixteen different drugs, all they want to do is tear the hair out of their heads. They just lose it. I had one the other day, bit his tongue clean off."

Susan pushed her new empty tray up next to her full one, took a saucer of green beans, a saucer of asparagus, a saucer of broccoli, and a saucer of fried zucchini and headed on down the line. The first of the men who had spoken was speaking again. He sounded jealous as hell.

"Marsha Deverborn gets all the luck," he was saying. "You know what she had the other day? A locked dick case."

Susan piled four cups of coffee, thirty creams, and enough sugar to sweeten Australia onto her tray and headed for the cash register. In between there was a display of desserts and she took one piece of chocolate cake with chocolate frosting, two brownies, and a cupcake. Then she pushed the whole mess up to the black woman sitting on the swivel chair at the end of the line and said,

"What in the name of God is a locked dick case?"

The black woman was staring at the ceiling. She was heavy without being fat and pretty in a late-nineteen-fifties sort of way. Her hair had been straightened and teased into a flip and she was wearing too much eye makeup.

"Well," she said, "there are these women out there, they say they want some man to get close to them, they don't really want some man to get close to them. So they get right to the point, if you understand what I mean, and there he is, stuck straight in, and these women have this kind of spasm, it's psychological, and they lock down and they don't come open—"

"Marvelous," Susan said.

"They always talk like that," the black lady said, looking up the line to the two men in white, as if she had overheard the entire conversation. She couldn't have. "They put these intern people in the emergency room for six months, it's six months without sleep, they all get crazy. Don't get many locked dick cases, though. Somebody must have got lucky."

"That's what the man said."

"You got a lot of food on those trays," the black lady said. "You gonna eat all that?"

"I'm going to take them up to PICU. There's a woman up there waiting for a sick child to wake up. I don't think she's eaten in days."

"PICU is the worst," the black lady said. "I just hope you have the money for all that, because subsidized or not, honey, this place ain't cheap."

Susan had the money. She also had a skill very few people had, that came in very useful under the circumstances: she could carry up to four fully-loaded rectangular trays at a time without dropping anything. It was something she had learned as a canonical novice when she, like every other canonical novice, had been assigned to waiting on tables for the professed sisters at dinner. At the time, she would not have said it was an experience she would ever be grateful for. Now she was.

She hitched the trays across her shoulder and arm and headed for the elevators, walking her nun walk, as fast as a run but not so jerky.

4 Upstairs, Susan Murphy came out of the elevator with both trays still perfectly poised on her left arm, put them down on the coffee table without spilling, and said, "I won't make you eat all of it, but I may make you eat half of it."

She was so charged up by her run to the cafeteria, she had noticed nothing except for the fact that Denny's mother was still in the waiting room and still pressed against the plate glass. She had certainly not noticed that the cop shift had changed, or that the cop who was standing in front of her now was recognizable to her as a cop only because she knew him.

"What the hell," Pat Mallory asked her, "are you *doing* here?"

CHAPTER
FIVE

1 In the beginning, he had not been worried about when they
found the bodies. Once he had killed them they were out of
his hands—consigned to God, as Sister Mathilde would have said—
and he had felt that there was something wrong with taking an
interest in what would happen to them next. Now, it was different.
He was so very close to the end, but the end couldn't come unless
all the bodies had been found first. His charism was more than a
gift from the Holy Spirit. It was a work of art, with parameters
and brush strokes and a source of light. It started with Susan Murphy and it ended with her—because she was *his* sister, *his* link with
the evil that caused the pain. In the middle there were examples
and expositions, necessary judgments. If they had all been found
together, or at once, there would have been a manhunt, too much
publicity, too much danger. If they weren't found at all, nobody
would know what he was doing. It was necessary in the long run,
that everybody know what he was doing.

He had just come from The Apartment—or, to be exact,
from a hole in the ceiling of The Apartment, accessed from a hole
in the floor of the empty apartment above—and he was finding it
hard to walk. Even now, free of them all, on his own and untouch-
able, he was never *entirely* free when he went to The Apartment.
He had to be careful not to give himself away, which meant he had
to be careful not to move. He had only a small slit in the ceiling
cover to look through, which meant he had to hold his eye steadily
against it or miss seeing what he'd gone to see. What he'd gone to

see this afternoon was the destruction of a boy named Stuart Harding, who was seven.

Now he was down on the Congo again, feeling jumpy. He had stolen a paper at the newsstand on Chapel Street and read it by the light of the only street lamp on Amora. There was a lot inside it about Marietta O'Brien and a piece on the boy who had lived that basically said nothing. There was nothing about the other one, lying in her apartment in that Spanish neighborhood across town, and he was beginning to be afraid. She had been a mean woman and a lonely one, not a mess of ineffectual sadness like Margaret Mary McVann. When he had knocked at her door she had snapped at him, and then given him a long lecture on what a sin it was to go slumming. It had almost made him laugh. What she had seen of him was just his skin. He was white and that was all she had wanted to know. She had simply assumed that he must be from a rich family uptown, down in the barrio looking for drugs—*she* called it the *barrio*, the Spanish people he had met up to then had called it the *neighborhood* or the *parish*. He had stared at his sneakers and sucked in his cheeks to keep from screaming at her. His sneakers were full of holes. He had pulled them out of a trash can on Prospect Street the day after he had escaped from The Apartment. On that day he had been dressed in beautiful clothes, expensive things from the troves that had arrived at The Apartment's door every week, via one of the johns who went out of town to buy it. The johns liked the boys to be well dressed, well fed, well washed, well groomed. They wanted to think they were giving the boys a Better Life than the one they would have had if they'd stayed where they'd been found. The johns never asked about where the boys had been found, or if they'd wanted to leave. Asking questions like that made things too complicated.

He hadn't dared keep the clothes once he left The Apartment, because they stood out. There weren't that many boys on the streets of New Haven wearing sixty-dollar sneakers and two-ply cashmere sweaters. He hadn't wanted to keep the clothes, because they were like a brand. Walk down the street dressed like that and everyone knew you were a whore. Every john in creation perked up his antennae and followed them to your door. Johns popped out of gas stations and police stations and restaurants and put their hands on their wallets. He had needed some old clothes. He had found them in the only place he knew of where old clothes lived: the Salvation Army. He had broken in there after dark and taken what he needed, everything but the sneakers, because they hadn't had any sneakers in his size. Then he had stripped to the skin and changed. He had not, however, thrown the expensive clothes away. He had other uses for them. He had been on his honor to give them back to the man who had bought and paid for them.

The woman down in the barrio, or the neighborhood, or the parish, or whatever you wanted to call it, had gone bitter from thinking she was trying to do good. She had been one of those people who think they know what everybody else in the world needs. Like all those people, she had been angry when she found out that nobody else in the world agreed with her. He had waited until she turned her back on him, reaching for a book to prove her point about everything, before he went for her neck. She had had a thick neck and he had found it hard to break.

Later, on his way to see Marietta, he had wondered if he had made a mistake. He couldn't believe that woman had ever had a vocation to reject. He couldn't believe she had ever even believed in God. Who she had reminded him of was the old lady that had lived behind their house in Oxford. The old lady had been abandoned by her husband and deserted by her children, and his mother always told him the old lady was on her way to Hell.

2 What Stuart Harding was was the new boy, the one they had picked up out in North Branford only a week ago. He was an ordinary one, born to a mother who abandoned him, fostered out to a pair of jerks who liked to beat him up. When he had first arrived at The Apartment, he had been covered with bruises from his neck to his knees. There was nothing at all on the parts of him that showed, on his face or hands or neck. It was possible

that the man who had brought him in didn't know about the bruises at all. It made for something of a dilemma when they first stripped him down. No boy was ever allowed to stay at The Apartment if he was damaged. Scars and cigarette burns were a death sentence. Lots of the johns liked to spank and some of them liked to whip, but the equipment kept for those purposes was carefully and custom made. The leather straps made welts when they hit hard enough, but not the kind of welts that lasted. It was the same with the restraints. There was always some john or other who wanted to use handcuffs. For some reason he had never been able to figure out, johns had a positive affinity for handcuffs. They were never allowed to get any near the boys. Instead, the closet in the extra room was full of leather cuffs, leather masks, leather gags—soft leather all of it, beaten until it was pliable, strong enough to tie a boy still but not sharp enough to cut or chafe him.

With Stuart Harding it was touch and go. They stripped him down and checked him over, but with all that black and blue it was hard to tell. Anything could have been hidden under those bruises. He remembered standing in the doorway of the room he shared with five other boys while the men talked it over, the men who were not johns but who brought the johns. On the street they would have been called pimps, but that was not quite accurate. On the street, pimps took a girl's money and disappeared. They didn't drum up business. As far as he could tell, all these men did was drum up business. He stood with the door open and the light out in the room behind him, holding his breath. He was already planning his escape and there were things he needed to know.

"Look," one of the men said, "he's not circumcised. Finding one that's not been circumcised is like finding gold."

"I thought they had to be circumcised," one of the other men said. "I thought the hospitals insisted on it."

"Maybe he wasn't born in a hospital," the first man said. "Maybe his mother popped him in an alley somewhere between junk hits. Who the hell cares?"

"If his mother had been a junkie he wouldn't be so bright."

"All I care about," the first man said, "is that he hasn't been circumcised, and we got half a dozen guys who'll pay a hundred-dollar premium for that."

"If we keep him for a week, all it will cost us is food," a third man said. "Then the bruises will have worn off and we'll know."

As it turned out, they had had to keep him for more than a week. They had had to keep him for over two months, which was why Stuart was still not turned out when he had escaped, and why he had had to go back today to watch it happen. He could remember with absolute clarity the day it had happened to him—not in the car, but later, in The Apartment, with the man who had first spanked him and then rammed an orange neon dildo up his ass—and from that day to this he hadn't been able to stay away from it. It was a kind of ritual slaughter. For Stuart Harding it had been less than that, because Stuart Harding had been psychologically dead long before he ever got back to The Apartment. He had blown all his fuses as soon as he had been raped in the car.

3 He was out on that street again now, the one with all the roosters in the windows. A few more blocks, a few more turns, and he would be back at the church. He wanted to find a church tonight and he would, but not until he had done what he had come to do.

He came to an intersection, checked the street signs—Sullivan and Vane—and turned down Sullivan toward the main drag and Saint Raphael's Hospital. The houses on Sullivan had mostly been broken up into apartments and were mostly dark. He had recognized on his first trip here that this was a street of single people, never married or widowed or just out on their own. A lot of the nurses from the hospital lived here. So did a little group of nuns, who—according to the one he had talked to, asking directions on the way to that woman's house—were trying out "an experiment in new forms of living in community." He had liked the nun very much, even though she wasn't wearing a habit. She was an older woman with a big mop of hair and a job at Saint Raphael's as some kind of nurse. A lot of the people who lived on Sullivan Street worked at Saint Raphael's as nurses.

He went down a block on Sullivan Street, and then another block, and then another, and stopped in front of the house where he had killed her. Her apartment was on the second floor, and it was dark. He had left it dark after he cut her, because although he needed her found he didn't want her found right away. Now he saw that all the other apartments in her building were dark, too. If she disappeared for a while, nobody would notice, except to be relieved. Nobody would go out looking for her.

There was a phone booth up at the far end of the block. He hesitated for a moment more, staring at her windows, wondering what she was like up there, if there were mice that had come out of the walls and eaten her. Then he walked down the street to the phone and dialed 911.

PART SIX

CHAPTER

ONE

1 From what Pat Mallory could remember, in the old days there had been places in the city of New Haven where it had been possible to take a girl for dinner, spend between thirty and fifty dollars, and make her feel as if she'd been transported to one of the nicer sections of New York. Of course, in the old days—in the days when Pat Mallory was more interested in girls than women—he hadn't been able to afford to take a girl to dinner. Now he thought it might be impossible to find the kind of place he was looking for at any price, especially in the center of the city proper. He had to be in the center of the city because he was on call, as he had been on call now for over a month. He had to keep his beeper within range of the call room at police headquarters, or he had to go home, where he could be reached by phone. He supposed he could go to one of those fancy restaurants out in the country and then call in and leave the number, but he didn't like the idea. There were too many people in the New Haven Police Department who would love to know where and when he was having a date.

Assuming that what was going on here was a date.

He looked across to the other side of the car and saw Susan Murphy take a pack of cigarettes out of her jacket pocket and light up. He didn't mind, but he thought it said something about how long she had spent in a convent and how recently she'd come out. She obviously didn't know there were people out here—men as well as women—who went totally insane at the very idea of someone smoking tobacco.

She was fumbling around on the dashboard, looking for the ashtray and not finding it. He leaned forward and got it open for her.

"I'm going to tell you now what I told you back at the hospital," he said. "If I was your brother Dan, I wouldn't let you go wandering around the streets at night."

"I'm going to tell you now what I told you back at the hospital," she said. "If you were my brother Dan, you wouldn't have anything to say about it." She leaned toward the windshield and looked out. "Is that the Payne Whitney gymnasium? Where are we?"

"We're not near the Payne Whitney gymnasium. We're around the other side near the cemetery. That's a Yale something."

"Everything in New Haven is a Yale something."

"Except the stuff that's a Catholic something."

They looked at each other and laughed. "Oh, well," Susan said. "I'm sorry I gave you such a shock. I'd had a fight with Dan and I was restless—I told you about that. I just wish life was like television a little, with resolutions."

"Do you like television?"

"I don't know. We weren't allowed to have them, in my order, except that the sister superior always had one locked up in a closet just in case of an assassination or an earthquake or something. I watched for about an hour a couple of days after I got home—my brother Andy has a whole list of shows he watches every week— do you know my brother Andy?"

"You know I do. You were with him the first time I met you, at Damien House."

"That's right. A lot of people find him invisible. Anyway, after he went to bed I jumped through the channels for a while, on this cable box, and there were things—"

"Sex," Pat said solemnly.

"Sadomasochism with genitals," Susan said. "One of the things my reverend mother always told me was that it was a mortal sin not to call a spade a spade. This particular spade that I saw ought to have been rated triple-X. And do you know what was odd?"

"What?"

"I'd always been told that the point of pornography was to arouse the passions. That's how they would have put it in my moral theology class. But good grief, Pat, that thing put my passions into a deep freeze for a week. I don't *believe* there are women out there dreaming of having some man urinate on them."

"There aren't. Those things aren't made for women."

"Are there things like that made for women?"

"Well, I'll tell you," Pat said. "I've been a cop for I don't remember how long. Seventeen, eighteen years. I've seen the evidence in hundreds of obscenity raids—back when we had obscenity raids. I've been in a thousand porno shops for one reason or another, usually to look at a corpse. People tell me they make porno for women, but I've never actually seen any."

"Maybe it's lesbian porno. I went to a conference once where this woman talked about lesbian feminism."

"Three-quarters of the videotapes in any porno store are lesbian videotapes. Men love to watch them."

"Marvelous."

"If I wasn't so sure this guy we've got is picking his victims in advance, I'd fill you full of dinner and then take you home and lock you in your room. Every time you blow smoke in my face, I keep thinking of Marietta O'Brien."

On the other side of the car the cigarette went up to Susan's mouth, down at the ashtray, up to Susan's mouth again. The car was filled with a thin haze of smoke that Pat liked the smell of, although he didn't usually like the smell of smoke. Susan had cracked her window a little and most of it was drifting outside, being replaced by sharp cold air that was doing its job of keeping them both awake.

He felt rather than saw her turn away from him, struggling under the restraint of her seatbelt. He felt rather than saw her turn back. He wondered if she was thinking about their talk at Damien

House. Tacitly, they had decided to forget about that, at least on the conversational level. She hadn't mentioned it, and he wouldn't. He couldn't believe she wasn't at least thinking about it.

Her cigarette was out. She dumped the butt in the ashtray and got another. He wondered if she'd been a heavy smoker before she entered her order.

"Pat," she said, hesitant, "you think you know who killed those women, don't you? You think it's the same person who killed those boys."

"No. I think it's connected to the killings of the boys. Two different murderers with two different reasons."

"But connected."

"Oh, yes. I've been half sure of it for a couple of weeks. Then I had that talk I told you about, with Bishop Riley." He hadn't mentioned the lecture he ended up delivering. The memory of it made him feel like a jerk. "Now I don't have the names and addresses of anybody—except I've got the alias of one of them—this is getting convoluted. I know who in the sense that I know what: what they are, what they're involved in. In the case of the boys, I even know why they're doing what they're doing. And, yes, they're connected."

Susan nodded. "This conviction you've got that they're all connected, it doesn't rest on the idea that the man who's murdering the ex-nuns is picking them out in advance, does it? I mean picking them out of announcements in the diocesan newspaper or because he knows them and they've told him they were nuns or anything like that."

"I don't understand what you're getting at."

"What I'm getting at is, would it ruin your theory if it turned out that the man who was killing the ex-nuns was just picking them up off the street, seeing them and just knowing they used to be nuns."

Pat jerked his head around, away from the traffic, away from everything he ought to be looking at. He nearly ran into the back of a city bus.

"How the hell could he do that?" he demanded. "How the hell could it be possible?"

Susan Murphy sighed. "I'm not saying he did do it," she said, "but trust me, with an ex-nun of a certain age, or an ex-nun from a certain kind of order, it would be easy."

2 He took her to George and Harry's. Partly he took her there because he knew it, it was close and convenient. Partly he took her there because it was the kind of place he'd always dreamed of going when he was young—a Yale place, for rich Protestants. What all that meant now, he didn't know. What he did know was that George and Harry's didn't look so exotic, or so rich, now that he'd reached the exalted position of chief of Homicide.

He let the waitress sit them down in a booth, ordered himself a Perrier, and ordered Susan something called a Rusty Nail. He didn't know what was in it and he didn't ask. He just waited until she got it and then he said, "All right. Tell me all about it. How could this man know a woman was an ex-nun just by seeing her on the street."

Susan had her cigarettes out again. "It would have to be more than just seeing her," she said. "He'd have to follow her for a while. But you've got to understand, Pat, that traditional formation practice—"

"Formation practice?"

"The process of turning a twentieth-century teenager into a model of sixteenth-century sanctity." She grinned. "It's not that bad, really. It's not that stupid, either. There are a lot of orders these days that have chucked traditional formation altogether, right along with traditional habits and the rule of silence. If a woman had entered one of those in the last ten or fifteen years and come out, he wouldn't have been able to tell. There wouldn't be any difference. But most of the women you've found have been older, haven't they?"

"Three out of the four."

"Then no matter what order they were in, they were all trained the same way. That's the key. What about the young one? What order was she in?"

"Franciscan," Pat said.

Susan threw her hands in the air. "There are probably five hundred orders of nuns in this country with 'Franciscan' in their names somewhere. What kind of Franciscan?"

Pat hesitated, then reached behind him for his jacket and the notebook he kept in the inside breast pocket. It took a while to find what he was looking for. His notes on these two cases were all jumbled up and overexamined. He found the reference and dropped the notebook down on the table.

"Franciscan Sisters of the Holy Name of Jesus. Does that help?"

"Very much so. Was she at least thirty years old?"

"Thirty-three." That was in the notebook, too, right under the name of the order.

"Did she enter her order when she was younger than, say, twenty-two?"

"She was," he had to search for that one, "nineteen."

"Wonderful," Susan said. "FSH has gone completely over to social gospel lunacy by now, but they were late starters. When your young one entered, they were still trying to train real nuns. Excuse me. It's extremely bad form for those of us on the traditional side to admit that we don't consider those of us on the modernist side real nuns."

"I won't report you. You still haven't told me how he could have known."

"Okay. Guess what I'm doing right now. With my feet. Under the table."

"I don't know."

"I'm keeping them flat on the floor. Absolutely flat. Have you ever seen a woman who isn't a nun do that? Unless they're too fat, they cross their legs. If they're too fat, they sit with their knees jutting out. My knees are together. Do you know what I do when I'm waiting for the bus?"

"No."

"I sit on the bench, if there is a bench, with my feet flat on the ground and my knees together. I keep my hands in my lap and I look down. I don't read. I don't look at the other people waiting with me. I don't check out the traffic. It's called custody of the eyes. Until a month or so ago, I'd spent seventeen years working very hard to practice it."

"But it was only a month ago," Pat pointed out. "Except for Theresa Cavello, all these women had been out of their orders for—well, for years."

"I know. I don't think it matters. I started looking around, you know, after I started going to Damien House, because every time I walked into that place someone I'd never seen before in my life would look me up and down and say, 'nun.' At first I thought it was just that people had heard about me—they knew I was Andy's sister, they knew Andy's sister was a nun. Later I realized it couldn't have been that, because I ran into people who just knew on sight that I'd been a nun, who didn't know who I was. So, like I said, I started watching."

"And?"

"And," Susan said, "as far as I can figure out, most of the traditional formation is impossible to get rid of. It gets to be too much of a habit—excuse the pun. It's not just the way they—we—sit. Hands close to the sides, not swinging and not stuffed into pockets. Close to buildings or the edges of sidewalks. I can make myself look around at things while I'm walking, if I've got something interesting to look at and I decide I want to look at it. When I'm just walking, thinking about something else, I do the custody-of-the-eyes thing again. Then there's the way I eat—"

"*Eat?*"

"When I first entered the convent, we had rules for eating every kind of food you could imagine. Actually, that's a lot less stupid than it sounds. When you have to live in community with a bunch of women you don't know, day after day, and you've got nothing in common with any of them except a vocation, little habits can get to be very irritating. So the traditional order used to—and I do mean used to, almost everybody has given this sort of thing up—anyway, we used to train everybody into the same habits. It reduced friction. I eat oranges with a fork—"

"With a fork," Pat repeated.

Susan smiled again. "It's worse than you think. I don't just eat them with a fork, I very carefully dissect them into quarters with a knife first. Then I peel a quarter. Then I eat it with a fork. Then I peel another quarter. Then I—"

"Good grief," Pat said, "Do you eat potato chips with chopsticks?"

"No, but I'm totally incapable of not taking something that's offered to me at dinner, and eating it, even if I hate it. I have an almost impossible time with small talk. I carry practically nothing in my purse. I have a very hard time shopping and when I do make myself shop I have to force myself to try things on. I feel so guilty when I look in a mirror, I put on makeup without the use of one. I—"

"All right," Pat said. "All right. What about these ex-nuns you've been looking at? How much of this stuff lasts?"

"A lot. You can't spend ten or fifteen or twenty years developing habits without having a hard time getting rid of them. The mirror thing especially. I don't know what it is about the mirror thing, but we all have it. A phobia for glass."

"Fine," Pat said. "Fine. But what does this mean? *Is* he picking his victims up off the street at random? Just running into a lot of ex-nuns?"

"You're the policeman," Susan said. "Maybe I'm looking at it backward. Maybe he's not picking on women he doesn't know. Maybe he knows a lot of ex-nuns and he's only killing the ones who do this kind of thing, the ones who were real nuns."

"What?" Pat said.

"What's that noise?" Susan said.

The noise was Pat's beeper. He grabbed his jacket and pulled it into his lap. He got the beeper out and stared at it.

He was going to have to answer his beeper, because it was blinking red.

"Excuse me," he said to her. "I've got to go find a phone."

CHAPTER
TWO

1 What he should have done, Father John Kelly thought, was to have stayed safely home at the Jesuit rectory and read a book. After his evening with the bishop, what he was doing— standing on Dan Murphy's doorstep in the dark, ringing the bell and getting more agitated by the minute—made no sense at all. Still, he was on Dan Murphy's doorstep, and he was ringing the doorbell, and he had no urge to go home. At home there would always be the chance that the bishop would call and give him another sermon about briefing the visitors before they were shown into the Presence. Pat Mallory, it seemed, had not been well enough briefed—and neither had the bishop. He'd ended up having to listen to a lot of information he hadn't known the first thing about. There was something in Father John Kelly that was very pleased with that, a kind of fierce exasperation very much like anger. The bishop sat there in the chancery, spiritual leader of a see that included one of the most violent and degraded cities in the United States— meaning Bridgeport, which was what Riley was supposed to be bishop *of*—and there was no damn reason on earth why he should have found child prostitution, police corruption, and the structural malevolence of the juvenile protection services a shock. It was Father John Kelly's private but so far unexpressed opinion that the vast majority of the Catholic bishops in the United States lived in a time warp where FDR was still president, Al Smith was still a hero, and good Catholic laymen wanted nothing more exciting in their lives than a chance to meet the Pope.

He pressed the buzzer again, waited, got nothing, and tried the door knocker again. He couldn't hear any sounds coming from inside the house, not even the sound of the bell. He had no idea if the damn thing was working. He picked up the door knocker and pounded that, just in case.

The bishop was on his way back to Bridgeport, riding in a big black car his predecessor wouldn't have been caught dead in, with a car phone next to his hand and a bug up his ass. John Kelly rubbed his face with the palms of his hands. A bug up his ass. That was probably some kind of blasphemy. He didn't really care. He tried the buzzer again, tried the door knocker again, stamped his feet. Somebody had to be home. Dan had to be home. John Kelly had called Dan Murphy's office and confirmed that.

"Son of a bitch," he said, to the air.

That was when he got an idea. He reached for the doorknob and turned it. He had expected to find the door locked. Instead, he found it open.

This was most definitely a sin of some kind, but he was too worked up to put a name to it.

2   In the foyer, standing on the black-and-white checkerboard marble, his agitation began to ebb away—and that was bad. Without it he lost what little self-assurance he had. He looked up the great curving staircase, to the dark on the landing. He looked through the pair of fifteen-foot-high double doors propped open in front of him, to the dark of what he thought must be the living room. He wasn't sure. He had never been in this house before— odd to think of, considering how constant his relationship with Dan Murphy had been—and he didn't have the first idea of where anything was. Or where anyone could be.

"You want to know who Victor Coletti is," he said aloud in the silence. "You want to know who really owns WNHY-TV. You want to know what all that business is about."

He was whispering.

He clamped his teeth shut, tight, hurting his jaw. He advanced to the double doors and looked into the room beyond them—a living room for sure. On the other side of it, curtains had been pulled away to expose a great wall of glass. Arc lights were lit across the long, narrow expanse of back lawn, illuminating a fountain and a garden house and a gazebo. There was a statue in the middle of the fountain, mock-Greek, a woman in flowing robes with one arm raised. He felt along the wall inside the left-hand door and found a switch.

It was when the light went on—an elaborate chandelier, spreading out over his head like George Orwell's infamous chestnut tree—that he became sure he was being watched.

"Dan?" he said.

Dan didn't answer, and neither did anyone else.

Out on the lawn, wind was rippling sluggish snow over the lawn. A line of pine trees was shivering and shaking at the back. The surface of the water in the fountain had hardened into ice. John Kelly reached for the pocket where he usually carried his cigarettes and found that he had forgotten to bring them.

"I want to know who Victor Coletti is," he said again, and knew that was a mistake.

3 When the blow came it hit him squarely on the back of the head, like a flat thing falling, even as he knew it wasn't a flat thing but a bullet. Sound and feeling wouldn't mesh. Life and death wouldn't mesh either. He felt himself suspended in time, half here and half there, like on that Christmas day when he had walked and walked until he had gone into a church. The priest was still waiting for him there, in the same black robes, with the same tired expression on his face—but what the priest was offering him was much clearer. Not an education. Not a life of safety. Not a vow of poverty with its secret promise of never, ever allowing him to get himself in debt. Not Victor Coletti, either, because Victor Coletti was a ghost.

There was a light up at the top of the world now and John Kelly could see it. It had started as a point and was spreading across all the darkness of space. In that light there was not only his history, but the answers to all his questions. He could turn back and see the man who killed him as surely as he had been able to see the chandelier the moment before he died.

The man who killed him was standing in the middle of the living room, tucking a gun into the waistband of his pants with one hand. With the other he was holding on to the shoulder of a small boy who looked frightened and frozen. There was no movement in the boy's body at all, not even the rise and fall of breath. The man pulled the boy closer to him and spun him around.

"Stuart," the man said. "Stuart, wake the fuck up."

Stuart didn't move.

"Crap," the man said.

He spun Stuart back around again, pressed the nozzle of the gun to the base of the boy's skull, and fired.

Up in the light, spinning away from it all, Father John Kelly thought how strange it was—that he had known this man and not known that he liked to dress in women's clothes.

THREE

1   If there was one thing Pat Mallory knew he couldn't do, it was to bring Susan Murphy where he had to go. It was one thing to take the woman out to dinner and pretend she wasn't who and what she was—a civilian and the district attorney's sister. It was another thing to haul her along on what was going to be a royal mess. Pat Mallory knew about the messiness because he knew every possible intonation in Ben Deaver's voice, and Deaver had sounded close to hysterical.

"You aren't going to believe this," Deaver had said, "you're not going to believe what he did this time."

"What did he do this time?" Pat had asked him.

Deaver had been in no mood to talk. There was a lot of noise going on in the background, police noise. Pat heard someone laughing and was sure it was Dbro. Dbro was enough to make Deaver nuts all on his own. Pat wished he could think of some way to get Dbro off the force, or transferred to Miami, or wounded in the line of duty. Even watching Dbro getting cited for heroism wouldn't hurt if the bottom line was that he'd no longer be carrying a shield. Unfortunately, Dbro was the kind of cop who never got wounded in the line of duty. He didn't give enough of a damn to take any risks.

"Ben?" Pat said.

Ben didn't answer.

"*Ben,*" Pat said again.

Somewhere in the distance, a man was shouting, frenzied

and angry and close to violence. "Cordon it off," he was screaming. "Cordon it all off. Do it now. Get those goddamned civilians off the goddamned crime scene and do it goddamned quick you fucking assholes what does the city pay you for?"

"Pat?" Ben said. "We're out on Sullivan Street. Do you know where that it?"

"Yes."

"You better get out here fast. There's a patrolman named Dunbar who's lost it completely, I think he's going to shoot someone, for God's sake."

"What's the—"

"Pat, just get down here, will you please? You can see it when you get here. Just get here."

"I'm with a woman and I'll have to—"

"Put her in a cab."

Ben Deaver hung up.

2   In the end, Pat Mallory didn't put Susan Murphy in a cab. Edge Hill Road wasn't exactly on the way to Sullivan Street, but it was in the same general direction, and this was another ex-nun he'd just gotten a call about. It didn't matter which theory he used, his original one or the one he'd been developing since Susan gave him all that information about ex-nuns. Neither theory exempted her from attack. Neither could, because they both ended up at the same place, except that the second one gave him a name and a face, a name and a face he had heard and seen for the last time on the day he met Susan at Damien House.

Coming back across the restaurant, he grabbed their waitress and threw a wad of money at her—too much money, but it didn't matter. Coming back to the table he grabbed Susan and pulled her to her feet.

"We've got to get out of here now," he said. "I'm taking you home. I've got to be someplace."

"Is it another one of the boys?"

Pat shook his head and pushed her toward the door. "Another

one of the women. Run, Susan, we've got to move it. Something's gone haywire."

She was a good girl, a good woman, a brick, whatever. She practically ran out onto the street and down the sidewalk to where he had parked the car—parked it illegally, too, for once not caring who got upset. He found something funny in the fact that he had always refused to do that when he was on official police business, and had finally fallen when he was on his own time.

She got to the car before he did, waited while he came up with the key, and then climbed inside without expecting him to help her in. He let her get on with it, and climbed into the driver's seat himself. As he started to pull away from the curb, she got her cigarettes out and lit up again.

"One right after the other," she said. "That's—faster than he usually is, isn't it?"

"I don't know," Pat said. "The first body was destroyed before we made the connection. I think he's always been pretty fast."

"I wish I knew what he was doing," she said. "It seems so crazy, killing women because they used to be nuns."

"He is crazy," Pat said. "He has every right to be crazy."

"What?"

He didn't answer her. It wasn't that far from George and Harry's to Edge Hill, and he was pushing it—not running the siren, but definitely pushing it. He wasn't afraid of being stopped. There wasn't a patrolman in the city who didn't know his car. He went down one one-way street and then another, around corners, around curves, automatically taking the route most likely to be clear of traffic. He went across Prospect Street with his horn blaring but his eyes straight ahead. He didn't have time to check on what might be coming at them through the intersection. A few seconds later he was sitting in front of her house with his motor still running and his gear still in drive.

"Go inside and lock the door," he told her. "Don't come out until I come to get you."

"Pat—"

"Go."

She went. He watched her run up the walk, fumble with her keys, stand back and look at the front door. For a moment, he thought he was going to have real trouble. She was going to have brought the wrong keys and there was going to be nobody inside to let her in. Then she went back to the door, fumbled around for a few moments and got the damn thing open. He jerked the steering wheel to the left and took off again.

It was nine o'clock at night and the city of New Haven was dark and cold and crazy—and deserted. If he'd been down in the Congo, the streets would have been packed. In the respectable parts of town there was nobody. He got to the bottom of Edge Hill, and finally hit Chapel Street. He also hit his siren.

3 From the sound of Ben Deaver's voice on the phone, Pat Mallory had expected at least a minor riot. That happened sometimes, either because the crime scene was too public and the civilians in attendance stampeded, or because the crime scene was in one of those sections of the city that didn't like cops on principle. Sullivan Street was not a dislike-cops-on-principle sort of place. Pat had heard that other cities had trouble like that in their Hispanic neighborhoods, but New Haven never had.

Pat Mallory definitely expected to find civilians stampeding. It was disorienting to turn off Chapel onto Sullivan and find only a small knot of old women in bathrobes, clutching rosaries and looking near tears. In the face of that, his siren felt ridiculous. He turned it off.

The old ladies were not only clutching rosaries, they were saying them. One or two of them had looked up when they'd heard him coming—they could hardly have helped hearing him coming—but by the time he had parked the car and was climbing out, they were bent over their beads again. Pat looked at the building they were standing in front of and saw that there was a uniformed patrolman there, doing sentry duty. The patrolman's lips were moving, as if he were saying a rosary, too.

Pat walked up to the building, then up the steps of the stoop—why was it all the buildings in New Haven had such high stoops?—and said, "Ben Deaver in there?"

The patrolman didn't ask his name, or for any kind of identification. Pat didn't remember ever seeing him before, but he supposed he must have.

"Lieutenant Deaver's in the hallway," he said. Then he swiveled his head around until his chin was practically on the back of his shoulder and said in a puzzled voice, "*Everybody's* in the hallway."

Pat went past him and through the building's front door.

Everybody really was in the hallway—not only Ben Deaver and Dbro, as Pat had expected, but half a dozen patrolmen and a man from the medical examiner's office and three techies. The techies were holding their equipment bags and looking mutinous. Ben Deaver had his back against the staircase and his arms crossed over his chest. He looked determined.

"Pat," he said, when Pat came in. He moved a little away from the staircase, and as he did the techies moved toward it. He moved back again. "Pat," he said again. "God, I'm glad you're here."

"I thought we had a riot on our hands," Pat said.

"We've got a problem on our hands, at least," one of the techies said. "He sent the ambulance away."

"We didn't need an ambulance," Ben Deaver said.

"He won't let us call for the morgue car," one of the other techies said. "He won't let us into the scene. He won't let anyone do anything."

"*I'm* not going to take the responsibility for this when the shit hits the fan downtown," the first techie said. "And you know it's going to."

An explosive wheezing sound came from one corner. Pat turned and saw that Dbro was there, doubled up, laughing so hard he couldn't breathe. There were tears in the corners of his eyes that threatened to spill down over his face and start a deluge.

"Oh, God," Dbro was saying, "Oh, God. The shit hits the

fan downtown. You better believe the shit hits the fan downtown on *this* one."

Pat turned back to Deaver and raised an eyebrow. Deaver shook his head.

"Come upstairs, Pat. There's something I've got to show you."

4   The stairway was steep and narrow. The hallway it ended at was long and narrow and led to a single closed door and the stairs to the third floor. Pat hadn't known what to expect this time— after the riot that never was, he didn't want to guess—but part of him was vaguely confused by the cleanliness of all of it. Part of him thought the place ought to be covered with great globs of blood. Deaver stopped in front of the single door on the landing and got out the white gloves.

"I don't know why I'm doing this," he said. "The outside knob is hopeless. The uniforms that caught the call came blasting through here with guns drawn or something, I don't know—"

"What call?" Pat said.

Ben Deaver sighed. "He called, Pat. He went down to a phone booth someplace and he dialed 911 and told us she was here."

"Tonight?"

"Of course tonight."

"He killed her tonight and then he called?"

Deaver hesitated. "I think maybe he killed her yesterday. Not too long ago, anyway. She's—you'll have to see her."

"How do you know he was the one who called? Pat asked.

Ben Deaver hesitated again. Pat began to feel uneasy. Ben Deaver was not a hesitant man.

"The thing is," Ben said, "I don't think it could have been anyone but him who called. When the uniforms got here the door was locked, bolted from the inside. He must have gone out the window in the kitchen onto the fire escape. I can't see any of the ordinary people on this street doing that."

"It could have been an ordinary sneak thief doing that. Coming in, finding something he wasn't prepared to deal with, getting on the phone to 911."

"I know. Pat, I talked to the dispatcher at 911."

"And?"

Ben Deaver didn't answer. He turned his back to Pat and faced the door, so that he was blocking it as he had blocked the stairs.

"Pat," he said, "I know what I sounded like on the phone. I know you must think there's carnage in there. There isn't. She's just like all the other ones. Amber rosary on her coffee table. Strangled and then cut on the forehead with that Catholic thing. There really isn't anything weird about the body except that maybe it gives you the feeling he didn't like her much."

"What's that supposed to mean?"

"With the others, he always seemed to be really careful about the way he laid them out," Ben said. "He *positioned* them, sort of. With this one, he just stuffed her into a chair. She looks uncomfortable."

"She's dead, Ben."

"I know. I'm just telling you it isn't anything he did with the body that's the problem. It's not—he hasn't gone on a frenzy. He hasn't popped his cork that way. I know you've been worried—"

"Ben, what the hell *is* the problem?"

Ben Deaver turned the knob, pushed the door open and stepped back.

"Go ahead in," he said. "Go ahead in and take a look."

For one split second, Pat Mallory resisted. Everything in him resisted. He felt as if he'd been slammed into one of those force field walls his nephews were always so excited about on "Star Trek." Then he made himself push through it and walk into the room.

In spite of what Ben had said, Pat had expected blood, a lot of blood, not this tired old woman crunched up in an overstuffed chair, the carving on her forehead as clean and crisp as the acid etching on a lithograph plate. She was right in front of him, just beyond the door's swing, almost blocking his path and his view to the rest of the room. Almost, but not quite. As soon as Pat Mallory raised his head, he saw it. Saw *them*.

Someone had turned on all the lights in the living room, overhead fixtures and table lamps, making the room look like a photograph gallery—because that was what there were, photographs. Dozens of them. Everywhere. Taped to the curtain that covered the front windows. Tacked to the walls. Strewn out over the tables and the couch and the floor. Black-and-white photographs taken with a good camera by someone who knew what he was doing. Black-and-white photographs with perfectly balanced contrasts and sharp, unmistakable images. Black-and-white photographs of grown men and very young, very naked boys.

Ben Deaver came up behind him. "Look at this," he said. "Remember that talk we had? How you liked the street rumors, the business about that kid Charlie Burton escaping from a bugger house and then they were killing the others to warn him off—except that sounded too extreme, killing so many of them just because one had run off? Well, Pat, take a look at this. Of course they killed the others to warn Charlie Burton off. Of course they did. They had to do something."

"Right," Pat Mallory said.

He reached out and took the photograph closest to him. It was a photograph of Billy Hare and a man he didn't have a hard time placing as the hot-shot psychiatrist Dan Murphy had sent down to the scene on the death of Ellen Burnett.

"When Charlie Burton left his stable," Pat said, "he took their goddamn blackmail file with him."

CHAPTER

FOUR

1 What had held Susan Murphy up at the door, when Pat
Mallory dropped her off, was the simple fact that the door
was unlocked. It had never in her memory been unlocked before
at night, even when her parents were alive and New Haven was a
relatively safe place. She pushed the door open, went into the foyer,
and looked around, feeling a little afraid. There were so many robberies these days, and so many crazy people committing them, she
thought anything might be inside. Nothing was. The foyer was
empty. When she walked across it and looked into the living room,
that was empty, too, although there was something about it—.
She turned on the chandelier and saw nothing. The furniture. The
floor. The rug. There was a sour smell in the air, sharp and anti-
septic, that reminded her of the heavy-duty cleaners they used to
use to clean the floor of the cellar in the convent. Certainly convents
were the only places where people still cleaned cellar floors.

She walked around the living room, confused, and then
walked out, turning off the chandelier behind her. The foyer was
still empty and the house was still quiet. She thought for a moment
about going to the kitchen to get herself a cup of tea. Part of her
imagined Pat coming back, late but before dawn, to talk to her. It
was stupid and she knew it. Things hadn't gone that far—they hadn't
even mentioned that thing she'd said, that morning at Damien
House—and she knew enough about police work from novels and
movies to know that Pat wasn't likely to be free anytime in the next
twenty-four hours.

She might have made herself a cup of tea anyway, but, strangely enough, she was finally tired. She went upstairs instead, wondering vaguely why it had finally hit her now. The upstairs hall was dark and she flicked the switch that turned on the small lights that lined its ceiling. At the door to Andy's room she hesitated. She didn't want to talk to him, but she wanted to talk to somebody. There was nobody on earth she could call. That was what seventeen years in a convent would do for you.

She went down to her own room, opened the door, and turned on the light. She saw the rosary right away, lying in the middle of her pillow like the chocolates the maids on cruise liners left for passengers before bed. It was the amber one that had come in the mail on the day she left the convent for good.

It was an amber one just like the amber one someone had given Marietta O'Brien.

Susan walked over to the bed, picked up the rosary, and stared at it. She was just about to put it down again when she heard her brothers in the hall.

2 "Be quiet," Andy was saying, "be quiet, for God's sake, that light's coming from Susan's room."

"I don't give a damn where that light's coming from," Dan said. "You're out of your mind, do you know that? You're crazier than Daddy was."

"I can't be crazier than Daddy was, I'm sober."

"You're drunk on blood, you stupid, psychopathic asshole."

In her room, Susan put the amber rosary carefully back on her pillow. They were coming down the hall, the two of them, and one of them—Dan, she thought, it would be Dan—was pounding his fist against the wall as he walked. They were whispering but they were loud. The odd acoustics of the house took care of that.

"I had it all set up," Dan was saying. "I had the whole goddamn thing set up. It took me months to work it out. It took me weeks to put together. I had that bastard neutralized—"

"You had that bastard on television."

"I had him where he couldn't do anything to save Tom Burne's neck, you fuck."

"He still can't save Tom Burne's neck."

"He's a dead body, you roaring fool. And we've got another dead body we don't even know what the hell to do with—"

"Stuart went over the edge on me. He was useless anyway."

"Stuart wouldn't have been God damned useless as a corpse if you hadn't offed him in my own living room."

"Fuck that," Andy said. "Fuck everything. As soon as I get my gear together, I'm going to go over to The Apartment and fuck my brains out my ears."

"You fucked your brains out your ears when you started all this."

Tom Burne. Dead bodies. Somebody Dan had put on television.

Tom Burne.

Susan was sitting on the edge of her bed. The rosary was back in her hands. She couldn't remember how it had gotten there. Down the hall she heard a door swing open and then stop, dead, as if someone had cut the thread of sense and put an end to sound.

The next thing she heard was Dan, part howl, part scream, a stream of words coming out in no particular order whatsoever.

"Dear sweet Lord fucking Jesus Christ in heaven what the hell is going on here dear sweet Christ fucking—"

Andy burst out laughing.

3 A moment later there was nothing, nothing, no words, just the sound of feet moving heavily on the floor of the room down the hall and then the sound of something tearing. Move, Susan told herself. You've got to move. She got off the bed and went to the door, opened up, and looked out in the hall. There was nothing there but the light streaming out of Andy's room. Shadows moved through that light that she knew were her brothers, but they might as well have been ghosts. Move, move, move, she told herself again. Move, move, move. And then she did.

She went out into the hall. She went down the center of the runner, moving carefully, moving slowly, making no noise. She was at Andy's door before she wanted to be, standing just to the side of it so that they didn't see her. She could see them, pacing in and out of view. Andy's room looked different, but she couldn't put a finger on why. The walls seemed to be the wrong color. She moved closer to get a better look, still going impossibly slow, impossibly silently, and then it clicked—

Photographs.

Hundreds of photographs everywhere.

Photographs on every surface, on every piece of furniture, even stuck into Andy's mirror like prom invitations on a popular girl's vanity.

Her eye caught one and stuck to it, held to it, made her mind take it in.

It was an eight-by-ten glossy black-and-white of a tall man bending over a child. The child was on his knees and doubled over at the waist, his rear end in the air. The man's pants were open and down around his hips. The man's penis was sticking into the air, dark and erect, but he wasn't doing anything with it. What he was doing was bringing a thick leather strap down on the boy's behind.

The man was her brother, Daniel Robert Murphy.

She did what she did next without thinking about it. If she had thought about it, she would have run. She walked instead, up to the open door, up to the empty place where they would have to see her, where she would be exposed. She rounded the doorjamb and stopped, practically slamming into Dan's chest. He was pulling photographs off the recliner and tearing them to shreds.

Andy was all by himself in the middle of the floor, holding a set of boy's clothes that looked rumpled and dirty and crusted with blood.

When Andy saw her, he smiled, reached into his pocket, and came out with a gun.

"Did I ever tell you," he said, "that I always wanted to shoot that goddamned *look* off your face?"

CHAPTER

FIVE

1 It was odd, Pat Mallory thought, how quiet you got inside, when you finally knew what you had to do.

He was standing in the middle of the woman's apartment, looking not at the corpse but at the photographs, as he had been looking at nothing but the photographs since he first saw them. By now he had identified the figures in most of them. The figures of the adults would have been hard to mistake. The children were sometimes identifiable and sometimes not. All the boys who had been killed showed up in one of the photographs or another. So did a few boys Pat knew nothing about. So did Denny Grissom, the boy now in the hospital. The adults were a kind of honor guard of New Haven city politics.

He had picked out the photograph of Dan Murphy almost first thing. Actually, it was a photograph of Dan and his brother Andy, good old harmless, ineffectual Andy, getting together to beat up on a single terrified little boy. All the boys looked terrified, except the ones that looked dead. The impression was so overwhelming Pat thought he could drown in it. What would happen if they went to wherever these boys were and got them out? What could happen? For most of them, the juvenile system would take over and they'd be lost. For the rest, there would be years and years of therapy that probably wouldn't work, and they'd be lost anyway. Reality was a paralyzing thing. So was realism. He was looking at the yearbook album of an army, an army of men with power—and, in one case, of a woman with power, too. Half the prosecutor's

294

office was tacked up on these walls. So was a good proportion of the Special Investigative Unit of the police force. So was the head of New Haven Social Services and the man who was supposed to supervise the city's homeless children's shelter. So was the chairman of the board of directors of New Haven's leading private action group for Children's Rights. If he found that apartment and got the boys out, if he arrested all the adults in these photographs— who the hell would prosecute them? There were three judges up on those walls. Who the hell would supervise the trials? Did everybody do this, everybody on earth, or was it just New Haven, just here? His muscles were locked into place and his mind was frozen solid. The whole world had been taken over by pod people.

And then, of course, it hit him. What he had to do.

"Ben," he said.

Ben was next to him in a second, babbling nonsense. "They couldn't have been hers, these pictures, he must have brought them here, they couldn't have belonged to her because—"

"Of course they couldn't."

"The lawyers will say—"

"Never mind the lawyers, Ben. Who else has seen what's in this room?"

"Dbro."

"Just Dbro?"

"I haven't let anyone else in."

"Has Dbro *talked* to anyone about this?"

"I don't think so. I think he's—keeping it. To spring on people later."

"All right," Pat said. "The first thing you're going to do is, go down to your car—you and Dbro came together?"

"Yes."

"Good. Go down to your car and disconnect the radio. Get your hand up under the dash and pull the wires straight out and stash them someplace. Not in the car."

"Dbro will—"

"You tell Dbro I'm sending him off someplace, this is an

emergency—he'll believe *that*—he's going down to Danbury or someplace on total blackout. I don't care what you make up to get him out of here but get him out of here, is that clear?"

"Yes."

"The next thing you do is you start making some phone calls," Pat said. "Roger Farnum, the crime guy from the *Register*. Jack Meskowitz, who strings for the *New York Times*—"

"The *New York Times*? Pat, what the hell—"

"I'm covering our asses," Pat said. "I'm making sure we put these people out of commission once and for all—"

"The evidence will be contaminated—"

"The evidence is fucking useless under the circumstances. I'm going to take some of it, Ben. Any of these guys wants a nice clean photograph, you send him to me and tell them I'm handing them out."

"But—"

"*Do* it. Meskowitz also strings for *Time*. Then there's that woman, what's her name, Linda somebody who does the true crime stuff for *Connecticut* magazine and Diane Smith from *Action News*— oh, crap, Ben, you know who's honest."

"Yes," Ben said, "I know."

Pat was taking photographs off the couch and stuffing them in his jacket pocket. He took the one of Dan and Andy and the boy. He took the one with the smug, self-righteous bastard of a psychiatrist in it.

"You can make those telephone calls from here," he said. "When you get done with Dbro I want you back in this room and I want you to stay here until those reporters have seen what they're going to come to see. Nobody else in or out. Nobody. Not techies. Not police photographers. Not even Anton Klemmer."

"Pat, for God's *sake*."

"*Do* it," Pat said again, "and do it fast. I've got to get out of here. There's something I forgot."

2   There *was* something he'd forgotten, forgotten completely, lost in the blackout. Even staring at that picture of Dan and Andy and the boy hadn't made him remember it. Even the picture of Denny Grissom hadn't made him remember it. Remember, remember, remember. Remember what?

Remember that he had sent Susan Murphy back to that house, back to her brothers, back to a pair of psychopaths who could be trusted only to make sure that anything they touched turned to blood.

Remember that the very last time he had seen her, she had been having trouble with her front door.

CHAPTER
SIX

1 The first time he shot, he aimed at her foot. The bullet went wide and buried itself into the rug, a gorgeously colored, red, green, and black Persian that must have cost ten thousand dollars when it was bought in 1956. She didn't understand why she was thinking of the color and price of rugs. She didn't understand anything.

The next time he shot, he aimed at her head—and came closer. She felt the breeze of it along her cheek and heard the impact on the door frame behind her like an explosion. Not a mini-explosion, but a real one. It was that close and that loud. It hit her that she had to get out of here and get out of here now, or she would be dead.

She was spending so much time thinking about Andy, she had forgotten that Dan was in the room. He came up on her right side and reached for her, his long arms outstretched in the air like sticks with claws, his face the mask of something that was not really an emotion. She saw him just in time and stepped back. Her movement put her just out of the range of Andy's third shot, aimed at her chest.

If she had not moved, she would have been hit.

In the dark of this night the house was too quiet and too big. There was rain coming down outside and beating against the window at the end of the hall. She ran and ran and felt like she was getting nowhere, but knew she was. She had only one chance and it was this: that years ago, when they were all being ground to nothingness beneath their father's drinking and their mother's craziness, the boys had been allowed to escape into the outside world and she had not. There were a hundred places in the house that they knew nothing about but she did.

Andy was standing in the doorway to his room, firing and firing. She could hear the sharp whine of bullets in propulsion in the air around her. The gun never seemed to run out of ammunition and Andy never seemed to run out of steam. A bullet hit the jade porcelain vase her mother had brought back from Venice in 1959 and shattered it. Another bullet hit the feet of the crucifix that had hung at the top of the landing for as long as Susan could remember. The feet splintered into a hundred pieces that flew into the air like magic darts.

She reached the landing and turned, blindly, heading downstairs. She got halfway to the foyer and stopped.

Standing in front of her was a small boy, no more than ten or twelve, with a face like a Botticelli angel. At any other moment in her life she would have been able to place him: the boy who had been with Francesca that first morning at Damien House, the boy Francesca had called Mark.

At this moment the only thing she could place was the identity of the object he was holding in his right hand, jutting it up into the air at her as he came toward her, cutting through the thick fog of this wonderland she had fallen into and smiling while he did it. It was a stainless-steel carving knife with a sharp point at its end and it was covered with blood.

"It was your fault," he said, as calmly as if he were reciting sums in an arithmetic class. "The Holy Spirit told me so. It was your fault because you got a divorce from Holy Mother Church."

Susan turned, headed up the stairs again, and prayed to God she made it to the attic.

2 "This is a seven-oh alert," Pat Mallory was saying into the radio, "this is a seven-oh alert. Edge Hill Road. Murphy house. Number seventeen. This is a seven-oh alert and we want—"

"Stop," the patrolman beside him said. "Mallory, what are you doing?"

Pat wasn't entirely sure what he was doing except driving, except running the siren at full blast. He was in a patrol car instead of his own, because he hadn't wanted to even chance getting stopped by the one cop in the city who didn't know what he drove. He was keeping the police band open and not giving the dispatcher a chance to ask the usual questions. He was doing a hundred things that would have been appropriate only for the start of a nuclear holocaust and he didn't give a flying fuck.

He came up Chapel Street at eighty miles an hour. He came up Prospect at eighty-five. By the time he was on Edge Hill Road he was doing ninety, and the car was damn near out of control. The nightly freeze had set in and the rain was turning to sleet. The whole street was paved with ice.

"Lieutenant," the patrolman said, "you've got to give them a chance to answer you. They may have questions. They may need to know—"

"They know what they need to know. Number seventeen Edge Hill Road."

"Lieutenant—"

Number seventeen Edge Hill Road was just ahead. The lights in the foyer were lit. So were the lights on either side of the door. Nothing else was. He pumped his brake frantically, skidded, righted himself again, and then pulled up to the curb.

The place looked as quiet as a Catholic church.

3 In the attic it was not silent, and Susan knew that if she had heard the sirens, the rest of them had heard them, too. She drew her knees to her chest and tucked her head under a rafter. She was in the hollow place between the attic ceiling and the underside

of the roof. She had gotten there just in time. When she had come back up to the landing, running from Mark and the knife, Andy had been waiting for her, gun in hand, legs apart, set up like a SWAT raider ready to burst through the door of some drug lord's apartment. She had ducked at the last minute and the shot had gone over her head, down the stairs. She had dived between his legs and gotten to the other side. Dan was there, hands out to catch her like a quarterback ready to catch a hiked ball. She rolled to the side and headed back the way she had come, running as she had never run before in her life.

The door to the attic stairs was at the far end of the hall. It locked from the inside like a bathroom door. The lock was useless at keeping anyone out. She had never understood why it had been put there to begin with. She ran up the narrow curving flight and pulled the door shut behind her, locked the door anyway, even though it wouldn't work.

She had just made it into her hiding place when she heard them coming up behind her, not just Dan and Andy, but the other one, too. The one she knew as Mark.

"Charlie," Andy was saying, "Charlie, for God's sake, what are you doing, what's wrong?"

Susan stuck her head between her knees and tried very hard not to laugh.

4 Down on the street, Pat Mallory was out on the pavement, running up the sidewalk, opening the front door. He stopped in the foyer under the light from the chandelier and listened to silence that was not silence. The house was quiet but inhabited. He could feel it. He went to the double doors that looked into the living room, turned on the light, and saw nothing. He went to the windows that formed the wall at the living room's back and looked out at nothing again. The patrolman came up behind him with his gun drawn and pointed it at the statue in the fountain.

"Listen," Pat told him. "Listen. Someone's walking."

Someone was walking. Far above them, someone was walking. Far above them, someone got off a shot that sounded as loud as a shot on an indoor firing range.

Pat Mallory ran out of the living room and up the stairs.

5 It had finally happened. Susan realized it as soon as the sound of the shot had died away. It had finally happened. Andy's gun had run out of ammunition. *Andy* had run out of ammunition.

The quiet in the attic was so deep it might as well have been the quiet of a well. They might as well have been underground. Susan felt as if she had a rock pressing down on her, squeezing the air out of her chest.

She put her eye next to the only crack in the wall beside her and tried to look out into the attic. She saw the legs of Dan's pants and nothing at all of Andy. She saw Mark.

He was standing in the middle of the floor with his legs spread apart and his arms out, in just that same position Andy had used when he fired on the landing, except that instead of a gun Mark was carrying the knife. There was light coming in from somewhere. It caught the blade and made the clean parts of it gleam. The clean parts were like stars in a dark night. There weren't that many of them and they were small.

"My name isn't Charlie," Mark said. "My name is Mark Harrigan and I'm from Oxford, Connecticut, and I remember *everything*."

6 Down on the second floor, Pat Mallory had stopped in the hallway—stopped to look at the shattered vase, the broken crucifix, the aftersigns of bullets that had gone into the walls and the floor. There were casings everywhere. It looked like there had been a war up here, to the death. The soldiers had all killed each other and disappeared and left their battlefield empty.

He walked slowly down the hall, stopping at every door, opening every door. The rooms were all empty.

Behind him, the patrolman was repeating the process, just in case.

Two doors from the end of the hall on the left side, Pat Mallory got to Andy Murphy's room. He didn't know it was Andy Murphy's room. He only knew it was full of photographs, just like the room of that woman down on Sullivan Street. He looked on the floor and saw the crumpled heap of boy's clothing, the mess on them that had to be blood. He raised his head and heard the sirens coming up outside.

He had just decided to go back down and meet them when Susan's voice exploded over his head.

"No," she shouted. "No, Dan, no, don't you dare *touch* him."

7   She had only been able to see a little sliver of space, but she had seen this. Andy coming for the boy named Mark and Mark with the knife out, with the knife ready. She kept thinking that it was right, not Christian, but still right, she wanted to see Andy dead and bloody on the attic floor at this boy's hand. Then the sliver was clouded with a blacker thing and she realized in shock that she had forgotten again, forgotten about Dan.

Dan was coming up on the boy's other side the way he had come up on hers. The boy was paying no attention. He was too crazy to pay any attention. Even in her hiding place, she could see that. Dan was reaching out for the boy and Andy was backing up, backing up, putting the boy in position.

Susan grabbed the loose board she had used to get into the space and pulled it, hard, so hard that she cracked it in half. The sharp smack of it went across the attic as if another gun had gone off and they both turned. Both her brothers turned. The boy did not. Susan could see the boy coming up on Andy, moving steadily, not changing plans at all and she let him come.

"No," she shouted at Dan. "No, Dan, no, don't you dare *touch* him."

"Fucking holy *bitch*," Dan said.

That was when the boy's knife came down on Andy's neck, slashing into the side of it, cutting across the windpipe and coming through the other side.

8 A second later the attic door burst open and Pat Mallory launched himself in, went down on his knees, and fired.

He caught Dan Murphy in midair, with a shot to the heart that went in clean.

He caught Mark Harrigan with the knife in his hands, staring at the damned thing as if he'd never seen it before.

He caught Susan Murphy fainting.

EPILOGUE

1 At four o'clock on the morning of Tuesday, December 23, Denny Grissom woke up. Pat Mallory was there to see it— although he didn't. He was sitting at the back of the PICU waiting room with his legs stretched over a coffee table, fast asleep. It had been a long night after a month of long nights, made even longer by the realization that he had panicked, just a little. Those photographs they had found in Martha O'Connell's room had not really included every public official in the city of New Haven. They hadn't even included most of them. What he hadn't noticed in his first shock he noticed later: there were a lot of repeats. Now he had two major problems on his hands and no idea what to do about either of them. There was the Case itself, not quite ruined by all the publicity he had made sure it got. It had a special prosecutor down from Hartford, an investigative unit from the state police, and little clots of men from the U.S. Marshal's office and the FBI, all swarming around, trying to work it into something they could understand. Then there was the Fallout, as Susan persisted in calling it: the body of Father John Kelly, found in a window seat on the first floor along with the body of the very last boy; the boys they had found when they had finally raided The Apartment; and Mark Harrigan. Any civilian bright enough to spend his Saturday nights watching reruns of "Hill Street Blues" would have thought that Mark Harrigan was part of the Case, and no cop would have expected him to be. He was not only a twelve-year-old child, but crazy as a loon.

On the other side of the waiting room, Denny Grissom's

mother had fallen asleep with her head against the plate-glass window that looked in on Denny's bed. She began to slump and caught herself, grabbing onto the windowsill with one hand and locking her knees. When she was upright again, she looked through the glass and swallowed hard. God only knew where Ken was. This had gone on so long it could have been going on forever, time before time and time after, like God in the Athanasian Creed.

On the couch, Pat Mallory stirred and wondered, in his sleep, what Susan was doing.

On the other side of the plate-glass window, Denny Grissom moved his head very slowly from side to side, from side to side, from side to side. His eyes were a camera panning a movie-set hospital scene, but he didn't know that. He only knew that his eyes were open and that when his head was flat back against his pillow, he caught sight of his deliverance. He wanted to look at nothing else, but he couldn't make himself stop moving.

On her side of the plate-glass window, Karen Grissom was rubbing her eyes with her fists. Her eyes stung and she kept wishing they would stop. She kept feeling full of salt. She put her hands down at her sides and blinked, willing tears. She turned toward the plate-glass window and stopped.

Denny's head was just the way it had always been, lying back, pointed toward the ceiling, but there was a difference.

He was staring at her.

2 Susan Murphy didn't know when she had first realized that Mark Harrigan was the boy that nobody wanted. Even his parents, who had been brought up from Oxford three days after the Mess had gone down, didn't seem to know what to do with him. They couldn't bring him home, not after everything he'd done. They couldn't make him fit the picture they had of the son they'd lost, either. He'd been eight when he was picked up. He was twelve now. In a little while, he would be a man. In the meantime, he was on a locked ward at the hospital, cleared for visitors under observation, waiting for disposition of his case.

Susan had started spending her time with Mark partly because she was interested in him, and partly because where he was was the only safe place she knew—safe from the police. She didn't want to talk about Dan or Andy, or what they had done. She had been living in Pat Mallory's guest room since the night her brothers had died. She supposed that, after a while, she would move across the hall to Pat's own room and they would finish what they had started. Pat Mallory's guest room was no place to keep the book she was reading. It would certainly be no place to dispose of it when she was done.

She dog-eared the lined page she had just finished reading for the third time and put the book down on her lap. It was one of those sewn-binding, cloth-covered "keepsake books" you could buy in any Hallmark outlet, and it was crammed full of Andy's handwriting. Andy's handwriting was so small, she sometimes wished she had a microscope to read it with. Mark was sitting cross-legged in a chair on the other side of the room, holding her copy of the breviary, reading Lauds. She had offered to say the hours with him, even to let him read the declamations while she prayed the response, but he had turned her down.

When she put Andy's book on her lap, Mark closed the breviary and looked up at her. "Is it still what you told me it was?" he said. "All about your father?"

"Yes."

"Will they say it was your father who made him do what he did—do what he did to us?"

"Not if I don't give them this."

They looked at each other and almost smiled—almost, because the mirror on the north wall of the room was two-way, and there might be someone behind it. It was a long shot at four o'clock in the morning, and an even longer shot in the case of Mark. For all the vaunted interest of psychiatrists in studying "unusual" cases, there wasn't one in the city of New Haven interested in studying Mark. They shied away from him, the doctors did, and the nurses did, too. Susan and Mark both noticed it. The people in white filled Mark full of Thorazine and disappeared.

Susan picked up Andy's book again and looked at the cover, back and front and spine. She had found it where she knew no police officer could, in one of those places—in the walls and under the floors and God knew where else—that the house on Edge Hill Road was full of. There were things of hers up there in places like that, too, bits and pieces of her adolescent privacy, when privacy had been a treasure and revelation an act of suicide. She put the book back in her lap and said, "I thought, you know, at the time, that it was Dan who'd killed him. That he'd gone into one of his drunken insanities and things had just gotten out of hand, and then that Dan and Andy had worked it out together and covered it up. But things didn't get out of hand at all. For once in his life, Daddy was stone-cold sober."

"He was just a bad man," Mark said, "your brother Andy."

"Dan was no prize either. They were both men who looked at people as assets and liabilities, and nothing else. Our father was the worst possible kind of liability."

"That's how I know it really is the Holy Spirit who talks to me," Mark said. "That's how I know I have a charism."

Susan opened her eyes. "How?"

"Because I set out to kill you," Mark said. "You were the first one. I saw the notice in the newspaper, the little newspaper the church puts out—"

"*Connecticut Catholic?*"

Mark shrugged. "He put a sword in my hand," he said, "to cut down all the people who had betrayed Him. I was supposed to cut them down and leave them where they could be found, to let the others know, to let everybody know it was connected."

"Nuns who left their orders and what happened to you at The Apartment were connected."

"In times of great apostasy, the devil always has his way with the world. I read that in a book."

"It sounds like you did."

"When they decided not to be nuns anymore, they gave the devil their energy. They were like batteries. Making him go."

"Who?"

"Your brother Andy. Your brother Dan. All the rest of them."

"That's a 'them.'"

"I thought you were one of them," Mark said, "but I never made any real mistakes. The Holy Spirit kept me from that. He gave me a charism, and then when we were all together, us and them, in the attic, He made me *see*."

"Yes," Susan said, "I know He made you see."

"He's gone away from me now," Mark said. "Did you know that?"

"Yes," Susan said, "I know that."

"I hope they let you do what you asked them to do," Mark said. "Send me to that place your order runs. I think I'd like it there. Like being a monk forever."

It was getting on toward four-thirty and Susan thought it was time she went down and got herself some coffee to drink. Mark's last Thorazine had been delivered half an hour ago. It was beginning to get to him. She could see that his eyes were growing heavy and his shoulders were beginning to slump. Thorazine was not supposed to put people to sleep, but it always did just that to Mark. Maybe the doctors put something in it to make sure it did just that.

The place that her order ran was called a mental hospital, but what it really was was an old-fashioned insane asylum, a hospice for hopeless cases.

She picked up the book again, put it down again, picked it up again, put it down. When she finally abandoned it and looked back at Mark, he was asleep.

It was time she got rid of this book, and found Pat, and tried to talk him into going home.

3 Up in PICU, Pat Mallory was in no position to go home. He didn't know what he was in a position to do, because he didn't know what was going to happen. Karen Grissom had just done a very odd thing. She had leaped for the door of the back unit, pulled it open, and raced inside. It was equipped with an alarm that had to be blocked before the door was opened. The alarm was set whenever the receptionist was away from her desk, to make sure no one in the waiting room did anything stupid. Since the waiting room was usually full of parents the people in it often felt called upon to do something stupid. Now the alarm was going off like the fire-drill siren in a parochial school. Nurses were racing in from everywhere, running up to the door of the PICU and rattling its knob, yelling through the plate-glass window for Karen Grissom to turn around right this minute and come *out*.

Karen Grissom wasn't listening to them. She was standing over Denny's bed, looking down at his face, and he was looking back at her. From what Pat could see, Denny didn't hear the sirens any more than his mother did.

Karen Grissom put out her hand, touched Denny's forehead, and smiled.

Denny put out *his* hand, touched *her* hand, and said, "Mama?"